To Lexi-Lee!

The Sword of Demelza

An Australian Fantasy Adventure

J. E. Rogers

Best Wishes

Cover and back plate, Guy Atherfold
Copyright (C) 2012 Acadia Publishing Group LLC
All rights reserved.
ISBN: 061570994X
ISBN 13: 9780615709949

Library of Congress Control Number: 2012951314
CreateSpace Independent Publishing Platform
North Charleston, South Carolina

ILLUSTRATIONS

Cover, Guy Atherfold

Dragon Lizard, Guy Atherfold

Flitch, (thylacine) Guy Atherfold

Devon, (fox) William Hulbert

Ackley and Amber, (echidnas) Guy Atherfold

Hector, (gang-gang cockatoo) Guy Atherfold

Bede, (bilby) William Hulbert

Aldon, (numbat) Guy Atherfold

Oswin, (masked owl) Guy Atherfold

Cynric, (fox) William Hulbert

Erik and Emma, (kowaries) Guy Atherfold

Gorgon, (dragon lizard) Guy Atherfold

Sebastian, (quoll) Guy Atherfold

Pearce, (quokka) Guy Atherfold

Moloch, (thorny devil) Guy Atherfold

Stokley, (echidna) William Hulbert

Durward, (goanna) Guy Atherfold

Babble, (sugar glider) Guy Atherfold

Byrnie and Lazlo, (kowari and wombat) Guy Atherfold

Back Plate, Guy Atherfold

AUTHOR'S NOTE

I have always been told that one should write about what they know. That statement would confine a lot of authors. What about writing for the sheer enjoyment of it, and in the process learning something you hadn't known before. The adage, 'you learn something new every day,' is very true. I did learn while writing this fantasy for middle graders. I learned that there is a way of combining passions to make a point, and to make it in such a way that it is enjoyable and educational.

The Sword of Demelza introduces middle graders to a number of animals. Some of these animals are unheard of by children here in the USA (including this child). Most of the animals in the book are indigenous to Australia. The more important fact is that many of them are endangered. Many species of animal and plant life as well, are gone from the planet forever. They have become extinct for many reasons, some natural. Sadly, man has played his role via encroachment, greed, and negligence.

If a young person reads my book and is inspired to learn more about the animals who roam the pages, then I have accomplished a worthwhile goal. Maybe, just maybe, they will be the generation dedicated to making a change. If they enjoy it while they are learning, well, what more can I ask.

One does not write a novel in solitude. There are people who I bugged, bothered, annoyed and generally aggravated in every way imaginable.

First to Lorri, who actually helped to conceive the plot, and stayed with me when it got a little rough. Lorri, how can I thank you?

Secondly, Karen, who spent countless hours reading the book and then reading it again, and again, and even after she had reached the point where she could recite it by heart, she read it again. Karen, I couldn't have gone on without your unwavering belief in me, or the love you showed for the story.

Third, to my editors, they showed me the error of my ways, and were always quick to offer support for my writing ability and my story. I sincerely thank Gavin Doyle, and Beth Bruno. Also, a quick thank you to my beta readers, Pat and Marie.

Finally, to my children, Erik, David and Katie, they listened as I read. They put up with papers all over the floor, and the computer moved to different places, wherever I was comfortable that particular day or moment. They offered wonderful constructive criticism and splendid suggestions when I thought I had hit a brick wall and that my muse had left me forever. And to my husband, I thank you for buying the paper shredder. It came in handy.

Just one more thought. The characters actually bugged me. They were alive in my head, and they wanted out. Not a day went by that I didn't think of a way to put them onto a sheet of paper. They were so much happier there!

J.E. Rogers
September 2012
Danbury, Connecticut
Copyright © 2012 Acadia Publishing Group LLC

Dear Readers,

You are about to embark on an epic adventure with some of Australia's most endangered animals. More than likely, you will not recognize these animals, but they are very anxious for you to get to know them. So, they ask kindly that you do not let the fact that you don't know what they look like bother you. Instead, after you've read their story, and if your curiosity is piqued, and you want to see what they **really** do look like, check out this web site:

http://australian-animals.net

Also, I have added a glossary at the back of the book so you can read a bit more about the unusual flora and fauna of Australia!

Thank you, from the bottom of our furry, feathery and scaly hearts, for choosing *The Sword of Demelza!*

PROLOGUE

The sun was setting over Sunderland and Acadia Abbey. Devon had fallen asleep on the lookout above the manicured grounds. His auburn fur rippled in the summer breeze, and the white star on his forehead gleamed in what remained of the late afternoon sunlight.

He was still young, but he was maturing quickly. Although he was rash at times, he was a strong and clever fox. He loved the monks of the abbey, especially Colum. The old bilby monk had taught him many things about the wild world and soon he would be old enough to leave the abbey and be a part of it. After the tragic death of his mother and father, Colum had taken him in.

Devon looked after Colum now that the small mouse-like marsupial was beginning to age. The young fox was dedicated to him and the other monks of the abbey as well. But he often thought of the father and mother he lost. How different life would have been if the tragedy had never happened, if he had never lost them. Still, he was happy here at Acadia. He had all he needed, and life was peaceful. Peaceful, that is, until today.

In the soft rustling of sleep, Devon thought he heard the warning bell of the abbey ring. Startled, he sprung to his feet. *The warning bell*, he thought. *Did I really hear it?* Drowsy from his nap, he stumbled as he sprinted toward the tower door. The bell rang again. He stopped to glance over the wall. Cries could be heard rising from the grounds below. Flames shot out from the windows of the scriptorium. The monks of the abbey were running in every direction.

A troop of dragon lizards approached on great hind claws, running up the slope from the billabong toward the abbey. Devon had heard of the lizards but had never seen one. Colum once told him about how they traveled alone in the western lands of Sunderland, but these lizards were not loners. They were organized, clad in thick leather armor and carrying flaming torches as they ran across the lawns from the forest. Stunned, he placed his front paws on top of the rampart wall. Leaning over it, he scanned the grounds below, trying to understand what was happening. He gasped as one lizard threw a lit torch through an open window. Across the lawn, near the gardens, two lizards laughed as they tossed a small monk between them. One monk was being dragged across the lawn and down to the banks of the billabong, where he was thrown into the water. Several lizards had broken through the main gate. *They are in the abbey.* The thought terrified him. Colum, he must reach Colum.

Devon pushed away from the wall and ran. Flames and acrid smoke met him as he opened the tower door. He buried his muzzle in the crook of his arm and took a step inside. Fire was consuming the wooden stairs. He began descending the steps, leaping over the flames, but the steps and railing were burning. He could see that the framework of the staircase was breaking away from the stone wall. It began to shake beneath him, and the center pole holding it in place was burning. He would not be able to descend the steps any farther. He threw himself out toward the center post, grabbing it just as the stairs broke beneath him. Flaming pieces of wood fell to the floor below, and hot embers drifted up around him. He pushed away from the post and dropped the final distance to the floor.

Huge wooden pillars and a series of immense wooden beams supported the high-arched ceiling of the nave. He watched in horror as the blaze grew from the floor toward the roof. The entrance to the scriptorium was down a corridor at the far end of the nave. Devon sprinted toward it. As he turned into the scriptorium's outer hallway, he found his way blocked by a pile of smoking timbers.

"Father!" he screamed as he began to climb over the debris. "Where are you?" There was no reply. A cracking sound came from above. Startled, Devon lost his footing and fell to the stone floor. Over the noise of the crumbling roof, Devon heard an evil, guttural growl. Turning toward the sound, he saw a

DRAGON LIZARD

creature creeping toward him through the smoke and flames. It was a thylacine. Its mouth, full of saber-like teeth, hung open and its wicked yellow eyes drilled into his. From somewhere in his memory, Devon recognized the knifelike canines, heard echoes of its malevolent growl, and felt the same hatred he had felt years before emanating from the evil beast. The wolf-like body was thin and half-striped like that of a tiger, and its thick tail trailed behind it, scraping the stone floor. Frozen with fear, Devon's heart beat as though it would burst from his chest. He shook his head in disbelief as he scrambled on all fours, backing away.

"The Demon," Devon whispered under his breath. Shivers crept up his spine as memories came flooding back. Demon is what his father had called the thylacine back on that fateful day.

"Yes, you can call me that. But my name is Flitch!" The thylacine spat out his name like a curse. "I remember you!" he hissed with satisfying surprise. "You are my unfinished business." Flitch took a step closer to Devon. "It's so nice to see you," he said with an evil grin. "You got away once, but it won't happen again."

A loud crack from above warned that a rafter was weakening. Devon ducked into a small alcove as a beam crashed to the floor. It broke into hundreds of sharp shards, sending burning projectiles in all directions. One struck the thylacine in his hind leg, and he let out a scream of pain that echoed throughout the abbey. He limped toward Devon, who scrambled up the pile of smoldering wood to get away from him. The injured thylacine attempted to follow, but he could not climb the debris.

"Another day, Fox!" he snarled. Turning, he staggered away.

Devon climbed over the debris and continued on into the scriptorium. Desks were overturned, and smoking remains of illuminated texts covered the floor like snow.

"Father! Answer me!" Devon frantically peered through the smoke and scanned the ruins of his father's beloved library. He spied a small paw sticking out from under a large desk at the far end of the room. The wall behind the desk had partially fallen in and the stained glass window hung precariously in its frame. The setting sun shone through what remained of the image of the sword and created beams of light that covered the room in shades of blue and green. The center stone on the sword's hilt cast an eerie glow on the top of the desk. Holding his breath Devon crossed the room and braced for the worst. With all his strength, he groaned as he lifted the heavy oak desk. It toppled over, sending ashes flying into the air, where they floated slowly, like phantoms, in the shafts of the setting sunlight. Colum's small body was curled in a ball seeming somehow even smaller in death. Lifting his father, Devon's tears flowed shamelessly. With his father's body resting in his arms, he left the abbey through a gap in the wall where the dragons had torn down the stones.

Bilby monks ran frantically across the grounds and fields outside the walls, putting out fires, attending to the wounded and gathering the dead. He could see the dragon lizards heading away from the abbey in the distance, their cruel laughter reaching his ears as they disappeared into the forest. It was a vision that Devon would never forget. Once, long ago, Colum had carried Devon to the safety and warmth of Acadia Abbey. He would now carry his father away from the wreckage of the abbey and lay his body down on the banks of the billabong.

FLITCH

As he knelt beside Colum's body, he tried to recall the lessons he had been taught. "See not with just your eyes, Devon, but with your mind and heart as well. You are a part of this wild world, and cannot separate yourself from it."

His thoughts drifted back to their talk earlier in the day.

He was leaning over Colum's shoulder. He had stood there with his paws clasped tightly behind his back watching Colum's quill move smoothly across the parchment. The illuminated texts produced by the mouse-like bilby monks of Acadia Abbey were beautifully drawn and painted with vibrant colors, etched in gold leaf. The texts were a treasure known throughout Sunderland. They not only contained the history of the abbey, but hinted at its mysteries as well.

For Devon, the greatest mystery was the image of the sword in the large stained glass window. Devon glanced up; the window dominated the scriptorium and the grounds of the abbey. In the middle of the window an image of a magnificent sword pointed toward the earth. The glass was stained a deep green at the center of the sword's hilt, where the legendary emerald stone of Demelza was depicted. No one at the abbey was certain where the sword was, but Devon knew that many stories of its powers had been told. Tinted rays of light poured down into the scriptorium from the colored glass panes. Colum had yet to tell Devon the significance of the sword, though he had asked about it many times. Why would a sword in a stained glass window dominate a peaceful abbey such as Acadia? What was its importance?

Had Colum become shorter over the years, or maybe I have become taller, Devon thought. He now towered over Colum.

He wore a golden muslin vest over dark blue pants. A belt was cinched tightly around his vest at the waist. A small dagger and leather pouch hung from the belt.

"Father, you said you would tell me about the abbey's beginnings." With his eyes still lingering on the sword's image, he rested his chin on his father's shoulder, continuing his quick chatter. "How did the bilbies become monks and build the abbey?"

The small scratching of Colum's quill hesitated briefly, and Devon's eyes were drawn to the parchment. Encouraged by the pause, Devon pressed on. "You promised to tell me about Aldon, the Great Numbat that saved them—how they built the abbey to honor him. And the sword, Father, it was his sword, wasn't it? Aldon's sword would be a better weapon than that old wooden staff you found with me all those years ago."

"Yes, yes, my son!" He laughed. "I did promise to tell you of the sword, didn't I?" Colum placed his quill in the inkwell and shifted the worn brown fabric of his monk's habit. Dropping to the floor from his stool, he stood before Devon. The top of his head came to Devon's waist. "When did you grow so tall?" He laughed, tugging playfully on the tip of Devon's vest. "You are certainly not the small kit I carried from the forest so long ago; along with that old staff, as you call it. You may yet find that ancient staff to be useful, my son. I have a feeling that it may have more meaning, and more power than we know."

Devon bent down and hugged his father, lifting him off the floor. Releasing him from his arms, he set him back down. "Power in a wooden staff?" Devon chuckled. "All I know for sure is that it was a lucky day for me and a terrible one..." A shiver passed through him as he thought of the terrible creature that had killed his father and mother. He recalled the horrifying image of the beast attacking them. He could see its sharp teeth. Its frightening voice shook him to his very core. The memory haunted his dreams. "I don't know what I would have done if you hadn't happened along."

"It was the will of Aldon that I found you that day," Colum said quietly. He shook his head as he looked up at Devon. "I am as lucky as you, my dear boy. I am lucky to have had you by my side all these years." He took Devon's paw in his. "Alright, my son, if you want to know more about the abbey, I'll tell you." Touching a claw to his forehead in contemplation, he said, "What have we discussed thus far? My memory is not as good as it once was."

Devon barked a laugh. "You bilbies may as well have taken a vow of silence for all that you told me thus far. All I know is what I see; it's a building of stone and wood and it overlooks the waters of Kakadu Billabong." He thought about the lovely red lilies covering the surface of the lake, about how the monks of the abbey spent many hours lost in meditation along its banks. The bilbies, small animals with pointy inquisitive noses and long ears that stood up stiffly on their heads, were quick and lively, and took great pride in their abbey. Not only had they been his family all these years, they were also known by many of the forest inhabitants for their charity and caring nature.

"I love it here. But, still, I have so many questions, questions that you promised to answer for me."

"You're right, my son. But right now I would like to finish my work while the sun still shines on my parchment. Tonight we'll have dinner on the banks of the billabong and we'll talk." Colum hopped back up onto his stool. "I have a few more hours before the sunlight leaves the scriptorium. Then I'll tell you everything." He grinned at Devon, his bright eyes sparkling in the light that shone down through the stained glass window.

"Ok." Devon grinned. Placing one arm gently across Colum's back, he said softly, "One day soon I'll leave the abbey. I'll go out on my own. You know this." Colum looked up at Devon and Devon saw sorrow in Colum's eyes. "I'll visit the Wingcarrabee Swamp. And perhaps I'll make it as far as the Pinnacles Desert. I'll visit all the places you've told me about, and I'll tell everyone I meet about the wonderful monks of Acadia Abbey."

"Yes, yes, you are certainly old enough to set out on your own." Colum looked down at his paws and rubbed them nervously. "I was hoping you might stay one more season."

"We don't have to talk about that now, Father."

Colum hesitated for a moment then waved at Devon, shooing him off.

"Run along now, you young rascal!"

Devon turned and walked toward the doors of the scripto-rium. "I'm going up the tower to the parapet walk," he said over his shoulder. "I'll be back for dinner." He listened to Colum laugh as he walked out the immense double doors.

Heading through the nave of the abbey toward the tower, he noticed two monks coming toward him. The parapet walk was high enough above the abbey to serve as a lookout, and the monks took turns watching over the grounds.

"Brother Alfred, Brother Edgar," Devon nodded, acknowledging them, and they nodded in return, smiling up at Devon.

"Taking watch on the parapet this afternoon, Devon?" Alfred asked. "Or will you just be napping up there?" The two monks chuckled to themselves, holding their paws in front of their snouts, trying hard not to laugh out loud.

"You know me too well," Devon replied with a smile and a wave of his paw.

At the top of the tower he opened the door and stepped out onto the walk. He strolled toward the crenellated wall. Leaning over the wall, Devon looked out across the grounds of the abbey. A wide expanse of grass gradually ended at the edge of the waters of the billabong and the hills of Sunderland rose up on the far side of the lake. From his vantage point he could see several monks working in the gardens, while others were engaged in quiet conversation or reading beside the sparkling water. It was peaceful. He moved to the other side of the walkway and settled down. Leaning his back against the stone wall, he closed his eyes to rest for a bit.

Now, Colum rested on the banks of the billabong. Raising his eyes toward the ruined monastery, Devon saw a small group of monks gathering on the lawn. They spoke quietly with one another, a mixture of fear, worry, and sadness etched on their faces.

He continued to gaze at the abbey and the remains of the stained-glass window. The sword's colors were dark now that evening approached. What was the purpose of the sword? The image of a terrible weapon meant only to bring harm and pain had always seemed a strange object for the peace-loving monk's abbey. The sword seemed to shimmer with a life of its own in the evening light. For a moment, he thought he saw the thylacine standing beneath the tip of the sword, but it was just his imagination. He drew in a deep breath, and then dropped his head to look at Colum. He vowed to find out why this happened and who had brought this destruction down upon the abbey. He would have to look deeper, as his father had taught him. The mystery of the sword would remain for now. There were other questions that needed answers. He may never understand why a sword was emblazoned in the stained glass window, but that didn't matter anymore. Colum was gone. The time for stories and mysteries was over. He furrowed his brow and narrowed his eyes as anger took hold. There was only time for revenge. He would take up his own weapon, the ancient wooden staff that Colum had found with him so many years ago. Devon knew nothing of its powers, but he would wield it against those who had brought pain and terror to his home. He would hunt down the dragon lizards. He would kill the thylacine. He would make them pay for what they had done this day, for what they had done to his father.

The screech of an owl echoed through the woods beyond the billabong, and a feeling of dread came over Devon. The time had come for him to leave the place he had come to know as home.

DEVON

CHAPTER 1

E rik Grassley sat on the flat boulder at the top of the path.
His light-brown fur blended well with the rock and his
intense, dark-brown eyes studied the little hamlet of
Digby. Short pointy ears and a sharp pink nose twitched and
crinkled as he absorbed his surroundings. His teenage years
were approaching, and he spent much of his time imagining a
day when he could venture into the wild world outside Digby.
But that day was not today—he was still a young kowari. He
sighed as he watched his twin sister Emma kiss their mum
good-bye. It was berry-picking day and Emma held a basket in
each paw, one for him and one for her.

A slight movement in the brush at the base of a tree caught his eye. Amber and Ackley, two echidna puggles, were trying their best to hide. The puggle babes had found their feet this summer season and used them to follow Erik and Emma everywhere. Erik was sure they would follow today, as usual.

Erik took a moment to think about his forest home, and consider the possible berry patches they could visit. He slowly traced the winding path beneath the aged tingle trees that led into Digby. All the woodland creatures that lived in and around Digby knew it well. Low hanging branches, fallen logs and twigs sometimes hid the path, but there were treasures of every kind to be found. All varieties of berry bushes, wild mushrooms, and scallions lined the path. The exploding orbs of the golden wattle would catch the rays of sun that splashed through the trees. Blossoms of kangaroo paw grew alongside the pathway, creating a riotous display of color.

He thought about Calder Stream. It ran alongside the pathway into Digby, flowing over moss-covered rocks. He enjoyed standing by the sparkling water watching dragonflies as they flew in and out of shafts of sunlight above the creek. Further upstream, Calder Bridge, a small

bridge painted blue and red, crossed over the creek. Fragrant flowering vines hung over the railing of the bridge, cascading like a living waterfall to the stream's surface. Once one crossed the bridge, they were no longer in the safe haven of Digby. They were entering the realm of the wild wood, where dangerous creatures stalked the thick undergrowth.

Erik and Emma trundled along, swinging their baskets. Erik raised his nose, snuffling the clean fresh air as he went. "We'll bring the best of the berries home to Mum," he said to Emma as he walked by her side. As the twins strolled through the forest surrounding Digby, Amber and Ackley followed in their wake. Erik listened for them to make sure they didn't fall too far behind.

Chewing a blade of grass as he walked, Erik turned to Emma, and said, "Let's go up Calder Stream this time. We've picked all the berry bushes by the lily patch clean away."

"Okay, the stream it is," Emma said, glancing at her brother. "I'd like to see what condition the old bridge is in. I wonder if the red and blue paint has worn off." She chuckled softly. "I remember the last time we painted it with Papa. And Uncle Durward was there too," she added. "We had so much fun. You were blue and red for days afterwards. Mum just couldn't get the paint out of your fur." She tried not to laugh as she raised one paw to cover her mouth, but her eyes sparkled with the smile hidden underneath it.

"Yeah, yeah. As I recall, you certainly were no help. You never could hold a paintbrush, and you spilled more paint in the stream. We were supposed to paint the bridge, not the water! And Uncle Durward got paint beneath those scales of his. Mom had to use a scrub brush to clean him up." Erik laughed out loud at the thought of it.

"Yes," Emma said breaking out into laughter along with her brother. "I don't think goanna lizards are built for painting. Every time he turned around, his tail would knock over the pail of paint."

"Durward certainly makes a better soldier than a painter," Erik said. "He's much better with a sword than a paint brush!" The twins laughed together at the memory.

AMBER & ACKLEY

Erik stopped and cocked his head. "Hey, where are Ackley and Amber? I don't hear them anymore."

Erik and Emma turned and walked slowly back down the trail. They found the two echidna babes off the path, standing and staring into the black beady eyes of a deadly brown snake.

Amber leaned toward her brother and giggled. "Look at 'em. He's got some kinda funny kinda tongue, kinda. What ya say, mister funny kinda snake?"

"Silly, silly Amber, you can't talk to that snake," Ackley said with a complete look of disdain.

Emma gasped, dropping her basket to the ground, but the puggles seemed to be ignorant of the danger. Erik gestured silently for her to keep still. He set his basket down on the path, and slowly stepped toward Amber and Ackley. Taking them by the paws, he began to back up with the babes in tow. "You're not interested in us, Mr. Brown Snake," Erik said. "We're just little tidbits, and a big strong snake like you doesn't bother with small pickings like us."

"How would you know what I want?" the snake hissed. "Sssooo sssure of yourselves, are ya?"

Finally realizing they were in danger, the puggle babes began to tremble while Erik tried his best to move the two away from the serpent's reach.

Amber whimpered. "I don't wanna be kinda eaten by some kinda old brown snake." She sniffed and wiped her nose with the back of her free paw. "I wanna see Mum. I wanna go home, please!"

"Silly, silly Amber, you're the one that stopped to talk to 'em. Not me!" Ackley teased.

"You can see, Mr. Brown Snake, these here are just babes. They're not worth your time or effort." Erik did his best to sound confident and convincing so as not to appear afraid, which he most certainly was.

A voice called out from above, "Hey, Snake! Move on! There's nothing here for you."

Daring a quick look up, Erik spotted a large grey bird with a red-feathered head sitting on a tree branch. The Gang-gang Cockatoo looked menacing with his chest puffed out, as he spoke with a threatening tone.

The snake lowered its head while mumbling under its breath, "You guys are always ruining my meal. How's a sssnake supposed to survive with the likesss of you around?"

"Just move on, move on!" The bird screeched, waving a wing toward the forest. "You have no business here. Get going or I'll peck your eyes out!"

"Aaaaa . . .." The snake coiled, making itself as small as possible. It turned to move away, but not before looking back at Erik. "Watch your ssstep. You're too big for your britches, ya are. Think you can stand up to the likesss of me?" With a disgusted look it slithered off into the forest hissing under its breath. "And I know where you live."

Erik and Emma breathed deep sighs of relief as the snake disappeared into the underbrush. Amber continued to whimper, gripping Emma's skirt hem, and Ackley rubbed his sister's back, trying his best to comfort her.

"Silly, silly Amber. That'll teach ya. No more talking to them nasty snakes." Ackley mumbled without any sense of embarrassment that he'd been doing the same.

Erik looked up at the bird sitting on the branch over their heads. The cockatoo spun upside down and looked at the four friends with a silly expression on his face. The stern look he wore for the snake was gone.

"So, me mates, where ya headin'?" the bird asked. He kept moving his head back and forth, spinning it almost completely around as though he could not make up his mind who to look at first.

"Huh?" Confused, Erik gawked at the bird, who had just sent the snake crawling away. The cockatoo looked like the dizziest creature he'd ever seen, and it didn't make sense. One minute he was stern and the next his eyes were rolling around in his head.

"Where you tikes headed?" the bird asked again. "Bet you're going berry pickin'."

"How would you know? Maybe it's berry pickin' day, and maybe it's not."

"Why, we been watching ya. That's how we know. Sometimes you pick 'em by the lily patch, and other times you pick 'em by the stream. I think they grow sweeter by the stream."

"Oh my!" Emma exclaimed. "They've been watching us! And anyway, who's *we*?" Emma's eyes narrowed as she looked up at the cockatoo.

"Why, me and me lads, of course." He pointed his wing at the tree limbs overhead. With that, five more birds stepped out from

HECTOR

behind the foliage. They bobbed their heads, flashing their beautiful feathers. Black eyes rolled around in their heads, making them all appear just as silly as the first bird. They glanced silently at one another, and then burst into raucous, cackling laughter.

Erik looked up at the cockatoos and noticed the leader of the group holding his feathered wing over his mouth, whispering loudly to his pals, "Follow me lead, boys." He glided noiselessly down past the kowaries and snatched Emma's basket from the ground behind her in his beak. Back up to the trees the bird went with the basket. As he hung the basket on a high branch, another bird flew down with a great deal of encouragement from his mates.

"Hey!" Emma shouted. "Stop that, you silly birds!"

The second bird swooped down, repeating what the first one had done, this time grabbing Erik's abandoned basket.

Erik's fright at their dangerous encounter with the snake was quickly turning to anger at the birds' behavior. "Now get out of here." Erik waved his paws in the air. "We'll have nothing to do with you thieving birds."

The heckling from the trees began in earnest.

"Got ya!"

"Caught you off guard, didn't we?" another bird called.

"Should always be aware of what's happening around you, little ones," squawked another of the bunch.

The first heckler added in, "You're much too small to walk these woods alone."

"How about some security? Looks to me like you'd benefit," commented the bird who'd scared off the brown snake.

Erik seethed. The birds scurried back and forth on the limbs above them, laughing and holding their bellies with their wings. Erik thought if he waited a minute or two, maybe they'd fall right out of the trees. As if thoughts could make it so, the leader of the group—who laughed so hard he could barely catch his breath—stepped the wrong way and fell toward the forest floor. Just when it looked as though he might crash to the ground, he spread his wings and landed on two claws facing Erik. With the most foolish look on his face, the bird said, "I'm Hector. Glad to meet you, cobber." Erik and Hector scrutinized each other. It was difficult to tell what the cockatoo saw with those eyes since they didn't stay in one place for very long. Erik couldn't stay angry. The bird looked too ridiculous. He started to laugh, and then so did Hector.

"I'm Hector." The bird introduced himself again with a triple-bob of his head. He was very odd, but the bird had been there for them when they needed him.

Erik nodded to the bird in return. "Thank you for helping us. I do hope we meet again sometime. But... before we leave, do you think we could have our baskets back?"

Hector let out a loud amused squawk as his mates nudged the baskets free from the tree.

"Just a lesson, little wingless ones. You shouldn't be messin' with us. We have powerful skills."

"Skills?" Erik asked. "What kind of skills?"

"Well, if we wanted to we could bring the fog around you, or make it rain on your heads. Couldn't we, mates?" He nodded to his buddies in the branches above.

"I don't believe that for a minute," Erik said. "Show me."

"I don't feel like it right now," Hector said indignantly.

"Yeah, that's 'cause you can't!" Erik turned and began walking away when he felt something wet drop on the back of his head. When he turned back, Hector's pals were laughing uproariously, and Hector had a trail of drool hanging from his beak. "Spit doesn't count as rain, Hector!" Erik said angrily. Then he turned back and continued on down the path toward Calder Bridge, determined not to look back at the dizzy birds.

"We will meet again." Hector bobbed his head up and down. "Right, boys?" He looked up into the trees where his five companions sat, all nodding their heads in unison. "Right, mate!"

Hector took flight and his group of birds followed him quickly into the distance.

"Well, that was weird," Emma, said as she gathered up the fallen baskets. "I've never seen the likes of them."

"Gang-gang birds!" Erik said offhandedly. "These guys are the goofiest bunch of birds I've ever seen. They are always making up stories about mist, rain and fog." He paused and said, "Still, we were lucky they happened along. I wasn't certain how to deal with that snake. I don't want to run into him again!" He shook his head as he walked and waved to the two puggles, urging them to keep up. "Don't lag behind any more, ya puggles. We want no more trouble, and I don't wanna be telling your mum that you were eaten by a snake or some other nasty creature."

The two young echidna babes looked at each other, eyes wide, and ran fast to close the distance between themselves and the kowaries.

Emma was the first to spot the blue and red bridge through the bushes. "The bridge is almost as shiny as when we first painted it! And look at all the berries!" She spun with her arms outstretched motioning to all the fruit laden bushes. "We'll have such a feast this evening."

Emma and Erik placed their baskets on the ground and began picking the berries. For each berry they put into their baskets, one went into their mouths. They were so juicy and sweet that they couldn't resist eating them. Several hours later, with their baskets and bellies full, the two kowaries and puggle babes started on the path homeward. The excitement caused by the snake and the cockatoos had faded into memory, and the comfort of their cozy homes was their only pressing thought.

CHAPTER 2

Edlyn Grassley was chatting with Aida Whateley in front of the old tingle tree when she spied the bilby monk approaching from the top of the path. It had been some time since Bede's last visit, but his wisdom, kindness, and healing skills made him always welcome in their little village. Bede's light-brown fur gleamed in the afternoon sun, and he waved hello. Stopping and leaning heavily on his rough-hewn staff he smiled warmly.

"Good day, Mrs. Grassley. Good day, Mrs. Whateley." The wandering monk nodded. "How are you lovely ladies today? It's another sunny day in Digby. Summer is such a pleasant time of the year, don't you think?"

"Good day to you, Bede," both women said in unison.

"It's been a while since your last visit," Edlyn said.

"Yes, it certainly has." Glancing behind the women, he asked, "Where are the young ones? I don't see the twins or their two little puggle shadows. I'm sure they've grown since my last visit to Digby."

"My two have gone berry picking, and we're certain the puggles are following along," Edlyn said nodding in Aida's direction. Aida smiled back. "And, yes, they are indeed growing quickly. The twins enjoy watching over the young puggles. It makes them feel as though they are doing something important, which they are."

"Yes, your twins are maturing into fine kowaries. Their father would be proud." A thoughtful expression crossed Bede's face. He hesitated a moment, then continued in his usual bubbly manner, "Berry picking! Did you say, *berry picking*? How wonderful!" His stomach rumbled loudly.

"I am hoping they will pick enough berries to serve with sweet cream this evening." Edlyn said with a smile, as a look of expectation crossed Bede's face.

"How long will you stay in Digby?" Aida asked.

Bede turned to Aida and scratched his snout. "I'm not sure, but I have some news." His stomach interrupted him as it rumbled again. "Oh my, I think I'm a bit peckish," he said with a grin. "I've traveled such a long way, and I'd really love a cup of tea and a bite to eat."

Edlyn noticed the tired look on his face, and exclaimed, "Oh, where are our manners? You must stay, even for a short while - a cup of tea, a bit of cheese. Please come in, and rest a moment. We can talk more."

"Yes," Bede said, "we can talk more. Cheese, did you say cheese? Oh, I do recall that fine blue cheese that Mrs. Kenwick makes. Do you have some of that?" He licked his lips expectantly. "And the children, when do you think they will be home with the berries?"

Edlyn ushered him through her front door at the base of the tingle tree. The quaint living room glowed with warm sunshine that filtered in through a small window over the kitchen sink. Cheerful paintings of family decorated the wooden walls. A vase filled with colorful flowers adorned a small table surrounded by four tiny chairs, and a ladder led up to a loft bedroom. Dried cooking herbs hung from beams above the mantle.

Edlyn crossed the room and stopped before the warm glow emanating from the fireplace. She lifted a kettle and hung it from a hook over the burning logs.

"Tea in just a moment," she said as she placed a tray with cups, saucers, a honey jar, and creamer on a tiny table in front of the sofa.

"Wonderful, wonderful," Bede said, rubbing his paws together in anticipation. He turned to Aida, who arranged herself on the seat beside him. She primly straightened her apron as she settled down. "Aida, tell me more about those little puggles of yours." Bede said, as he patted her paw.

"They are just fine. Thank you for asking. Quite the handful at times, I must admit, but they keep me young. And, of course, Erik and Emma are truly a blessing. I do declare, I don't know how I would do it all if it weren't for those two young kowaries watching over my little ones." Aida's little paws moved quickly as she spoke. Edlyn smiled at her from across the room, and Bede nodded his head as he listened attentively.

Edlyn retrieved the kettle from above the fire, walked to the sofa, and poured hot water into the teapot to steep. The wonderful aroma of tea wafted into the air, as she perched in a small yellow chair opposite her company. She waved toward the paper-strewn desk that stood against the far wall. "Don't mind the mess. Those are the things Farrell was working on the day before he . . . he left," she stuttered. "No sense cleaning it, as he'll be back before we know it."

Bede caught Edlyn's gaze. "Have you had any word?"

Edlyn picked up the teapot and filled three cups with the steaming brew. "No, not yet. But Bede, you have known Farrell since he was a young kowari." She stopped what she was doing and gazed across at her friends. With a desperate and pleading look in her eyes, she said, "You know how resourceful he is. We must have faith that we will see him again. I'm sure I would feel it if anything untoward happened to my mate."

Bede smiled. "Yes, of course. He is one of the brightest and strongest kowaries I have ever known. If anyone can overcome a bad situation, it is definitely Farrell!"

"Bede is absolutely right about that, dear." Aida enthusiastically pointed her paw directly at Edlyn. "You know he's right. We both do. A fine kowari neighbor, he is. We couldn't ask for better." She lifted a cracker covered with fine blue cheese and popped it into her mouth.

"There is much turmoil in the wild wood," Bede said as he quickly grabbed a cracker and munched it down. Then he fell silent as he looked solemnly at Edlyn and Aida. "I'm afraid I've come with some bad news. Dragon lizards have attacked Acadia Abbey. Villages and towns within the borders of Sunderland have been burned." Edlyn watched as fear rose on Aida's face. "There is a shifting in the land - a movement within the wild wood." He rubbed his furrowed brow. Edlyn recognized the tone of dread in his voice. "There are sinister creatures about." The sun slipped behind the clouds and the room went dark. Fear crept up Edlyn's spine like a dozen spiders, as silence engulfed them. The sun appeared again shining, and shone in on them. Bede looked up at Edlyn and Aida. "Now, now," he assured them both, his paw raised in front of him. "Digby is quite a long way from the abbey, and it is tucked deep in the forest, but the villagers here need to be warned. That is my purpose, to deliver this warning."

"Of course," Edlyn said gravely. "We'll help you get the word out."

A sudden ruckus outside the house caused Edlyn to open the front door. Ackley and Amber were at the top of the path, teasing one another. Erik and Emma grinned as they watched the two puggles.

"I'm first." Ackley taunted. His stubby legs moved as quickly as they could carry him, while his spikes trembled on his head. Amber followed him, and in an effort to catch up, she moved too close to Ackley. Her little feet tangled with her brother's. The two young echidnas fell to the ground and rolled down the path together, ending with a loud thump at the base of the tingle tree.

Amber hopped to her feet first. "You, you—" She pointed a stumpy little digit at her brother. "You, trip-tripped me. I know you did!"

"Me?" Ackley stared at his little sister in disbelief, his paw resting on his chest. "You're ridiculous. I ought to pull your spikes out one at a time until you beg for mercy!"

"Now, now, that's just about enough." Aida stood in the doorway looking down at her two little echidnas. "To your rooms, quickly, before I conjure up a punishment for you both!"

"Aw, Mum!" both babes said together.

"No arguments. I won't have it. You've had a good time today, I'm sure, but the fun is over. Let's go, the both of you." Aida turned to Edlyn and Bede, a concerned look on her face. "What will you do now, Bede?"

"I will go to the center of Digby, meet with the elders, and deliver my warning." Bede answered. He turned and walked over to Erik and Emma, patting each of them on the head. Then his fatherly mood disappeared as a troubled look crossed his face. "These are dark times," he muttered. He moved slowly on, staff in paw. A feeling of eminent danger passed between the twins and their mother. It was a feeling not even the prospect of berries and cream could overcome.

BEDE, THE TRAVELING MONK

CHAPTER 3

E rik placed his basket of berries on the table and looked around his home. He supposed he'd be in Digby forever. And since his father had gone missing, Erik's dreams of seeking adventure in the wild world had come to a screeching halt. Leaving was becoming a frightening thought, not an adventure, and the courage he once had was flagging. His thoughts went back to his father. He hadn't been missing long, but it seemed like forever. He sighed, as he gazed at the fishing poles leaning in the corner near the fireplace.

"What are you thinking, dear?" his mother asked, smiling at him.

"I was thinking of papa," he said in a whisper. "I miss him."

Edlyn walked up to her son and hugged him tightly. "No worries, Erik. He'll be back. You'll see." She turned to Emma. "Isn't that right, sweetheart?" She moved to the sink and busied herself with the dishes. "Of course I'm right," she murmured to herself. "Farrell will be back."

Erik sensed a change in the weather. He went to the open window and looked out. The skies had darkened to a steel gray. The wind had kicked up. Leaves on the trees were inverted, revealing their silvery undersides, shaking as they clung desperately to the branches.

"Looks like there's a storm brewing," he said to his mum. Leaning out the window, Erik watched as neighbors scurried about the small hamlet, securing loose items, and seeking shelter from the oncoming tumult. "Everyone's preparing for this one. But it's strange, mum. There's no rain." He pulled his head in and closed the shutters tightly. "I do hope that Bede is safely indoors," he added. Candlelight bathed the room as the natural light of the day was shut out. The sound of the crackling fire intensified and strange shadows danced eerily on the walls.

Edlyn waved her paw at her son. "It's just an early summer storm, and I'm certain Bede will find shelter at Digby Inn."

The air bristled with electricity. Edlyn turned to Erik. The concern on her face made him shudder. None of them had ever seen day turn into night this quickly. The wind howled, and thunder shook the branches of their home, but not a drop of rain could be heard falling against the bark.

A sudden clap of thunder caused the small family to stop and look at one another with shocked expressions. In the stillness following the thunder, Erik noticed a teacup vibrating on the mantelpiece. Moving to catch the cup before it fell to the floor, a brown streak shot by his face, brushing his cheek as it passed. Leaning away from the blur, he lost his balance, falling against the table and sending baskets of berries spinning into the air. The teacup crashed to the ground, and berries scattered in every direction as a frightening shadow crossed before him.

A high-pitched scream from his sister alerted him that this was no simple shadow. He jumped quickly to his paws, his jaws open, ready to defend himself and his family. It was the brown snake they had encountered in the forest.

Erik stopped; his feet froze to the floor as he watched the snake turn to look at him. The reptile raised its body off the floor as high as it could in an effort to intimidate Erik. Its fangs dripped with venom, and its forked tongue flicked in and out of its mouth tasting the air. Erik knew that to make one false move could mean the worst. The snake slithered toward him, and Erik slowly moved back, keeping his distance from the venomous creature.

"Ssso, you think you can challenge me!" The snake spat its words at Erik. "You have made one mistake today. Don't make another! I am here to teach you a lesson." He coiled himself tightly, staring directly into Erik's eyes. "So sure of yourself. Think you can meddle in everyone's business. I will put you in your place!"

The snake struck out, and Erik dove to the floor to avoid the deadly bite. The snake's strike missed Erik completely, but his fangs found a mark. Erik watched in horror as they sank deep into his mother's shoulder. He heard Emma shriek as his mum collapsed to the floor. Anger consumed him. He flung himself at the snake, grabbed hold of it just beneath its head and shook it mercilessly. The snake's tail whipped up and curled about Erik's neck, tightening, choking. *I must not let go*, he thought. They dropped to the floor and rolled in a mutual death grip. Even after the snake had gone limp, and it was clear that Erik had killed it, he continued to strangle it. Tears rolled down his cheeks as he roared repeatedly, "My mother, my mother! You've bitten my mother!"

"Let go of him!" Emma shouted at Erik. "He's dead! You need to listen to me. Mum is hurt. She needs you. Please stop!"

Erik opened his paws slowly and watched as the lifeless snake fell limply to the floor. "He was trying to strike me and hit Mum instead." He looked up at Emma with sorrowful eyes. "This is my fault," he whimpered.

"Don't think about that now. We have to do something right away. We have to get help."

Erik stood up and ran to his mother. Carefully, he lifted her head and placed it into his lap. He could see that she was barely conscious as he spoke softly to her, "Don't worry, Mum. We'll get help. It will be all right. I promise."

Edlyn opened her eyes and gazed at Erik. "Get Bede. He will know what to do." Her eyes closed as she slipped into unconsciousness.

Wiping away his tears, Erik turned quickly to Emma. He had to be strong, no matter how helpless he felt.

"You stay here. I'll go find Bede. Hopefully he's still at the inn."

"Hurry, Erik!" Emma yelled at him as he raced out the door.

Erik ran out into the storm and raced to the center of the hamlet. The wind blew angrily and leaves rushed by him in the whistling air. He covered his face with his arm as he leaned into the fierce storm. Soon the inn came into view. He sprinted across the town square and entered the inn with a gust of air and a cluster of flying leaves swirling about him.

"I need to speak to Bede," Erik cried as he ran into the dining room. "Is he here?" He glanced quickly about the room and saw Bede sitting at a table in front of the fireplace.

"Erik! What is it, my boy?" Startled, Bede grabbed his staff in one paw, as Erik ran toward him. He rose abruptly from his chair, sending it crashing to the floor.

"We need you, Bede." Erik gripped Bede's paw tightly. "Mum's been bitten by a brown snake. Come quickly!"

"Oh my, oh my!" Bede headed toward the door with Erik close behind. "We must lose no time, Erik." He looked deeply into Erik's eyes for a moment, and said, "No worries, young man. It will be alright."

As if it recognized their urgency, the wind pushed them along.

CHAPTER 4

E vening was closing in when Erik and Bede arrived home. Aida had moved Mum to her bed. She was bent over Edlyn, applying cold compresses to her forehead.

"She's running a high fever," she said. "And she's trembling with chills. We need to move her closer to the fire to help keep her warm." She nodded at Bede and Erik, and then looked at Emma. "Emma and I have disposed of that disgusting snake." She shook her head sadly. "What a terrible tragedy," she sighed.

"I'm so frightened, Erik," Emma choked out.

"Try not to worry. Bede knows what to do."

Bede made his way to Edlyn's side. He felt for her pulse and placed his paw on her brow.

The small group gathered round, waiting expectantly to hear what Bede would say. The silence in the room was deafening as the rainless storm continued to rage outside. With his eyes shut, Bede took several steps away from Edlyn's bedside. He stopped and brought his staff down to the floor with a loud thump. Standing in the center of the room with eyes closed, he raised his staff into mid-air.

Erik's gaze darted to Emma and then to Bede. *What's happening?* Everyone stood motionless, staring at Bede as he spun his walking staff perpendicular to the floor and brought it down again - this time louder than the first. Thump!

In the glow of the candlelight, Bede spun his staff once more, raising it as high into the air as his arm would allow. He slammed the staff to the floor for a third time. The sound vibrated the floor and paintings on the walls shook, threatening to fall.

Suddenly, the winds of the raging storm subsided. Everything became eerily silent and the atmosphere grew as still as death, both inside the house and out. The forest was quiet except for the screech of an owl.

Bede opened his eyes. Looking around the room, he gazed into the frightened faces of the friends gathered there. "He's here," he said, sighing with relief.

As he walked through the front door, the storm clouds cleared, the winds turned into a gentle breeze, and the moon could be seen in the night sky. He looked over his shoulder, and motioned for everyone to follow. Curiosity overcame Erik's fear, and he fell in step behind Bede with Emma at his side. In the small clearing in front of their arbor home, a yellow mist churned in a circular motion moving from the tops of the trees toward the ground. Its light filled the clearing, wrapping them in a warm glow. As the mist settled, the largest numbat Erik had ever seen appeared at its center. Once again, the eerie sound of an owl echoed through the forest, and two glowing eyes appeared on a branch above the numbat. The numbat stood tall on his hind legs, his thin face ending sharply in a small black nose. His eyes were banded with stripes of black and white fur and a white robe fell around him. He held a rough-hewn wooden staff in his right paw.

Erik reached for his sister, drew her near, and whispered in her ear, "He looks like a kowari, only much bigger and more regal."

Emma couldn't take her eyes off the numbat. "He seems to be a part of the mist itself," she said.

"Aldon, my teacher," Bede said. He bowed and approached the majestic numbat. "It has been too long since we last spoke."

"Bede, my dear friend, it has indeed been too long." When the numbat spoke, his voice was gentle, warm and kind.

"We have called upon you, Guardian of the Forest, because we are in great need," Bede said. "Edlyn, the mother of these young kowaries, has been bitten by a brown snake. She lies unconscious within." Bede raised his arm and pointed to the tingle tree.

Aldon smiled down upon the twins. "Well then, how can I refuse? It appears your mother needs the both of you now more than ever." Aldon bent toward Erik and Emma. "You must be strong and brave." He straightened, stretching himself to his full height. "For your mother to survive, she must have medicine. A special medicine that will require several ingredients, all of which you must gather."

43

ALDON

Erik couldn't believe his ears. His jaw dropped and he looked to Bede for answers.

"What does he mean by this?"

"Just what he says, my dear boy."

Aldon shifted his staff from one paw to the other and pointed it slowly at Erik and Emma. "The ingredients can only be found in the Wild Wood, beyond the red and blue-painted bridge." He gazed into the dark forest. "You will gather the ingredients, and then you will bring them back here." Aldon sighed deeply, bent once more toward the twins, and solemnly said, "Is this understood?"

"Us?" Erik raised his paw, and pointed at his sister then himself. "You think we will be able to do this?"

"Of course you will, Erik," Aldon said. "You and your sister will work together on this quest and complete it."

"I-I, well, we," Erik stuttered while his sister stood beside him, totally speechless.

Erik looked up at Aldon. His feelings were so jumbled. He was frightened, afraid for himself and his mother. He was concerned for his sister, and at the same time he knew what he needed to do in spite of all his fears. Finally, his gaze rested on Aldon.

"Of course, sir. We will do whatever it takes to save our mum. But we don't know how to begin."

Erik felt his sister move closer to him, seeking reassurance. He did his best to stand tall, to portray a strong manner, so she would have confidence in him. He worried about his own confidence and courage. He must not let Emma see his doubts.

"Ahh, my young man, I can see the fear in your eyes." Aldon peered down at Erik, pointing his finger at him. "You believe that you do not have the courage or skills necessary to accomplish the task before you. But, indeed, you have all the qualities you need and one more advantage that you may not recognize, even at this moment." Aldon's paw waved over their heads, pointing to masked owl. "Why, look here, you have friends. You can count Oswin as one of them." Oswin shuffled across the tree limb, stopping directly above Erik and Emma. He leaned down to the young kowaries, and with a low chirp, he inspected them. Satisfied, he strode back up the branch and took up his position above Aldon.

"Oswin, and others will be there to help you along the way." Aldon's soothing voice calmed Erik and gave him courage.

"You will travel to the land of the graveyard termites and their magnetic mounds. After you gather dust from those mounds, you will then travel to Wingecarribee Swamp where you will gather a blossom of loosestrife." He paused a moment before continuing. "Finally, you will journey to the Pinnacles Desert. There you will gather petals from the desert rose."

Erik looked up into the numbat's serious expression. "How will we find our way?"

Aldon took a pouch hanging from his belt. He opened his paw, and the pouch floated down, landing gently at Bede's feet. "This contains all that you will need to make your journey."

A warm wind blew, and the yellow mist began to rise. Aldon's robe rustled with the leaves on the ground around him, and he began to fade from sight. As he slowly became a part of the yellow mist, he said, "We will wait here for your return."

OSWIN

"But how much time will we—" Before Erik finished his question, the yellow mist surrounded Aldon, and he began to fade.

"Do not worry, Erik, do your best, travel as quickly as you can." Just an outline of the great numbat remained as he said, "The poison in your mum's blood has been slowed. She will sleep deeply until you return."

Soon, only the masked owl remained. He sat on the branch above their heads and let out an ear-splitting screech. With that the mist evaporated completely, leaving no trace of the regal numbat.

Erik looked up at Oswin, who was now leaning out from the limb as far as he could. His powerful claws gripped the branch as his head swiveled back and forth; his round yellow eyes reflected the moonlight.

"I think he likes you," Bede chuckled.

"That's a good thing, right?" Erik said hesitantly.

"Yes, my dear boy, that's a good thing."

Erik and Emma sighed with relief as they looked at each other.

"I suggest we go back inside now. We will see what it is Aldon has left for us and discuss what we need to do to help your mum." He began walking to the front door. The two young kowaries following close behind.

Bede settled at the table, placing the pouch before him.

"Now, let's see what we have here." Bede set the pouch down on the table and began to empty it. "There is a map, a small dagger and two quivers of arrows with bows. And here's a list of the three items we need for the potion. He glanced across the table to the siblings. "The Wild Wood is a dangerous place, but the termite mounds are not too far. The mounds will be your first stop." He smoothed out the list on the table with his paw, and clearing his throat, he continued. "We will need two types of flowers; loosestrife from Wingecarribee Swamp, and a Desert Rose from the Pinnacles Desert." He finished with a flourish of his paw. "Now that doesn't seem too bad. We'll get this done in no time. We'll leave as soon as possible. You can practice your archery on the way. I am sure your father taught you well."

"Yes, father did teach us..." Erik hesitated. "But, I'm not concerned about that. What do you mean by 'we'?" Erik asked.

"Bede," Emma said sweetly, "you can't make a trip like this. I don't mean to offend you, but aren't you a bit old to do this? And we will need to travel quickly." She glanced at her brother for support.

Bede waved her comment off with his paw. "No offense taken, Emma. I insist. You will need my help."

"Bede, I think you will be needed here, with Mum." Erik pointed across the room where Edlyn lay unconscious. "You must have medicine for her, to keep her well enough until we get back."

"True, true," Bede said, quietly nodding his head. "But I will not take no for an answer. I will go with you and that is the last of it. Aida will stay with your Mum."

Emma and Erik stared down in silence at the items on the table. "Ok," Erik said quietly. "If that's the way it must be." He took the pouch and returned the map, dagger, bows and arrows, and list into it. "I guess this ends the discussion. We will leave as soon as we can."

THE SWORD OF DEMELZA

"Yes," Bede agreed. "Just give me a moment to speak with Aida. I will tell her what she needs to do to keep your Mum comfortable until we return." He rose from the table and walked to Aida, who was sitting in a chair next to Edlyn. Taking a seat across from her, he began to chat.

"We'll be waiting outside," Erik said as he headed to the door with Emma. Erik shot a sly look at his sister as they went out.

CHAPTER 5

Erik walked quickly away from the house. Emma hurried after him, trying to keep up.

"Slow down, Erik," she said sternly.

Erik came to a stop behind a dense shrub, where they would be hidden from view of the house.

"What are you doing?" Emma asked angrily.

"We're leaving. That's what we're doing."

"I don't understand."

Erik gazed out into the dark forest considering what needed to be done. Trees stretched against the night sky twisting in the fitful breeze. Their arm-like branches seemed to claw at the air with bony fingers. Emma stood beside her brother, concern evident in her hazel eyes.

"We need to leave soon," Erik said firmly. "I know that Aldon said that mum will stay in a deep sleep, but we don't know how long. We can't waste time, and Bede will slow us down. He's too old to make this journey. And anyway, he needs to stay here. He will keep Mum safe until we return."

"You want to just go?" She hesitated, searching her brother's face for answers. "Just like that? I don't know, Erik. I'm not sure if Bede..."

"Emma, maybe you need to stay here." Erik looked down at the ground and shook his head. "I mean, if you're so unsure... The Wild Wood is dangerous."

Emma's mouth opened and her arms dropped to her side. "But, Aldon said we need to do this together."

"I know what he said. I'm just thinking about what would be best." He began pacing back and forth in front of his sister. "This is serious. Who knows what type of trouble is out there waiting for us?"

"There's trouble *here*." Tears welled up in her eyes as she spoke. "Look what just happened to Mum." She wiped a tear away. "This will not be easy, but we can do this together. There will always be challenges." She took a deep breath to calm herself. "I know you have always wanted to set out on your own, to leave Digby. This may not have been what you hoped for, but it seems to me we have to put our own plans aside now, and think about what we need to do for Mum."

"You don't understand. It will be hard enough just trying to take care of myself."

"I see. You think I'll be a burden." She grasped Erik by the arm, forcing him to look into her eyes. "I'll just get in your way. Is that what you mean?"

"No, no, that's not—"

"Erik Grassley, mind what you say." She shook her finger at him. "I may be small and a bit timid at times, but she's my mum too. Aldon says we have to do this together." She stomped her foot to the ground, and folded her arms across her chest. "I'm going. End of conversation."

He had never seen such defiance and resolve in his sister before. He looked down at her. She was so small, at least a head shorter. He paused for a moment as he made his decision. "It's settled then."

She unfolded her arms, and wrapped them around her brother, resting her head on his chest. "It will be all right. I promise." He felt her warm breath against his fur as she spoke.

"Ok, it's agreed," Erik said reluctantly. He was worried, but he would keep those concerns to himself. "We'll just leave. We'll travel light and fast." He patted his vest pocket, "I've got the map," he said. "And I've got the dagger." He grasped the pommel of the small knife at his waist and wrapped his bow and quiver over his chest. He handed the other bow and quiver to Emma.

"Good," Emma nodded. "We'll gather food as we go."

They took one last look down the path toward their home and turned. Calder Bridge was ahead, waiting for them to cross it.

THE SWORD OF DEMELZA

Erik stopped when the bridge came into sight. "This is it, Emma." He let out a deep sigh, feeling as though he was about to take a leap off a high cliff. His life's plan did not include leaving Digby this way. He rubbed his forehead with his paw, considering the task before them. He turned to Emma, and as if she could read his mind, she held her paw out and he took it in his.

They stood for a moment beneath the trees. A full moon drenched the bridge in light. With one step they would be crossing it. With a few more they would be on the other side of the stream, and would enter the wild wood. It was then that Erik noticed movement in the underbrush along the path behind them.

Erik peered down the path. "Come out," he shouted as he took a step toward the moving leaves. "I see you!"

With heads down, and paws clasped tightly in front of them, Ackley and Amber stepped out from their hiding place.

"What do you think you're doing? And how long have you been standing there?" Erik jabbed his finger at the air like a dagger in front of Ackley's face.

Ackley kept his gaze to the ground and nervously rearranged the leaves beneath his feet.

"Nothin', Erik. We doing nothin' here."

"We just kinda walking here," Amber added. She fidgeted, pulling at the flowered suspenders of her overalls as she spoke, looking from her brother to Erik.

"Well, go back home. It's late. You little puggles should be in bed at this hour."

Ackley turned to go, then suddenly spun back around and looked up at Erik. "We could help you and Emma, we could. We can gather food and watch out for bad critters. I knows how to read a map. And I got this here super slingshot!" Ackley raised himself up on his toes, trying his best to look tall, all the while patting the slingshot tucked into his pocket.

Erik looked at Emma, "The little blighters have been spying on us!"

Emma could not help but giggle. "Well, like Aida says, 'they are a handful.'"

Erik glared at Ackley, but the little puggle's eyes never left Erik's steely stare. Erik looked to Amber. She was nodding, agreeing with each statement her brother had made.

"No way." Erik waved his hand in finality. "What we have to do is dangerous. We cannot be responsible for two puggles." He walked away. "You two puggles go home!" he shouted over his shoulder.

"Are you coming, Emma? We're wasting time," he said. He looked back and saw his sister drop to one knee and talk with the puggles. They nodded their heads in unison, seeming to listen intently to what Emma said. After hugging the two babes, the puggles turned and headed back home, waving good-bye as they went. Erik sighed with relief.

He looked across the bridge. The forest was dark and mysterious to the two young kowaries, but they had a purpose now, and they were determined. After one last look over their shoulders, followed by a knowing look at each other, the two walked side by side across the red and blue bridge over Calder Stream and into the wild wood.

The door at the base of the tingle tree opened and Bede walked out. The empty pouch lay on the ground near the front door. "Oh my," he muttered to himself, "I should have expected this." He looked up into the tingle tree. The stately owl sat on the branch above him. "Watch over them, Oswin. Keep them safe from harm."

The owl blinked once, and spreading his wings wide launched himself from the branch and disappeared into the night sky above the hamlet of Digby.

CHAPTER 6

C ynric knew Flitch was close. Very close. He had to keep moving. Sounds of the forest reverberated in his ears. A loon's mournful cry, the chirping cicadas, and the breeze racing through the tops of the trees were like a chorus whispering: keep running, keep running. The thylacine closed in on him, growling *between great rasp-like breaths. He anticipated dagger-like teeth sinking into his neck. He stumbled for a second as Devon squirmed in his arms, then, regaining his feet, ran faster than before.*

"I can run, Papa. I can run."

"You . . . will . . . not," Cynric panted. The kit was strong and fleet of foot, yet Cynric knew Devon was much too young

to outrun the evil thylacine. This night began with one devastating loss; he would not survive another. It was then that Flitch pounced on him. The two animals rolled together hitting logs, rocks, and tree stumps as they tumbled over the ground. Cynric collided into a rock causing Devon to fly off his back. Cynric quickly leapt to his feet and lashed out against his foe. He attacked with all his might, trying to bite the thylacine in the throat. The two enemies glared as they circled each other, baring their fangs. Flitch struck out again. His claws cut into Cynric's chest, leaving deep furrows. Cynric fell back, striking his head on a large, jagged rock. Blackness enveloped him.

He opened his eyes and raised a paw to his throbbing head, wondering how much time had passed. His ear felt warm and wet, and he realized he was bleeding. He moaned and slowly rolled to his feet. Devon, where was Devon? He looked frantically about for his son. Devon was nowhere in sight. He closed his eyes, fell to his knees, and held his head in his paws as he rocked back and forth, crying softly to himself. How could he have let this happen? His leg was bruised, and he ached all over. He rolled onto his back and looked up into the night sky. His final thought, before he drifted into unconsciousness, was of his son. He must find Devon.

Cynric woke with a start. He had that dream again. A low roll of thunder rumbled outside. How many times must he re-live that awful night? His son, carried away from him by that grotesque demon. He shook his head in an effort to empty the dream from his thoughts. The familiar anger rose in him. His throat tightened as he clenched his fists. He looked around his chamber. The great bed was draped with red velvet; a goblet lay on its side on the table. One of the chairs was toppled over onto the floor. The leaded glass window was open, and the cool night air flowed through his room carrying the scents and sounds of an oncoming storm. His sword rested against the window ledge, the green stone of Demelza ensconced within its hilt. A single candle was lit, and the stone walls of his chamber glistened from the reflected light.

He was very tired, but he would not sleep again tonight for fear the dream would return. The dream haunted him. It summoned that dreadful night so long ago—the night he had lost his son and his mate. The memory consumed him and he could not let it go. He had become a wretched fox because of it. He dropped from his bed to the floor and walked across the chamber. Grabbing hold of the goblet from the table, he flung it into the fireplace. Slumping into a chair, he closed his eyes. A moment later, the sound of paws running down the corridor made Cynric look up.

"Sire." Braydon entered the chamber and saluted the fox. As captain of the guard, he was in charge of Cynric's quoll forces. He grasped the leather strap, which held his bow and a quill of arrows, across his chest. The powerful quoll stood as tall as Cynric. He wore a blue vest, and a broadsword was belted around his waist. Distinct white spots covered his reddish brown fur, running down the back of his head, and onto his long tail. His quick, intelligent eyes scanned the room.

Cynric rose to his feet, a snarl forming on his face. His great strength and presence were unquestionable. Combined with his bitterness and frightful wrath, the quoll knew that this fox, this King of Demelza, was not to be toyed with nor disobeyed. "What is it, Braydon?" Cynric roared.

The quoll stepped forward. "Sire, a small group of bilbies waits at the gate. They are asking for protection from the oncoming storm."

"Storm?"

"Yes, sire. The thunder is coming closer by the minute, and the winds have kicked up considerably. We expect it will be quite wild tonight."

"We have no obligation to protect or care for anyone other than ourselves." His voice boomed and echoed against the walls of his chamber. "Let them find shelter elsewhere!" Cynric turned on his heels and walked toward the window. The quoll hesitated for a moment. Cynric spun rapidly around and glowered at him.

"Do as I say!" he shouted.

"Yes, sire, as you say."

Cynric watched Braydon walk away. He heard the low growl. He knew the quoll hated him, but that didn't matter. Braydon walked from the chamber, glaring once over his shoulder at Cynric as he left.

Braydon would have to refuse shelter to the bilbies. Now was not the time to anger the fox. As Braydon walked down the corridor, he thought of his brother. His brother had been a fine warrior, but he should never have opposed Cynric's will. If Braydon had been there, he was certain that he could have prevented the battle between the two. His brother would still be alive. Braydon's hatred for Cynric was strong but he would have to wait for the right moment to avenge his brother's death.

He saw the dim light of a torch approaching from the end of the hallway. It was Luella. She was a quoll who had the unenviable position of caring for and fulfilling the king's every whim. She tended to him every day, from his morning meal to his evening glass of elderberry wine. A young quoll, with deep golden-brown eyes, Braydon was fond of her and concerned for her safety. She walked toward Braydon, her pink tipped claws holding tightly to the torch. Cynric was at ease with her, and Braydon assumed that the king confided in her. Nevertheless, he felt her responsibilities to Cynric were a heavy burden.

"How is Cynric?" Luella asked.

"He's his old miserable self. There's nothing further that can be done for him this evening. Unfortunately, I must go down to the gatehouse. Cynric has refused a request for shelter. I must turn the bilbies out into the storm."

Luella reached out and touched Braydon's arm, her soft touch easing the anger raging inside him.

"Somehow this must stop, Luella. Are we not all fellow inhabitants of this forest? Should we not care for one another?" He released a breath in frustration and turned away from her. "Ah, I don't know what I'm saying. I'm becoming a tired old quoll."

"Oh, Braydon, that's not true." Luella moved to face Braydon and she smiled up at him. "You're right, we should be good to one another, but these are trying times. I believe there is much more to Cynric than what you see on the surface." She reached up and softly touched his muzzle. "Trust me, Braydon. We will all see one day. I am sure." She turned to go, and Braydon reached out to stop her for a moment more.

"Will you be all right?" he asked as he leaned toward her. "I mean, you're obviously headed to his chamber. Do you want me to go with you? He's in a foul mood."

"I'll be fine, Braydon. Don't worry, my dear friend. I'll see you in the morning." With a quick smile, Luella continued on her way, and Braydon watched as she melted into the shadows, the light from the torch disappearing as she turned a corner.

CYNRIC

CHAPTER 7

E rik stood on a small outcropping of rock. He and Emma had left Digby and were well into their journey.

They had traveled without rest the night before and through the next day. Now the sun sat low in the sky. Night was approaching. Dappled light fell through the leaves to the forest floor. Erik watched as Emma paused on the path to catch her breath. He knew she wanted to be strong, wanted him to be proud of her. He was concerned and afraid for her; there was no doubt about that. But, he knew they were in this together, and although she was tiny, he had faith in her.

"We've covered a lot of ground," he said to Emma. "The termite mounds should be just ahead." Erik was studying the map, when a sudden movement from the underbrush caught his attention.

"Emma, come here. Stand beside me."

Emma's ears perked up and she looked around as she scrambled up the rocks and stood next to him. "What's wrong?" she whispered as she peered into the woods.

He scanned the dense undergrowth of the forest, looking for movement. "I don't know what it is, but we have to move. Now!"

The two kowaries jumped from the rocks to the forest path and began to run. They scampered swiftly, glancing over their shoulders at the path behind them. Erik was certain they were being followed, or hunted. His instincts took over as he reached out a paw and grabbed his sister's to help speed her along. He knew he must not allow his fears to get the best of him. They ran toward a large fallen tree and crawled into the old trunk, settling quietly in the relative safety of the darkness within.

"We'll hide here for a while," Erik said. He took a quick look around and decided that he had chosen a good place to rest. "I'm not sure what's out there, but I think we'll be safe here."

Emma merely nodded as she sat beside her brother.

Through a thin crack in the log Erik surveyed the surrounding woods. The sun was going down and the forest was growing dim. A thin veil of mist began to gather along on the ground and around the low shrubs. Erik watched as it thickened before his eyes. A small breeze moved the mist and it churned as it enveloped the forest around them. Soon, Erik found that he could not see more than a few feet into the woods. Above their heads, leaves rustled in the trees. Then an ominous silence fell all around them. He pulled his sister closer, wrapping his arm around her as he raised a finger to his mouth. His lips moved without speaking as he mouthed the word *quiet*. Emma nodded once in acknowledgment.

They both looked up as something landed with a small thump on top of the log. A knothole in the roof allowed a view overhead. Erik kept an eye on the knothole, his ears twitching as he listened intently to the sound of footfalls moving up the log toward the opening. He removed his dagger from its sheath, preparing to defend Emma as the 'tap tap' drew closer.

One beady black eye surrounded by bright red feathers filled the small opening above the kowaries' heads. "Whatcha doin'?" a familiar voice whispered.

Erik released the breath he was holding. "Hector! Is that you?"

"Yes, sir, it's me. Last time I checked, indeed it was."

Feet skittered along the top of the log. Their visitor dropped to the ground, strutted inside, and stopped before the two siblings. The grand, yet goofy bird sat, smoothed his feathers, and made himself comfortable. He eyed the interior of their hiding place and nonchalantly said, "Nice place you got here. I like it."

"So glad you approve." Erik could hardly believe that Hector was there before him. "What are you doing here?"

"Ah, you're wondering what I'm doing here."

"Yes, that's what I just said. Didn't I?" Erik shook his head in disbelief.

Hector hesitated, and for a moment and his goofiness seemed to disappear. "Well," he began slowly, "me lads and I heard about your mum. We're sorry that we didn't stop the snake. We meant to follow him, but the storm confined us to the trees."

"It's not your fault, Hector," Erik said. "And the snake is the reason we're out here. You see, we're going to gather ingredients of all sorts. We need to make a potion to cure our Mum."

"Ah, I see," Hector said, bobbing his head at Erik and Emma "Where will you go?"

"We need to go as far as the Pinnacles Desert."

"Hmmm... I'm already quite a ways from me lads, but I promise you that we will fly out often to keep an eye on you." With one wing stretched out, Hector pointed out of the log. "I brought the mist for you."

"You did what? What are you talking about?"

Emma and Erik were stunned. "You really can bring the mist!" Emma whispered excitedly.

"Yes," Hector said, puffing up his chest. Bending down, the red feathered curl on the top of his head unfurled, curving toward the twins. "We really can bring the mist. It will cover your movement and protect you as you make your way through the forest."

Emma reached out and held Hector's face gently between her paws. "You're wonderful, Hector. Thank you!"

Erik wrapped his arm around his sister. He peered through the knothole over his head, watching the pale yellow mist swirling above. "I'd like to think we can do this alone," he said to Hector, shaking his head in wonder. "I didn't believe you, about the mist, I mean. You have saved us twice. Thank you so much!"

"You have friends. We will do our best to watch over you both." He stretched out his wing, touching Emma's cheek. "You must take great care now. The woods are filled with dangers, and creatures who will do their best to make mischief for you, or worse, do you great harm."

"I thought I heard something moving in the wood. I knew it! There is something out there. Do you know what it was?" Emma trembled as she spoke.

"It's a demon named Flitch. A thylacine. Its cruelty knows no bounds." A stern look crossed the bird's face. "It is pure evil and has no conscience. He hunts the smaller animals of the forest like a coward!"

The anger flashing in Hector's eyes stunned Erik. It was obvious that the creature he described was one to be feared.

"You're safe here for the time being," Hector explained. "Wait until the sun goes down before you set out again."

Erik nodded.

Hector moved toward the opening in the log, preparing to leave. "Stay safe, and travel as quickly as you can!" Hector waved his wing, accenting each word with his grey plumage.

Erik and Emma watched as Hector rose from the forest floor and disappeared into the mist.

CHAPTER 8

T he moon, a bright orange disc, rose just above the treetops. It seemed so close that one could imagine reaching out and touching it. The two young kowaries emerged from the shelter of the forest into a field of magnetic termite mounds. The collection of large mounds, homes to thousands of termites, rose from the earth like oversized tombstones. Erik and Emma had to cross the field. They would need to enter the forest on the other side to continue their journey. But crossing would mean being exposed, and the fear between the two young kowaries was palpable. Emma sat down beneath the leaf of a great fern, nervously fingering the buttons on her jacket as she looked up at her brother. Erik lowered himself to sit beside her. He looked into her eyes. They were wide with fear, reflecting the light of the moon.

"We've seen the signs all evening, Erik. Hector warned us. You know what I mean. Movement in the trees of the forest, the rustling in a nearby shrub," she whispered. "If we cross the field, whatever it is that has been following us will surely see us and get us."

"We can't turn back now. We've come too far to give up. We'll just stay here for a bit." Erik wrapped his arm around his sister. "You'll feel braver in a minute. We're well sheltered under these ferns, and we can use the mounds for cover as we cross the field."

"Erik?"

"What?"

"Do you think we're going to get home in time to help Mum?"

"Of course we will." He turned away from his sister, concerned that the uncertainty he felt would show on his face. "Mum is counting on us," he said. The termite mounds loomed before them. "I know we can do this!"

The sound of snapping twigs came from the forest behind them. Whatever was in the woods was headed in their direction. The termite mounds were just steps away.

"We must move now, Emma. Head for the first mound and we'll hide behind it."

Quickly, they crossed to the first mound and huddled with their backs against it, putting it between themselves and the woods. Erik's pulse raced as he held his sister close.

He listened intently.

"Nothing," he whispered. "Let's move on."

They put another mound between themselves and the woods. The silvery light of the moon cast thick tombstone-shaped shadows all around, creating a chilling scene.

Then, a low growl drifted on the night wind. Erik felt certain a shadow passed between two nearby mounds, only to disappear behind a third. He touched the hilt on his dagger and removed it slowly from its sheath. The moon withdrew as clouds scudded across its face, and a thin wispy fog crept along the ground through the field.

Erik froze with fear. Could it be the thylacine? The same one Hector had warned them of? If so, they were in mortal danger.

The answer came soon enough. The thin, angular face of the thylacine appeared from behind a nearby mound. Sharp teeth glistened and dripped with saliva, its tongue lolling from the side of its mouth. Orange eyes pierced the fog and came to rest on the two kowaries.

"How nice! Two little morsels for my midnight snack." The creature's deep, sinister voice rolled like thunder across the gap between them. "Come to die in the termite mound graveyard, did you? How appropriate." He took a step toward them, lowering his head as he moved.

Erik pushed his sister behind him. Brandishing his dagger before the face of the thylacine he said in his most threatening tone, "Don't come any closer or I'll—"

"Or you'll what?" Flitch snarled.

ERIK & EMMA

Erik stepped forward, stabbing quickly at Flitch. With one swipe of his paw, Flitch deflected Erik's arm. Erik was quick. He gripped his dagger tightly and jumped above Flitch's head. In one movement, he sliced through Flitch's ear and returned to the ground in front of Emma. The thylacine screamed in pain. Blood from the wound dripped into Flitch's eye, blurring his vision. He dropped his head to the ground and covered his eye with his paw. Erik saw his opportunity. He grabbed Emma by the wrist and they ran through the termite mounds toward the forest. As they ran, the air above them resonated with the high-pitched screech of an owl.

"Keep running!" Erik shouted at his sister. Looking up, Erik saw what appeared to be a vast number of white wraiths passing overhead. The ghostly figures descended toward Flitch in a great circular wave.

Erik and Emma stopped to watch as an immense colony of ghost bats flew toward the thylacine. Hundreds swooped close to the ground. Their leathery wings beat at the air, creating gusts of wind that whipped up loose leaves and dust from the termite mounds, causing a small tornado to spin toward the night sky. The bats' white underbellies formed an image of phantoms flying in unison. They were attacking Flitch.

The colony circled, rose to the sky, and descended once more, aiming directly for the creature. At the front of the colony, a great masked owl led the ghostly crew. He stretched his wings to their full length, screeching a challenge to the thylacine as he flew over it. Flitch struck out at the owl, front claws swiping uselessly at the air as the owl and the bats flew swiftly over his head.

Bats came from every direction. They were too numerous and quick for Flitch, and he dropped to the ground, rolling over and over in the grass, trying to fend off the many wings beating at his head and back. Screeches from the owl grew louder with each pass of the colony. The thylacine roared at the sky in an effort to frighten away the onslaught. Finally, he flattened himself against the ground and scrambled toward the shelter of the thick undergrowth at the forest's edge.

Erik and Emma watched in amazement as the colony plummeted again and again from the sky, pursuing the thylacine as it struggled to reach the edge of the woods. Finally, the evil thylacine disappeared into the depths of the forest, its wails echoing on the night air.

Emma pointed to the owl in flight across the face of the moon. "It's Oswin," she cried. "I know it's him. He came to help us. Why won't he stay?" She kept her gaze on the great owl as it flew away, a cloud of bats in his wake.

"I'm not certain why he doesn't stay." Erik shook his head as he bent down and gathered some dust at the base of the termite mound, and put it into the leather pouch on his belt. "Let's move on." He pointed westward across the field toward a dark and unknown forest. "We'll rest as soon as we reach the woods. Tomorrow will come soon enough."

Erik held Emma's paw tightly as they turned and scurried across the field. *We'll be safe when we reach that forest on the other side*, Erik thought. In the distance, they heard the eerie cry of an owl. Erik no longer looked back. He would not rest until he found shelter somewhere within the woods.

CHAPTER 9

litch crept into the thick underbrush of the forest. The encounter with the bats infuriated him, and he shook once, trying to release his anger before settling to rest between the twisted roots of an old tree. His chest still heaved from his efforts to fight off the masked owl and his flock of leather winged cohorts. He expected to make a quick meal of the two kowaries, and was disappointed that he would have to look elsewhere for his dinner.

He had been traveling west, toward Demelza, for several days, hunting the young fox. He had not been successful in killing him, and thinking about it only made him angrier. Malfoden would not be happy. Then again, the evil sorcerer demanded too much.

The night's shadows embraced the forest with shades of grey, but his yellow eyes easily pierced through the darkness, and his ears twitched with every noise that carried on the cool breeze. A sound, like the snapping of a flag in a stiff wind, came from overhead and he looked up. High in the branches of the old tree, the great masked owl was settling. His long talons reached out for a branch as his wings beat the air. Slowing his descent, he grasped the limb.

Flitch's lip curled, baring his teeth.

"Come to gloat?" His sharp tone had no effect on the bird. "You have done your job tonight. Be on your way!" The owl was unmoved. He glared down at the thylacine with round yellow eyes.

Flitch growled again and rising to all fours, began creeping farther into the forest, leaving the owl behind. *I must continue to travel west, toward Demelza, ,* he thought. He scanned the forest trying to decide on the best route. With each step, the forest floor came alive with small animals, bugs and lizards scurrying away from him. He listened closely, waiting for movement that would signal some larger prey, some unwary animal he could catch. The rustling of dry leaves around a large rock alerted him. Slowly, he moved forward, his belly close to the ground, placing his paws carefully, avoiding the dry twigs and branches. Closer now, he heard whispering. *There is more than one. How wonderful. Perhaps I won't go hungry this evening after all.* His tongue moved over his sharp canines, saliva dripping to the earth as he anticipated devouring some delicious prey.

He rounded the rock. Two quokkas were arguing with one another, oblivious to their surroundings. One wore a dark brown duster over green shirt and pants. He was thin and carried a large pouch over his shoulder. The other, a bit smaller then the first, was short and round. He wore a brown cape buttoned up to the neck.

"You wanted to come this way," the taller of the two said. "This could have waited until tomorrow morning."

"Why do you always have to give me a hard time?" the short one retorted.

"Because you're stupid, and you don't think things through!" He removed the pouch from his shoulder and set it on the ground. Shaking his fist at the small fat quokka, he said, "I don't know why I listen to you. Now we're lost."

"We'll find shelter for the night, then we'll get our bearings when the sun..." The small one stopped and lifted his nose into the air. It twitched as he and his companion turned, coming face to face with the thylacine. Flitch stared at them, an evil grin revealing his sharp white teeth. The two small creatures started to run, but Flitch was quick. Stretching out his paw, he cut off their only path. Both quokkas stepped back until they were pinned against the rock.

"Going somewhere?" Flitch chuckled wickedly. The quokkas trembled together, fear taking their voices. They could do nothing but stare wide-eyed at the monstrous thylacine. "Come now," Flitch began, "I have always thought that polite conversation before dinner was a sign of good manners." He paused. "Have you nothing to say?" Hunching down on the ground, he laughed maliciously at the two frightened animals.

The tall quokka's eyes moved back and forth and his feet shifted in the dirt.

"Looking for an escape route?" Flitch asked, tilting its head to the side. The small animal's sudden movement amused him. The thylacine's paw flew out in a blurring motion, slapping the quokka as he tried to get away. The quokka flew backwards, landing against his companion. They both fell to the ground in a heap. The thylacine took a step closer and placed his front paws on the two helpless creatures. Pressing them tightly to the earth, he lowered his face toward them.

"Which one first," he said, sniffing the two whimpering quokkas. "What a delightful dilemma." He smiled, and a soft satisfying moan rose from his throat. His yellow eyes drilled into the thinner quokka. "You, tall and skinny one, tried to run. And yet, " he turned his attention to the short fat quokka, "you, my fat little friend, would be tastier. Not nearly as bony as your skinny mate."

The thin quokka shook his head a bit and swallowed hard before choking out, "You should leave us be."

"Oh!" Flitch snickered loudly. "You've found your voice! That's good. Now tell me why I should leave you be." When no answer came, he said, "I've always loved playing with my food. It helps the digestion." He gazed at the quokka and followed his eyes as they looked up. There, in the tree above him, sat the great masked owl. Flitch's eyes narrowed as anger welled up, his chest heaving with it. Pressing himself closer to the ground, one of the quokkas let out a shrill scream beneath the crushing weight of the thylacine.

"You!" Flitch shouted. Before he could utter another sound the owl dove at his head. With his great talons extended, his wings outstretched, the owl came down at Flitch, striking him. Flitch howled, batting the bird with his paw, rising up on his back paws to strike again. The owl's powerful wings held him in the air over the thylacine, and he continued to claw at Flitch's snout. A talon scrapped across Flitch's head opening a gash from its left eye to the base of his ear. Rising back up to the tree the owl settled on a branch well above the thylacine, its wings beating the air in mighty thrusts causing the leaves and small boughs of the tree to bend away from him.

Flitch rubbed a paw over his injured head and ear. He looked around, a momentary glimpse telling him that his meal had escaped into the forest. Casting a hateful glance at the owl, he leapt onto the rock and over to the other side. He skulked away, disappearing into the dark woods.

CHAPTER 10

"Gorgon! Where is Gorgon?" Cynric's shouts could be heard throughout the main keep of the fortress. Gorgon glanced across the table at his captain of the guard.

"Speaking of the devil." Gorgon grinned at the captain. The captain shot a quick glance at Gorgon. He could not hold his stare for long, because Gorgon's one scarlet eye unnerved him, as it did so many of the other dragon lizards in the fortress.

Gorgon slammed his mug of ale down and snarled. He pushed himself away from the table, lifted his black broadsword from the chair, and strapped it across his back. A massive dragon lizard, he towered over all the other creatures living in the fortress. His body was covered in dark-green thorny plates. Over his scales, he wore a black leather tunic trimmed in red. Numerous rings of yellow scales encircled his tail, which dragged along the floor behind him. Yellow stripes marked his throat, and a crest of pointed scales ran from the top of his head down his back.

He feared no one. He certainly didn't fear Cynric, King of Demelza. No living creature could remember how Cynric came into possession of the sword, not even Gorgon. But Gorgon knew that while Cynric held the sword he was protected. In fact, he seemed nearly invincible while he possessed the sword. Gorgon wanted to have the sword for himself. He wanted to rule the forests of Demelza so its inhabitants would answer to and serve only him. For that, he needed to take the sword from the fox. Anger and hatred grew inside him and his resentment toward Cynric was beginning to show. He must not allow his feelings to jeopardize his plans. He knew he had to be patient. He would wait for orders from a master more powerful than this wretched king. He would wait for Malfoden.

Malfoden, an evil and potent sorcerer, had been imprisoned at the top of Mt. Olga by a powerful foe. Gorgon had witnessed the battle between the two mighty creatures. The contest had taken them from the hills of Sunderland, across the desert sands and into Demelza to the top of Mt. Olga. Gorgon watched as Malfoden was overpowered, humiliated and imprisoned. Nevertheless, he remained loyal to and served Malfoden even after his defeat. Gorgon vowed to free him. In return, Malfoden promised to help Gorgon capture the sword and gain power over all the lands surrounding Demelza.

Gorgon laughed as he thought about the day he would hold the sword and rule as king. He would tolerate the miserable lowly fox while waiting for that day.

He thundered down the passageway; his steps shook the walls. Loose pieces of stone and dirt fell as each clawed foot landed on the stone floor. Bilbies, quolls, and other small inhabitants of the fortress scampered across his path, moving into any available crack or crevice in an effort to avoid his footfall. He curled his lip and growled at them as they scurried out of his way.

Crossing the threshold into Cynric's chamber, he watched as Cynric paced angrily back and forth before the flames of a huge fire.

"You called for me, sire?" Gorgon's deep voice roared across the room.

The fox stopped pacing and confronted Gorgon, speaking through gritted teeth. "I understand our minions have been out scourging the countryside. There have been reports of villages burned to the ground; women and children left homeless, food stores destroyed. I trust this was necessary, since I didn't order it!" His fist swung in front of Gorgon's snout, like a hammer preparing to strike.

"Why, sire, it's all for the good. My men must keep up their strength," Gorgon said in his most sarcastic tone. "They see these forays as a form of, uh, how should I say it . . . exercise?" His tone was controlled and his words were spoken slowly through clenched teeth; the bitterness was difficult to hide.

GORGON

"They need to stay strong so they are prepared to guard your fortress." Gorgon continued. "These incursions serve another purpose as well. They put down any thoughts of rebellion in the nearby towns." Gorgon glared at Cynric. "As you know, there has been much talk of revolt."

Cynric lifted his paw and in an uncharacteristic show of camaraderie, rested it on Gorgon's shoulder.

"Yes, yes. Indeed you are despicable, Gorgon. You have caused much murder and mayhem." He turned away, running his paw up his muzzle and over his tattered ear. Hesitating, he turned back to glare into Gorgon's scarlet eye. "Yes . . . revolt," he said with a smirk. "Speaking of revolt, we sent away a group of bilbies just the other night. They sought shelter from the storm. I believe they were part of a rebel army attempting to infiltrate my fortress."

Cynric moved to an open window and looked out into the black night. The Sword of Demelza leaned against the wall beneath the window. He glanced down at it. Gorgon followed Cynric's gaze to the hilt of the sword. The clear green stone had become clouded. Could this be a portent of impending doom? Could the time that Gorgon had long awaited for be approaching? The fox began speaking as though in a trance, as if controlled by some unknown force.

"Have you heard the whispers in the wind, Gorgon?"

"I have, sire."

"Are you aware that the forest moves at night?"

"I am, sire."

THE SWORD OF DEMELZA

"I am a harbinger of evil tidings, Gorgon. Whatever I touch dies." He looked down, staring at the stone floor. "Do you realize that there are myriad woodland creatures conspiring against me?"

"Yes, sire."

"I will not tolerate subversive behavior," the fox snapped.

"I understand, sire."

Cynric grasped the hilt of the sword and raised the weapon over his head. Moving toward Gorgon, he brought it crashing to the ground, embedding the point into the stone floor. Sparks flew in all directions. A chunk of stone broke away from the floor and struck Gorgon square in the chest.

He didn't move.

"And so you burn their homes!" Cynric's thunderous voice echoed off the walls of the chamber, and his eyes flashed with rage. "You will burn their homes when I tell you to! Not before!" He pulled the sword from the stone floor and held it tightly in his grasp, "We need to prepare. I feel the revolt will come soon. We must be ready."

"I assure you, we will be, sire."

"Double the guard on the battlements. I want reports four times a day."

"Doubling the guard will require taking my men from the dungeons."

"I don't care about the prisoners in the dungeons. They're traitors and rebels, and they're not going anywhere."

"As you wish, sire."

"You owe me your fealty. Do not let me down, Gorgon."

Gorgon stared at the fox, doing his best to hide his contempt and resentment.

"I won't...sire." His eyes locked on Cynric for a moment before he turned, strode out of

the chamber, and down the dark passageway.

CHAPTER 11

E rik and Emma scurried into the woods on the western side of the termite mounds.

"I don't think I can run anymore, Erik." Emma cried as she struggled to keep up with her brother. "And I'm so scared!" Erik stopped and Emma walked into his arms. She sobbed as he held her close.

"It will be alright. We'll find a place to rest and hide."

They walked, paw in paw, into the woods together. It was dark and the undergrowth was dense. Panting from exhaustion, Emma slipped from his paw and fell into a ditch. Erik quickly jumped in after her.

"It's a hollow," he said, as he took his sister's paw in his. "There, above us!" he exclaimed. "It's a root. A root of an old tree." He laughed in relief. "You tripped over it." The root rose out of the ground; a small trench underneath it would offer them shelter for the night.

"Some animal who knew nothing of windows and doors must have built this hollow. But, the leaves and branches hanging over this root will help to hide us," Erik said, settling in across from his sister. They could hear the wind whistling overhead, and the sounds of the forest filled the air as the two siblings huddled against the roots of the old tree. Erik looked up. Through gaps in the foliage he could see pale starlight flickering. He blinked and sighed, relaxing deeply. They were exhausted after their narrow escape from the clutches of the thylacine.

"We'll stay here 'till morning, Emma. We need to get some rest. Maybe have a bite to eat." Erik checked the map Aldon had given to him. "We're heading in the right direction. The swamp should be on the other side of this wood."

Emma leaned back; she folded her arms across her chest, trying her best to calm herself. She watched her brother roll up the map and tuck it into the leather packet on his belt. He was smiling at his sister reassuringly when a scuttling sound was heard and a shadow passed overhead.

"What..." Emma began.

"Quiet, Emma. Don't move." Erik slowly dropped his paw to his dagger.

"What kind of hideous rodents are you?" A gruff voice echoed off the roots around the hollow. A large spider sat on a leafy branch just above Emma's head. "Who are you?"

"We're not rodents. We're kowaries," Erik answered, as his paw curled tightly around the dagger.

"I apologize. I did not mean to offend. I'll accept that you know what you are. And knowing your limitations follows close behind."

Emma moved away from the spider and looked up at him with wide eyes.

"What do you mean by that?" Erik let out an exasperated sigh. "I'm not in the mood. Just say what you mean."

"Oh, I mean nothing, nothing at all." He waved four of his front legs at Erik. "However, it just doesn't seem right that two young animals such as yourselves should be here, in these woods at night, all alone." A slight grin formed on the spider's face.

Emma studied the spider and gasped. "Oh my! Six eyes!"

The spider lifted its two front legs in what appeared to be a gesture of surprise. "Six! Oh my, no, darling child. There are two more eyes on the top of my head. That makes eight alto-gether. Quite a few more than you have." He stared down at the two kowaries.

"Eight eyes! You must see everything!" Emma exclaimed.

"Well, not everything, my darling. I see just enough to catch my meals as they try to escape in the dark." Emma moved fur-ther away from the spider toward her brother. "Oh, don't worry, my dear," he chuckled quietly. "Tonight was a good night for hunting. I have just finished my evening meal, so you needn't be afraid of me. Besides, rodents are not on my menu. I have not had company in quite some time, and I was thinking how lonely I've been when I heard your voices in the termite mounds." He nodded his head toward the mounds.

"We're not rodents," Erik said. "What kind of spider are you?" He was wary of this new intrusion and he didn't want to confront another dangerous creature in the dark. He kept his paw tightly wrapped around the hilt of his dagger and considered ways to escape the spider if he became aggressive.

"I'm a wolf spider," he said.

"You seem to know a lot about these parts," Emma said as she peered at the spider, trying to see it better.

"Yes, indeed I do. You see, I'm a wandering creature." He tapped one of his legs on the thin branch beneath him. "Wandering is what I do. Since I left my mum, I've traveled alone, hunting for food and wandering." He paused and scanned the forest above his head with all of his eyes. "I know these parts very well. I'm familiar with the wood to the south, the desert, the swamp, and the woods to the west."

Emma's eyes widened. "Your mum?"

"Yes, my mum." The spider's two large eyes gazed deeply into Emma's. "Why shouldn't I have a mum? Don't you? Doesn't everyone?"

"Excuse me, sir, I didn't mean any disrespect. I just, well, it seems, I mean a spider—"

The spider chortled. The quiet giggle made his legs tremble ever so slightly. "Not to worry, my darling. It's hard to believe that a creature such as me would have something as lovely as a mum. The fact is, we all have them. They are so very necessary." The spider lifted a leg to his head and tapped it in a thoughtful manner as he continued, "Funny thing is, and I must admit this, some mothers are ever so much better than others. Now my mum, the dear lady, she would carry me to the ends of the earth, she would. On her back no less." He stared up into the dark foliage above, appearing to recall a lost memory. "It was a bit of a tight ride, as I remember, considering all the brothers and sisters who came along."

"Oh my!" Emma let out a little giggle. "You are very interesting, Mr. Spider. I am so happy you're not going to harm us. We've been told some spiders can bite. It's been a terrible night, and we want no more trouble. You haven't told us your name."

"The name's Perigrin, but you can call me Perry." The spider raised a leg and bowed slightly toward Emma. "Bite, yes we can. It's not pretty what a spider can do. You don't want to corner one of us." He shook his head. "We must defend ourselves. Don't you think?" He looked at Erik and Emma, and paused before continuing. "You said you had a terrible night. I know you did, I saw you. I watched as the thylacine came out of the woods. The creature would certainly have done you harm if the ghost bats and Oswin hadn't shown up."

Erik sat up. "You know Oswin?" He glared at the spider with narrowed eyes.

"Yes, I do. He is a friend to many night creatures. We respect his power and appreciate his skills as a hunter." The spider raised his front torso and leaned onto his back legs. "He is obviously your friend, and that is indeed a very good thing. Only Oswin can rally the ghost bats as he did for you tonight. I do, however, have to wonder why it is that Oswin would go out of his way to protect such small, seemingly insignificant rodents like you. I must remind myself that things are not always what they seem."

"Kowaries," Erik said, becoming more exasperated. Perry seemed to be a knowledgeable spider, but he knew nothing about kowaries.

"Oh yes, I'm sorry. Kowaries," he said, smiling teasingly. "Well, what is it that makes you two so important, and what are you doing out here in the forest? I've never seen you in these parts before, so I have to assume that you are far from home, and I'm wondering why. Considering the help you received this night, I'd have to guess that you are on an important mission." He opened his front two legs and asked with finality, "Am I right?"

"You are very clever, Perry." Relaxing a little, Erik released the dagger and pulled a mushroom cap from his leather pack. "I hope you don't mind if we have a bite to eat." He broke off a piece and handed it to his sister. "We're tired and hungry." He held out a small piece to the spider.

"Very kind of you to offer, very kind indeed, but none for me, thank you. Mushrooms are not my favorite. They give me gas."

Erik's eyebrows raised in surprise. "So," he said slowly as he popped a piece of mushroom into his mouth. "As I said, you are a clever spider, and you don't seem to be a threat to us either. And you ask what it is we are doing here. Should we confide in you? That's the question."

Emma nodded her head as she looked at the spider. "Of course we should. He means no harm, now do you, Perry?" Emma was warming up to the spider, and Erik reprimanded himself for judging Perry at first glance. His mum would never have approved of his judging another too quickly, but it was difficult not to, considering all the twitching legs and the dangerous fangs.

"We're out here because of our mum," Emma said sadly.

"Your mum? You have one?" Perry trembled all over as he laughed. "I'm sorry, I couldn't help myself." He laughed again and then his demeanor changed. "I'll be serious, I promise. Now tell me about your mum. Did I say how important mums are?"

"Yes, you did, Perry. Erik and I have a wonderful mum. Her name is Edlyn. She is home in our village of Digby. She is very ill." Emma's eyes filled with tears.

"Sick? Whatever from?" Perry asked. A glimmer of sincere concern crossed the spider's face.

"She was bitten by a brown snake." Erik couldn't keep the sorrow from his voice as he spoke. "It was my fault. We saw the snake in the woods, and he threatened me. He followed us home. I was the one he wanted to hurt, not Mum." Erik hesitated trying to push back the lump that caught in his throat. "I need to make this right. That's why we're out here. My sister and I have to continue on."

"We can't think about what happened. We have to do what Aldon instructed us to do," Emma added.

Perry gasped. "Aldon!" the spider uttered the name in a reverent whisper. He looked quickly down at the two siblings. "I should have known. If Oswin is protecting you, then Aldon must be involved in some way." Lifting one leg, he pointed at Emma and then to Erik. "There is more to you two young ones than can be seen at first glance. Maybe, just maybe . . ." The spider hesitated and fell deep in thought as all eight eyes glazed over.

"Maybe what?" Emma asked with some hesitation.

"Aldon is the keeper of the forest, the guardian. His intervention for such a small thing seems, how should I say this . . . unusual."

"Are you saying that our mum's life is not important enough for Aldon?" Erik said defensively.

"Your mother's life is very important indeed, young man. Do not misunderstand me. What I am saying is that as small as you two seemed to me at first, you may be playing a part in something much larger; a part that may become clear as you proceed on your journey."

"That's ridiculous." Erik brushed off Perry's comments with a wave of his paw. "We've already collected dust from the termite mounds. We need to gather yellow loosestrife from the Wingecarribee Swamp. Finally, we need to go to the stone desert and pick a blossom from the desert rose shrub. Once we're done, we'll head home immediately," Erik finished with determination in his voice.

"Hmmm, seems you have everything set in place for—"

"We most certainly do!" Erik said impatiently.

Perry gazed at Erik with compassion and strode out as far as he could on his branch, his long legs stepping carefully as he went. He looked intently at Erik. "Sometimes life gets in the way, Erik."

"I don't know what you mean by that, but I do know what we must do to save our mum. We cannot be distracted." He straightened his vest absently and moved slightly, settling in his place. "It is very nice chatting with you, Perry, but we really must get some rest."

"Before I go, may I suggest that perhaps an open mind is called for here?" Perry reached out with one thin leg and tapped Erik softly on his head. "Consider the possibilities. After all, you are a part of this wild world. No one lives totally alone." He shook his head and rested one of his legs on his chest. "Even myself, I am content in my solitude, but I am a part of the forest which has given me the opportunity to meet you. It is a forest that nurtured and protected me, and it will take me back some day." He let out a long sigh. "This much I cannot deny. You will see, young man, maybe sooner than you expect, that you too are a small piece of the whole and will play your part accordingly." He bowed to them both. "*How* you play that part is up to you. It has been my pleasure, indeed, to meet you both. I believe that I will hear about you again. Good evening and safe journey."

With that, the spider stepped into the foliage and disappeared from view.

Erik was unsure what the spider meant. He rubbed his forehead thoughtfully and sighed as he turned to Emma. "Get some rest, Emma. We will enter Wingecarribee Swamp tomorrow." The two kowaries snuggled together and closed their eyes, each one contemplating what the next day would bring.

CHAPTER 12

Thoughts of revenge drove Devon onward.

Holding his staff tightly in one paw, he wrapped his tattered red cape around his neck with the other. Colum had given him the staff. He told Devon that he had received it as a gift from a wise old numbat. Devon treasured it just as Colum had before him.

The young fox had been hunting the thylacine for days. He had seen his tracks, but the creature eluded him. Finally, in the dim light of early dawn, he came upon its tracks again. An occasional clawed paw print pressed into the dirt, led him through a stand of scraggy trees. The fresh tracks, a broken twig and a tuft of fur on a low branch told him that the thylacine might be close.

He followed the tracks until they led out of the trees into an open area. The ground beneath his feet was damp, the plant life was sparse, and an unusual putrid odor clung to the air. Tall reeds stood in bunches, and small shrubs dotted the landscape.

The snap of a twig caused Devon move behind the reeds for cover. He could hear his heart beating in his ears like a drum, and his breathing quickened. A solitary crow cawed at him from atop a scrawny tree. Soon daylight would make it difficult for him to conceal himself. Nervously, he rubbed the white star on his forehead.

As he rested in the weeds, his thoughts wandered to his mother. Only fleeting memories remained of the soft cuddling arms that once held him tight, and the tender voice that spoke to him. The sweet memory didn't last. Another deadly memory intruded and filled his mind.

They ran from the thylacine. Devon's little paws clung to the bristling fur on his father's back when suddenly they were struck from behind. His small body was thrown in one direction, and his father was hurled against a large boulder, falling limply to the ground. "Papa, help me. Get up, Papa." Devon froze in fear. He stared in terror as the beast approached. The monster's wicked grin and low, evil growl sent icy fear down Devon's spine. Then his father's voice snapped Devon from his paralyzed state. "Run! Run, Devon! As fast as you can!"

A sound in the nearby grass brought him back from the horrid memory. Slowly Devon edged out from behind the reeds and started toward the top of a small hill. The awful smell was stronger here and it mingled with another odor that he had become familiar with. The thylacine must be close.

Reaching the top of the hill he looked down a steep slope that ended in a swamp. This must be Wingecarribee swamp. This was the swamp he had wanted to see. *I did want to see it*, he thought to himself, *but not this way*. The snapping of a twig behind him made Devon instinctively duck. The powerful-clawed paw of the thylacine swiped past him, barely missing his head. He planted his back paws firmly in the soft earth and swung his staff, which connected with a second raised paw. He jumped quickly to his right, deftly evading the sharp claws once more. He blindly swung his staff again. A high-pitched yelp assured him he had met his mark. He watched as the creature rolled over in the wet grass and came up on all fours.

"Ah . . . the hunter has now become the hunted," the thylacine snarled. He circled Devon, studying him, an evil smile etched on his muzzle. "It's me, Flitch. Do you recall the day we first met?" he asked with sarcasm. "Are you still having nightmares about it? You see me in your dreams, you wake, and I stand before you. You run, and I am behind you." His tail flicked like a whip as he spoke. "It's quite the game, we're playing, isn't it? Your weakling father was no match for me either, boy. What makes you think you can hunt me down and defeat me?" He tilted his head to one side. "Our lives have been woven together ever since we first met." Devon could see a scar on its side. It was from the wound he had received at Acadia Abbey.

Flitch stared at Devon, displaying razor-sharp canines. A roar of rage rose from deep within Devon's chest and reverberated in the morning air. His arm and staff flew up and back down in one swift movement, but Flitch was quick. The two animals collided and rolled down the side of the hill. Rising quickly to his feet, Devon began circling the creature. The two combatants glared at each other. In one swift movement, both animals charged each other. Devon struck the thylacine soundly, his staff landing a direct hit on the thylacine's skull with a deafening crack. The thylacine roared in pain and attempted to hurl himself at Devon. One final thrust with his staff, and the thylacine fell to the ground unconscious. However, Devon's momentum caused him to slip in the muddy earth, and he fell into the swamp. He sank fast into the muck, his red cape wrapping around his legs.

Flitch lay motionless on the bank of the swamp. Though he didn't move, Devon did not trust that Flitch would remain that way for long. He had to think quickly. His staff was just out of reach, lying on the nearby bank. He struggled to free his legs from the thick mud beneath the water, until he was breathless. Devon looked at the thylacine. He was beginning to stir. A clump of water reeds would be his only cover. With all his strength, he slowly pushed himself until he was hidden behind the tall reeds. Again he sunk into the muddy earth at the bottom of the swamp until just his nose and eyes were above the surface.

On the bank, Flitch struggled to all four paws. He began pacing back and forth, shaking his head. Devon watched as the thylacine tried to steady himself. He sniffed Devon's staff and scanned the brown swampy water. With a low growl the creature shook, turned and began walking up the hill, disappearing over the top. Devon cautiously rose from the water and gazed at the spot at the top of the hill where he had last seen Flitch. All seemed clear, but how would he get out of the muck? He tried moving, but his movement only caused his cape to wrap more tightly about his legs, until he felt like a caterpillar in a cocoon. He grasped at a small bunch of reeds next to him and tried to pull himself out, but the reeds broke off in his paws. He was too far from the bank to reach his staff. His only solace was that he was no longer sinking, but he was stuck fast.

Time passed slowly until Devon thought he would go crazy. *I might be trapped in this fetid quagmire forever.* He had to get out, follow the thylacine, and kill it. The more time that passed, the harder it would be to catch up.

In the midst of these desperate thoughts, a small sound reached him on the breeze. Devon turned his head in its direction. He scanned the bank of the swamp and listened carefully. Yes, he did hear voices. Help might be on the way. Then a frightening thought came to him - *maybe dragon lizards were roaming the swamp.*

CHAPTER 13

Erik shook his head as he walked in front of his sister. "I don't think it matters how big the blossom is. We can argue about this all day. The important thing is that we get a blossom, just one, that's it."

"I'm just trying to make suggestions. I think a bigger and fuller blossom will be more effective in the potion. It might be best if we take some time to find a big blossom."

Erik released a frustrated sigh. "All right, we'll get the biggest one we can find. In case you haven't noticed..." He stopped for a moment and swept his arm in a circle indicating the surrounding swamp, "we haven't seen one yet! This *must* be Wingecarribee

Swamp." He took his map out, studied it and looked at Emma. "Well, at least we're going the right way." He tucked the map away.

They continued walking along when a barking noise caught Erik's attention. He froze. Emma, who had been looking around for a blossom of loosestrife, walked right into him. Both kowaries tumbled to the ground. Erik popped up quickly with one finger over his lips. Emma lifted her finger as well, mimicking his gesture. He then pointed farther down the bank of the swamp. She glanced at the spot and turned back to her brother with a questioning look.

"Over there, Emma," he whispered, "in the water, behind that bundle of reeds. Do you see it? I think there's something moving." Erik and Emma flattened themselves to the ground near the bank of the swamp, staring in the direction of the noise.

Emma held her paw over her eyes, peering out at the swamp. "Oh, yes, now I see it. It's red."

"Let's go a little closer. Be careful and stay behind me."

The two youngsters stayed low as they edged closer to the water.

"Hey, you two little rodents, over here. I need some help."

"Someone's in the swamp," Emma said.

Erik stood up and walked closer to the edge of the swamp, exasperated that they'd come across another uninformed animal who didn't know that the noble kowari had nothing to do with the lowly rodent. As he reached the bank, he could see a head sticking out of the water.

"Are you all right?" Erik shouted.

"No, I'm not all right. Can't you see I'm stuck in the mud?"

Emma stood beside her brother looking out toward the talking head. "What is it?"

"I think it's a fox. It has a very pointy nose, and it knows nothing about kowaries."

"Is a fox dangerous?"

"Stop with the chatting," the voice from the swamp yelled. "I'm not dangerous, not to friends anyway."

Erik laughed. "Well, since we don't know you, we're hardly your friends are we? Maybe we should leave you in there just to be safe."

"Erik, that's not nice," Emma said, scowling at her brother.

Emma took a step closer to the water. "You're too far into the swamp for us to reach you. How can we get you out?"

"My staff is on the bank. Get it and hold it out to me. Hopefully, you two little bits can pull me out of here with it."

Emma turned to her brother. "He is a teeny bit insulting."

"Ya think!"

Emma picked up the staff and walked back to her brother.

"Something always gets in our way," Erik complained as he and Emma attempted to reach the fox with the staff. The staff was not long enough even after both kowaries tried their best to stretch it out over the water.

"That's not going to work." The fox sounded disappointed and desperate. His efforts to reach the staff caused him to sink deep into the muck. "Look, you're going to have to find something else, something longer," the fox shouted. "Hurry!"

Erik searched the area for anything that might reach the fox. The caw of a large crow at the top of an old tree drew his attention. A dead vine curled up its trunk. Erik ran to the tree, gripped the vine and pulled with all his might.

"Let me help." Emma grabbed the vine just beneath Erik's paws. They pulled together and the vine tore free with a snap. Both youngsters found themselves on the ground holding a long piece of the vine.

"Here we are, on the ground again," Emma said as she stood and brushed herself off. "Well, at least this vine looks long enough."

Erik dragged the vine toward the fox and shouted to him, "I'll toss it out to you. Hopefully, you will be able to reach it."

"Quickly!" The fox's voice gurgled. He had now sunk so far into the muddy water that only the top of his head, his eyes, and nose could be seen. His paws flailed in a desperate effort to keep his head above the surface of the swamp.

Erik flung the vine as far into the water as he could. He watched as the distressed fox reached for it. It was not close enough. Erik pulled it back. "I'll try again. Stretch yourself out as far as you can."

Again Erik tossed the vine out over the water. This time it landed closer to the fox, and Erik watched as the fox grabbed it with his paw.

"Emma, grab the vine behind me," Erik yelled. "We'll yank together."

Erik and Emma pulled with all their might as their feet dug deeply into the muddy bank of the swamp.

"I'm moving." Excitement filled the fox's voice. "I can feel it!" The two kowaries pulled harder. Erik and Emma watched as the fox's head slipped under the water.

"Pull, Emma, pull!" With all the effort they could muster, they dragged the fox's limp, sodden body up onto the bank. He was covered with mud and spitting up water.

Emma knelt beside the wet fox, shaking him gently. "Can you hear me, Mr. Fox?"

The fox opened his eyes and stared up at her. "Yes, I hear you. Give me a minute."

The fox was covered with dirt and muck from the swamp, but the white star on his forehead was clean, and his amber eyes shone clear and bright. He slowly rose to a standing position and shook violently. Mud and water sprayed all around. Erik wiped a drop of mud from his eye, and looked at the fox with irritation.

The fox's shoulders relaxed as he released a deep sigh. "Thank you. Thank you so much. I didn't think I'd ever get out of there," he said. "But this is no place for discussions. We can't just stand out here in the open." Devon removed his cape and shook the water and mud from it. "Let's find a place where I can rest and then we'll talk. I'd like to know why you are walking through this swamp alone." He started walking and waved a paw for them to follow. "Let's find some shelter right away."

"So you're Erik and Emma. I heard you talking to each other. Hunting for flowers are you? My name is Devon."

The two kowaries glanced at each other as the fox led them down the bank along the swamp. Ahead, tall weeds and thick shrubs surrounded the trunk of an old boab tree. Devon disappeared into the thicket. The twins followed. On the other side of the thicket, at the base of the tree, was a hollow. Around its base, blossoms of loosestrife grew in profusion.

"Erik, look!" Emma pointed as she tugged on Erik's arm. "It's loosestrife." The tall stalks of the plant ended in yellow blossoms. Another group of loosestrife grew in a lovely shade of purple. The second ingredient stood waiting to be picked.

The fox poked his head out from the hollow. "Get in here. I've found a good place to hide. You can pick flowers later. It's dangerous out there right now."

Erik and Emma quickly entered the comfy, dry hollow. Dust motes danced in shafts of sunlight shining through cracks in the trunk of the old tree. The three animals settled down in a circle with their backs against the interior of the tree.

Erik's eyes narrowed as he looked at the fox. "Emma and I have traveling to do." He didn't want to waste any more time than he had to.

"Look, it's not a good idea for you two to be walking about out there. At least not right now." Devon removed his cape and hung it from a knot on the inside of the tree wall. "I have spent a lot of time hunting a thylacine named Flitch. It seems that when I get close, he slips away." He looked down at the ground and shook his head. "I was fighting him when I got stuck in the swamp. I thought I had the upper paw when we rolled down the hill. Unfortunately, I landed in the swamp." He sighed heavily, relaxing into the comfort of the old tree's hollow. "I stayed hidden until he left, and I am hoping that he assumed I drowned." He ran a paw across his head, rubbing his ears. A few drops of water and mud fell to the ground. "He could be anywhere, so I suggest we stay put." He squinted out of a crack in the tree wall and said, "You're obviously no match for Flitch, and I'm determined to catch up with him. Right now I feel waterlogged and tired. I can't go on just yet."

Emma drew in her breath. "Erik, he must be talking about the monster we saw in the termite mounds." She turned to the fox. "Why are you hunting him? That's a dangerous thing to do. You could end up dead."

Devon sat up and looked at the twins. "So you've seen him too." Surprise was evident in his voice. "What happens to me doesn't matter anymore. My story is a long one. The memory of what this thylacine has done remains fresh in my mind." He looked across at Emma. "So much time has passed and still it drives me on. I will catch up with him and I will kill him." He slashed the air with his paw in finality. "That's my plan. I don't expect two young rodents to understand."

Erik sighed in exasperation as he looked at the fox. "Devon, we're not rodents, we're . . . oh, forget it." Opening his arms wide, and with paws up, he looked hard at the fox. "It's obvious that we've had a confrontation with the same monster. I do agree. If he's in the area we need to lie low for a while." He dropped his paws and pulled on his vest, making himself comfortable. "Since we're stuck here, why don't you tell us what happened to you and how you came to hunt the thylacine?"

Devon relaxed again, leaning back against the old tree. Sighing deeply, he prepared to tell his story.

CHAPTER 14

Safe in the hollow of the boab tree, with evening falling over the swamp, Devon told his story.

"I have learned that sometimes things happen that we can't control, and that our character will be determined by how we deal with those things. For me, the darker side of life struck me at a very young age." He shifted slightly, moving the belt at his waist. "I was just a kit, not even a year old. I was sheltered in the arms of my mother, and protected by a strong and loving father." A slight smile crossed his face and his eyes shone in the dimly lit hollow. "My mother was kind and sweet, and I can recall her holding me gently while singing a forest lullaby or telling me a woodland story about the many creatures that lived in the forest around our den.

"My father was the largest red fox in all of Sunderland. He was renowned for his strength and regal bearing. His paws were huge, and he carried a longbow made of the finest ash." Devon's paws moved with the story and he smiled as he continued. "He was also an expert with a sword, and there were no challenges he would not meet. He was swift. Faster than any forest animal; he would race through the wood, and no creature could catch him." Devon gazed at Erik and Emma as he recalled his father. "He was wise as well, and many foxes came to him for advice." He rubbed his eyes and drew one paw over his muzzle. He looked down at his paws then back at Erik. "I have grown in the image of my father. I only hope that I can become as wise as he.

"That fateful day, my father had taken me out of our burrow for the first time since I was born. It was spring, and the trees were budding. Wildflowers bloomed everywhere. It was beautiful. He strapped his bow and arrows on his back as we left our home. He wanted to teach me about the dangers of the forest, and how best to keep myself safe." He dropped his head, staring at the dirt beneath his feet. "It was a much harder lesson that I learned that day.

"On the way back to our burrow, my father was naming the wildflowers for me." Devon grinned at Erik and Emma. "I was very young, but he spoke to me. He believed that I should know everything about the forest, both the creatures that roamed it and the plants that grew there. Our den was up on a slight rise above a stream where he would occasionally fish. You couldn't see the burrow until you passed through a large thicket of rose myrtle. I will never forget what I saw that day." He paused, searching for a way to describe his memories. "The purple rose myrtle surrounded us with its color and scent. Then the beautiful sensation dissolved into horror. My mother was lying on the ground in front of our home. Her throat had been slashed, and her amber eyes were glazed over with death." Devon stopped, swallowing hard.

"My father was distraught. Blinded with tears, he held my mother in his arms, rocking her back and forth. He did not see the thylacine creep up behind him. I saw him first, but I was frozen with fear." Devon leaned out toward the twins, his voice had become angry and he gritted his teeth as he spoke. "My father must have sensed my fright. He quickly gathered me up and ran into the forest." Devon wrapped his arms around his chest. "I know he hoped that he could outrun the beast, but he had me to carry." He blinked as his eyes dimmed with tears. His shoulders drooped and his paws dropped loosely to his lap. "I slowed him down. The forest passed in a blur before me as my father ran from the evil creature. I can vaguely remember the battle between them and my father yelling, 'Run! Run!' I ran as quickly as my young legs could carry me. I stumbled and fell many times, but I kept running until I collapsed."

"When I woke I found myself at the bottom of a small ravine. I could see that evening was beginning to fall. There was a huge owl perched in a tree above me. It was the largest owl I had ever seen. He was magnificent. A yellow mist surrounded him as he screeched up at the sky. I will never forget the sound." Devon

THE SWORD OF DEMELZA

looked at Erik and Emma, and his eyes narrowed. "It sent a shiver up my spine. Then I heard a strong, but comforting voice. It said, 'Stay with him. We must protect this young one. His future path is laid out before him.'"

"Maybe the voice you heard was Aldon," Erik proposed.

"And maybe the owl was Oswin," Emma added, nodding in agreement with her brother.

"I don't know. I was just a kit, a baby. It was my first time out of the den," Devon shook his head sadly. "Anyway, I didn't hear the voice again. I didn't know who spoke the words. I still don't know who it was or what he meant. I was exhausted and frightened. I couldn't move. The owl looked intently down at me. Somehow, I can't explain why, I felt safe beneath those watchful eyes." He glanced at the twins and scratched an ear. "Some time had passed when I heard a rustling in the underbrush. A bilby appeared and stood over me. He was clothed in a simple brown frock tied at the waist with a white cord. He spoke softly to me and lifted me into his arms. I remember the security I felt—the calm feeling that came over me."

Devon closed his eyes, allowing the memory to warm him. "The kind bilby carried me to his home, a monastery called Acadia Abbey. The abbey became my home." The fox stumbled over the next few words. "The bilby, whose name was Colum, became my father. There, in the abbey, he raised and protected me. Several months ago we were attacked by a roving band of evil dragon lizards. It appeared that they struck for no other reason than sport." He reached out and took hold of his staff, gripping it tightly. "They set the abbey aflame. They were led by this thylacine, Flitch. That beast is the same one I fought with today. It's the one who killed my mother, my father and my stepfather, Colum." He spoke Colum's name as if he were calling him, as if by invoking his name he would appear there, in the hollow of the boab to comfort him as he used to do.

Devon glanced over at Emma and saw tears flowing freely down her cheeks.

With a look of determination, he said, "My time for weeping is over." He gazed across the small expanse toward the two kowaries. "Now is the time for vengeance. I have vowed to hunt down this beast and kill it. It will not threaten another inhabitant in this land. I will see to that."

Erik studied the fox. "But how do you propose to do that? This is no simple hunter in the forest. This is a ruthless and cruel beast. We have come eye to eye with it ourselves. We know what it can do."

"I'm not certain how, but if I die trying, so be it."

Erik hesitated a moment before speaking again. "My sister and I are on a quest as well," he said. "We have to gather three ingredients for a potion to cure our mother. She was bitten by a brown snake." He touched his sister's arm lightly. "As soon as we have what we need, we'll head home. We would help you if we could, but we must continue on."

"Well," Devon said slowly. "It seems we each have our work to do. You have yours and I have mine. When twilight falls, I'll head out. You two stay here in the safety of this hollow until dawn." He reached for his cape and wrapped it around his shoulders. "Then you can both continue on your journey. As for me, right now, I need some rest." With that, the young fox curled up, wrapped his tail around him and fell asleep.

Erik and Emma cuddled together. Emma fell asleep quickly, but Erik's mind raced and he could not rest. They had a task to accomplish, there was an evil thylacine wandering the land, and they were short of time. Soon, the warmth of his sister sleeping beside him made Erik drowsy. His eyes began to droop and he fell into a fitful sleep.

CHAPTER 15

E rik woke to find Devon gone. For a moment, he thought of Devon, wishing him well and silently sending a request to Aldon to keep him safe. He stretched, reached for Emma, shook her and then walked out of the hollow. The morning bathed the landscape in various shades of pink and orange. Erik's focus returned to the task at hand: finding the ingredients for the potion. Emma stepped out of the hollow, yawning.

"I slept well, Erik. What about you?"

"It was okay, but I had a strange dream."

"What kind of dream?"

"It was weird. You know how dreams can be. I saw Papa, and Devon was there too."

Erik held his paw up to Emma. "Don't worry. It was just a dream. Forget it. It's not important. What *is* important is that loosestrife." He pointed at the blossoms. "You have plenty of flowers to choose from. Pick one and then we'll be on our way. I'd like to reach the stone desert before day's end."

Emma turned back toward the ancient tree. "Yellow or purple, what do you think?"

Erik stood with his arms folded across his chest, his foot tapping the ground impatiently. "Does it really matter? Just pick some!"

"Umpf. You got up on the wrong side of the rock this morning," Emma said. "Come on, grumpy brother of mine. We have some traveling to do." With that Emma picked a few yellow blossoms and handed them to her brother. He tucked them away in the leather pouch on his belt. They would stay there with the dust from the termite mounds until they returned to Digby.

Erik consulted the map Aldon had given him. "That confirms it. We need to go that way." Erik pointed toward the western side of the swamp.

They had been walking for most of the day. The land became drier with each mile that passed. There was less color too, more brown than green, and the sun blazed down on them. The terrain had become barren, desolate, and not a single animal was in sight.

An occasional shrub or scrawny tree dotted the brown landscape, and small willy willies, miniature whirlwinds of devilish dust, danced over the rocky earth. They stopped to rest at the top of a hill that sloped down toward the Pinnacles Desert below.

Erik was stunned by what he saw. Dark storm clouds were gathering on the horizon, while at the base of the hill the stone desert spread out before them. The pinnacles rose from great swaths of sand-like pillars protruding from the earth. Pointing toward the sky, hundreds of these stone sentries stood, casting long, slender shadows on the desert floor.

They headed down the slope and were soon walking among the pinnacles. Some of the pinnacles were triangular in shape; each spear was shaped differently at the base; some square, others round, but they all rose to a peak.

"Oh my, Erik, it looks so, so—"

"Pointy?"

"Yes. That's it. It looks pointy."

"Well, let's get this over with." Erik walked between several pinnacles, glancing up as he went. "Look! Up ahead in that rocky outcrop, I see an opening. Let's head for it. We'll need some shelter when that storm hits." Erik pointed to the dark clouds roiling in their direction.

In the distance, rain clouds streaked the sky, dropping torrents of water on the desert to the north of them. A dry riverbed cut through the desert, separating the siblings from the rocky outcrop. In the middle of crossing the dry bed, Erik's ears perked up. "Did you hear that sound?"

Emma was walking a few paces in front of Erik, climbing the small incline out of the riverbed. She took the last step up and turned to look down at her brother who stood below her.

"What sound? I don't—"

It happened so quickly. The sound came first. Then water rushed upon him. Instinctively, both young kowaries reached out, grasping each other's paws tightly. The deluge threatened to rip Erik from Emma's grasp, but she hung on to him from the top of the riverbank. Angry waters poured swiftly over and around Erik.

"Hold on, Erik," Emma shrieked. The noise of the rushing water drowned out her voice. She dug her back feet into the sandy bank, as she watched her brother gasping for breath, gulping in mouthfuls of water. Emma wrapped her free paw around a small tree next to her and pulled as hard as she could. The rushing current finally slowed, and Emma was able to drag Erik from the water. As she pulled him up onto the bank, the rain began in earnest. In seconds, Emma was as drenched as her brother. The soggy and exhausted siblings rose to their feet and made their way toward the opening in the outcrop.

They found a small cave beneath the rock, with enough room for the two of them to sit comfortably. It was warm and dry. They would wait out the storm, and rest for the night. Emma watched as the rain fell in sheets from the sky. The clouds clung close to the ground, touching and swirling around the tips of the pinnacles.

Water dripped from Erik's nose, and his ears drooped under the combined weight of weariness and water.

"Erik, are you hungry?" Emma said softly. "I think I still have some biscuits in my pack. A little tuck will help you feel better."

Erik looked at his sister. "You saved me from being swept away." He glanced down and shook his head. He didn't know what to say. When their journey began, he had serious misgivings about taking her along. Those feelings were gone. The realization struck him—he could not have done this without her. Her smile and easy ways bolstered him and made the journey bearable. He knew that this terrible storm would pass, and they would persevere.

Emma just looked at him. "You're my brother, Erik. You would do the same for me. Now, what would you like?" Her paw rustled in the tiny pack at her waist. "I have a biscuit, and I have a mushroom. Oh, and look, some dried berries."

"Maybe a biscuit," he said, shrugging his shoulders. "A bit of food would be good right about now." He took the biscuit from his sister and took a few sips from the water jug that he carried on his belt. He tore into the biscuit hungrily. Emma stared at him with surprise. "What?" he said with a full mouth as he showered himself with bits of biscuit. "I'm hungry!"

She began to giggle and could not stop. Before they knew it, they were rolling around in the tiny cave laughing and holding their bellies. Their feet kicked and twitched with delight. Oblivious to the storm, the two siblings laughed until they fell asleep.

CHAPTER 16

It was close to daybreak. Soon the feeble sun would try to penetrate the mist that always seemed to cover the fields surrounding Fortress Demelza. Swirling, black smoke could be seen rising from Mt. Olga in the distance. It curled and joined the dark clouds over the mountain's peak like the tentacles of a monster trying to escape the grip of its rocky adversary beneath.

Cynric stood on the battlements. A damp wind caught his cape and it snapped angrily around him in protest. Looking out across the field, his thoughts were vile and filled with a despair that was his constant companion. It was an evil shadow walking beside him. It made him do wicked things. Held in the clutches of the sword, he was aware of nothing else. *We must attack before the sun rises*, he thought.

The sword hummed in its sheath, and he took hold of the hilt. The vibrations crept into his paw and slithered up his arm. His feelings intensified. He unsheathed the sword and lifted it above his head. The sword rose toward the sky, the portcullis ropes stiffened and the great gate of Fortress Demelza slowly rolled up.

Cynric turned and looked down at his troops. The dragon lizards grumbled and growled at one another in their tightly packed formation. Baring their teeth, the lizards shuffled and pushed each other. A skirmish broke out between two soldiers and Cynric watched, an evil grin forming on his face. The two lizards lashed out at one another, their claws drawing blood with each powerful slash. Two more lizards stepped out of line and began to enter the fray. It seemed to Cynric that a major clash was about to break out. He pointed the sword at the two who had begun the fight and bellowed.

"Cease!" A streak of green flashed from the sword like a bolt of lightning, and the two lizards dropped to their knees.

Gorgon strode toward the two, picked them up by their necks, one in each of his powerful claws, and tossed them toward the group.

"Get back in line, you miserable worms!"

He glanced up at Cynric and nodded. "Your orders Sire."

"Kirby-Doane, Gorgon. I hear that it is a nest of spies and rebels. We must take care of them quickly. Burn the village. Once the village is gone perhaps they will see the error of their ways."

The great iron gate slammed into place. A clap of thunder shook the walls of the fortress. Cynric swung the powerful sword over his head once more. The clouds reflected the green light from the sword and it filled the air. Bathing the ground, the light created a path for the dragon lizards to follow. They raced through the fortress gate and spread out across the field. The humming of the sword grew louder and louder. In response, the snarling and roaring of Cynric's lizards became more frantic and ferocious.

Cynric watched from the battlements, his eyes flashing with hate and anger. *May you taste the bitterness of loss, Kirby-Doane.*

Gorgon ran alongside the troop until they reached the forest. He gave the order to halt and the troop came to an abrupt stop.

"We will enter the wood and proceed to Kirby-Doane. Follow in formation. Any one who dares leave the formation will taste the tip of my dagger." He slashed the air with his blade and lifted his head to the treetops. Opening his mouth, he tasted the air with his thick tongue. "The forest is quiet. Our attack will be silent and quick, before the sun rises." With a wave of his arm, he moved before the troop and led them into the forest.

Gorgon's claw pulled back a tree limb and he scanned the village of Kirby-Doane. It was so still that the sound of the rushing river running beside the village was the only noise that broke the silence. The village homes were nestled beneath the trees. Between the woods and the small village was an open field. The grass in the field swayed peacefully as Gorgon studied the scene. It was then that his inner ear began to vibrate with the hum of the Sword of Demelza. He quickly turned to look behind him. The sword's green light was approaching from deep in the forest and reaching out for him and his troop. Waiting for Gorgon's signal, the dragon lizards were hidden behind bushes and shrubs. When he finally lifted his claw, the troop rushed out from the wood into the open field. Running across the field toward the village, they let out a savage cry, their weapons ready.

The sound of pounding claws and the sight of the lizards alerted two quokkas sitting next to a tingle tree. Rising to their feet, they let out a blood-curdling yell in an effort to warn their neighbors. Villagers came to their doors and tried to defend themselves as best they could. The lizards were quick and powerful, and the villagers were no match for them. They were unprepared for the onslaught.

Confused by the noise and frightened by the flames, the villagers ran in every direction. One of the dragon lizards laughed as he scooped up two small echidnas and ran with them through the village.

A second wave of lizards emerged from the forest with flaming torches aloft. They threw the torches onto thatched roofs and flung them through open windows. Homes burst into flames as Gorgon watched, the fire reflecting in his scarlet eye. Tongues of fire lapped at the trees, and the fire ate hungrily as it climbed up into the leaves above the houses.

The sun was just beginning to rise over the hillside, matching the color of the burning village. The green glow twisted its way through the open field and rose into the trees around the village. Kirby-Doane was engulfed in flames. Gorgon threw his head back and laughed at the dawn.

CHAPTER 17

D evon had left the shelter of the old boab tree in the middle of the night. He thought of Erik and Emma, silently wishing them well. Tracking Flitch was foremost in his mind. He stopped and lifted his nose into the air. The morning breeze rustled the leaves in the trees above him. It was then that he smelled the smoke. He walked farther on, following the scent. In the distance he could hear frantic voices shouting for help. It was almost midday when he came upon the source of the smell. It was a horrendous scene. A small village, built on a hillside among the leafy trees of Sunderland's western forest, was burning. Quolls, quokkas, echidnas, and other forest-dwelling animals ran in every direction trying to save their families and neighbors. Some of the villagers had created a bucket brigade and drew water from a nearby river in an attempt to extinguish the flames.

Devon watched in amazement as a large group of sugar gliders barked orders from the trees, directing the efforts on the ground. A cluster of gliders flew to a burning tree, ignoring their own safety, scanning for survivors. A quokka ran past Devon, oblivious to the young fox's presence.

"Hey, wait! Wait! What happened here?" Devon yelled.

The quokka kept running, but shouted over his shoulder at Devon, "The king's guard happened here. Miserable lizards! You're lucky, they're gone now." The quokka continued on toward a burning building.

The king's guard? Miserable lizards? Could it be the same dragon lizards that attacked the abbey? Ahead of him, a large quoll was trying to move a huge tree limb that had fallen against the front door of a burning building. Flames engulfed the rear of the house, and the quoll sobbed as he attempted to lift the heavy limb. Devon ran to lend a hand. Working together, the two rolled the limb away and the quoll disappeared into the burning house. Devon followed him in. The smoke was blinding, but Devon could hear the cries of a child somewhere in the house. Staying low to the ground, he moved toward the sound. Through the smoke, he saw two tiny quoll babes huddled in a corner with their arms wrapped around each other. He lifted them, one in each arm, and headed back out the door. Shortly after him came the quoll carrying a small female. Both Devon and the quoll sat down beneath a tree, well away from the flames. They turned to look back at the house just in time to see it collapse.

The distraught quoll looked at Devon and slowly reached out a paw. "Thank you. Thank you so much." The little female coughed and started to come around. Shaking Devon's paw, the quoll said, "I couldn't have saved them all without—" The quoll paused. Devon watched as he rubbed his eyes, wiping away tears. "This is my wife, Stella, and my two children, Basil and Samuel. My name is Sebastian and I am forever in your debt."

"My name is Devon. You owe me nothing. I'm glad I was here and able to help."

The two baby quolls clung tightly to Devon, looking up into his face with adoration.

"They're so little," Devon said, peering at the two babes in wonder.

Sebastian smiled. "I think you've made two friends for life!"

Devon and Sebastian joined a group of villagers, who were gathering for a rest. They had worked hard all day. Devon labored alongside them, putting out fires and helping the injured. As twilight approached, they sat around a small campfire to share an evening meal and comfort one another. Devon sat next to Sebastian, watching Basil and Samuel playing in a nearby clearing. The two babes had attached themselves to Devon and would not wander far from him.

Devon and Sebastian stood as Stella approached them. She was followed closely by a matronly echidna who was whimpering and wringing her paws.

"Sebastian," Stella said, "Odelia says that the two young puggles are missing."

"Where were they last seen?"

"I'm not sure, but we have to find them. They were lost in the wood once. We can't let that happen to them again." Stella glanced at Odelia. Odelia had cared for the two puggles since the day they had wandered into their village, frightened, hungry and tired. They had been roaming the forest aimlessly, and could not find their way home. Odelia had taken them in, fed and cared for them.

"I can't find them," Odelia cried. "They have been in my care for just a few days. I turned for one moment and they were gone."

Stella patted Odelia on the back, trying to comfort her. "Don't blame yourself, Odelia. It was bedlam when the dragons attacked. We'll do everything we can to find them."

Devon watched as a large quokka and an old echidna, hobbling along with a cane, approached.

Sebastian cast a worried look at the old echidna. "Noden, what's happening?"

SEBASTIAN

Noden shook his head. "I'm afraid I have some bad news." He spoke gruffly, but his eyes were soft and kind as he glanced at the quokka at his side. "Pearce, here, says he saw one of the dragon lizards pick up the puggles and carry them off." He pointed at Pearce who stood next to him, nodding his head. "He also said that Slade and Stokley took off after them. It's obvious that Slade and Stokley were trying to rescue the puggles. Pearce says they headed southwest towards the fortress."

"Oh, no!" Odelia cried.

"Dragon lizards," Devon murmured under his breath.

Sebastian turned to Devon. "You know of the dragon lizards?"

"Yes, unfortunately I do. They attacked my home, a monastery on the far eastern side of Sunderland. I will never forget what they did. I am hunting them and the thylacine that came in their wake. Who are these lizards and what do they want?"

"The lizards are minions of the King of Demelza," Sebastian explained bitterly. "You are in the land of Demelza now. Although we are a part of Sunderland, the king has dominion over this forest and the surrounding lands." Sebastian swept his arms in a circle, indicating the forest around the small village called Kirby-Doane. "He controls the lizards and what they do. Before this king came, the lizards hunted alone. Now they travel in packs, destroying homes and plundering villages." His voice dropped as he looked from one creature to the other. "There is no telling where or when they will attack. We had no warning. The thylacine has been seen with them. I'm not certain, but he seems to be the leader. We have also seen that beast walking alone at the edge of the forest on the outskirts of the village."

Devon clenched his fists tightly, the rage rising within him. "Hasn't anyone tried to do something about this?"

Sebastian took Devon by the shoulders. "They are too powerful, and the king is powerful as well. The king seems to command these minions to do his bidding." Sebastian waved his paw indicating the group that had gathered around him. "How can we stand against such power? Our guards have been able," he hesitated, "up until today, to prevent an attack." He released Devon, dropping his arms to his side, frustration evident on his face.

Noden glanced up into the trees. "The sugar gliders have spoken to the gang-gang cockatoos. They speak of a rebel army forming somewhere in the western forest. They say this rag-tag army plans to storm the fortress to free the many prisoners being held within its dungeons. The rebel army vows to put an end to the reign of this evil creature who dares to call himself king of our land. He is not the rightful king."

Pearce stomped his foot. "Bah!" Fury shone in Pearce's eyes. The strong young quokka stood a head taller than Noden, who was old and feeble from battles long forgotten. "The rightful king?! No one knows who the rightful king is. And what do we know about the rebel army's intentions? I believe that if the rebel army wasn't threatening him, the king wouldn't have sent out the dragons."

Noden shook a clenched paw at Pearce. "You're out of your mind, Pearce! The rebel army is forming in response to these

THE SWORD OF DEMELZA

atrocities. Someone needs to find the courage to stand up against this cruel king. If I weren't so old and lame, I would seek out this army and join them myself!"

Pearce glared at Noden. The two were about to come to blows, when Sebastian stepped in. "Enough! This is not getting us anywhere, especially now, when Stokley, Slade and the two puggles are missing!"

"We should do as Noden says," Devon said solemnly. It all became quite clear to him. He suddenly realized that his troubles were not just his own. The trouble was bigger than what happened to him at the abbey. "Why don't we form a band of men, go into the woods, locate and join this army? You have forged weapons. Let's use them. You have many strong men here. We could—"

"Why are we listening to this fox?" Pearce's strong voice boomed in Devon's face. "Who is he to tell us what to do? We should leave our homes for him? Put our lives at risk? For what? For a *fox*?"

"I don't understand," Devon said, shaking his head incredulously at Sebastian.

"Of course you don't, Devon." Sebastian placed his paw on Devon's shoulder. Looking deeply into Devon's eyes, he said, "You see, the king of Demelza is a fox."

Devon stood in silence for a moment, the realization hitting him hard. Then he said softly but firmly, "Do not judge us equally. Fox or not, I am leaving in the morning to find this rebel army. Anyone who wants to put an end to this and has the courage can join with me."

Several individuals who had gathered around the campfire rose slowly. "I'm with you," one said. Another said, "So am I." More began to rise and a few others walked out of the darkness toward the campfire, willing to join Devon.

Sebastian turned to Devon. "It appears you now command your own group of rebels. I am with you as well. We leave at dawn."

Devon watched as Pearce, snarling under his breath, walked away into the darkness.

PEARCE

CHAPTER 18

Erik looked out over the desert in amazement. The morning brought a clear azure sky. His plan for the day was clear as well. "Wake up, Emma. You won't believe it!"

Emma rose and rubbed her sleep-filled eyes as she sidled up next to her brother. "What?" The two kowaries gazed out across the vast desert.

"Look at the pinnacles. They're sparkling!" The early morning sun caused the pinnacles to glisten, as though they had been sprinkled with thousands of gems.

"It's beautiful." She looked intently at her brother and smiled. "A few short days ago we doubted ourselves. We've accomplished so much since then." She hugged her brother and looked at him lovingly. "We've seen much more of Sunderland than we could have ever imagined. I'm proud of us, Erik. We did it!"

"Not so fast. We still have to collect the desert rose and return home safely." Erik gazed down on the sparkling monoliths. "That thylacine is still out there somewhere, and more enemies may cross our path. However, I don't think it will be too difficult to collect a desert rose."

"Why do you say that?"

Erik took her paw in his and grinned from ear to ear. "Look at the base of the rocks."

He watched Emma's gaze scan the hill where they had spent the stormy night. At the base of the rocky slope, among the rubble and sand, was a dense shrub. The shrub had dark green, oval-shaped leaves and amongst them grew mauve-colored blossoms whose centers were splashed with the deepest red.

Emma drew in her breath. "Oh my. They're lovely!"

"Yes, they are, and we're heading home." His eyes never left the dense shrub as he started down the slope. "Let's go pick a flower."

Emma followed close behind.

When they reached the bush, the two siblings stopped. Erik turned to Emma and said, "Go ahead, Emma. Pick one." The bush was a profusion of flowers. Some were far too high for Emma so she simply reached out to the one closest to her. As she did, a small shrill voice said, "Hey, what are you doing? Leave my roses alone!"

Emma quickly retracted her paw. "Goodness! Who's there?"

Erik stepped in between Emma and the shrub. "Come out so we can see you!"

"Don't you yell at me, young man. I've been around a lot longer than you, and I demand a modicum of respect from the young ones that roam this desert!"

A small thorny lizard appeared from the leaves at the top of the shrub. Its dark olive color helped it to blend well with the leaves of the rosebush. He was covered in sharp spikes, and glared at them angrily.

"Now that I look at you a bit closer, I can honestly say that I have never seen your kind in these parts." The thorny creature cocked its head. "What are you doing here?"

Realizing that he had offended the old lizard, Erik decided it would be best to express their intentions clearly. He wanted the lizard to know they meant no harm or disrespect.

"I apologize, sir," Erik said. "I'm sorry I yelled, but we were both startled. We couldn't see you, and we didn't know who was speaking." Erik cleared his throat, glanced at his sister, and then up to the lizard. "My name is Erik, and this is my sister, Emma."

"I'm Moloch." The lizard turned its spiky head to look at Emma.

Emma curtsied politely. "Erik and I are kowaries. We come from Digby."

"Kowaries. I thought you were just rodents." He brought a claw to his chin and rubbed it thoughtfully. "Digby? Never heard of it."

Erik shook his head. "Nope, nope, nope, we're not rodents, sir. We're not rodents." Emma giggled a little as Erik continued, "We would like to ask your permission to pick one of your roses."

"Pick one of my roses? Now, why would you do that?"

"We need just one, sir. It's for our mum," Emma said with pleading eyes as she gazed up at the lizard. "Our mum needs medicine to cure a snake bite and this rose will be part of a potion. We've traveled a long way, Moloch, and this is the last ingredient we need." She looked from her brother to Moloch. "We need to return to our mum in Digby. I'm certain if your mum were in need, you would do the same."

The siblings watched as the lizard slowly made his way down through the branches of the shrub, finally coming to a stop in front of Erik. He was eye level with Erik when he said, "Was she bitten by a brown snake?"

"Yes, she was. How did you know?"

"As I said, young man, I've been around a long time, and I am aware of the medicinal value of the desert rose. My roses are a crucial ingredient in a potion; a potion that will cure the bite of a brown snake." Moloch's thorny skin had turned from a dark olive to shades of light and dark brown, blending well with the desert floor.

Erik watched in amazement. "That's quite the trick!"

"What trick?"

"You changed your color. First you were the color of the leaves, and now you blend with the rocks and sand."

"Oh, that. I don't even notice it anymore." Moloch quickly lapped up a small ant that ran under his nose. Gulping the ant down, he continued. "I like you, and I like your mum too. I may not know her, it's true, but now I can see that you are caring and respectful rodents. We must give credit to the source, the mum, as well as the child!" He lapped up another ant as it crossed his path. "She must be very special to have raised such respectful children." He pointed up to the roses. "Pick a rose, my dear, and return safely to your mother."

MOLOCH

Emma smiled down at the lizard then reached up and pulled a flower from the shrub. She held the freshly plucked blossom in her open palm. As she and Erik looked down at the flower, the petals closed in upon themselves and swirled around one another until the blossom was tightly shut. Startled, Emma looked up, concern written on her face. "Should it do that, Erik?"

Moloch answered the question, "Yes. It will retain its potency for you in this form. No worries."

Emma looked down at Moloch with smiling eyes. "Thank you, Moloch. Thank you so much for allowing us to take the blossom. You are very sweet even though you appear a bit scary, clad in all those thorns."

"Well, I'll take that as a compliment . . . I think." He looked up at Erik.

Erik nodded. "Yes, it is a compliment, sir. And I thank you as well. My sister is right; you are not as thorny as you appear to be at first sight." He turned to Emma and said, "We should be on our way now."

Emma bent down and placed her paw on the lizard's spiny head. "You are a wonderful little lizard, Moloch. Guard your roses well. We will always remember you."

With that the two kowaries turned and began their journey home.

CHAPTER 19

Stokley followed the sounds of the dragon lizards as they ran headlong into the forest south of Kirby-Doane. Slade was close behind.

"Come on, Slade. I hear them. We can catch them if we hurry."

Branches snapped and dry leaves crunched under foot as the lizards, carrying the two young echidnas, slashed through the dense undergrowth. The sound of the puggles' cries spurred Stokley on. The louder the puggles screamed, the louder the laughter and taunts of the dragon lizards became.

"We'll throw you into the dungeons and have you for dessert when we're ready for ya!"

THE SWORD OF DEMELZA

"Sweet, juicy little puggles, perfect for me stew, ya are!"

"Ah, yes, but they're a wee bit prickly. We'll have to rip out those nasty pointy spines 'afore we boil 'em."

Stokley and Slade caught up as the dragon lizards slowed their pace. They watched from the underbrush as the puggle babes struggled in the arms of the largest dragon lizard they had ever seen.

"How many dragons did you see, Slade?" Stokley whispered. "I think I saw four of them."

Slade shook her head. "I'm not . . ."

"Sure?"

She nodded.

The bond between them was strong. The two young echidnas had never been separated. They seemed to know each other's thoughts. Slade's speech was slow. She always began a sentence, but was never able to complete it. Stokley always finished her thought for her.

As a puggle, Slade witnessed her parents being devoured by a saltwater crocodile. The crocodile had leapt out of the muddy waters of the river that ran alongside Kirby-Doane, and grabbed her mum. When her father went to her mother's aid, the crocodile grabbed him as well. Ever since then, she could not find her voice. Stokley would help her express herself, and she had grown dependent on him. He was always there for her.

"I think there are four," Stokley said again. The forest had gone still. Stokley cocked his head. "Do you hear that, Slade?"

"I don't hear—"

Stokley quickly wrapped his claw around Slade's pointy snout, but it was too late. A huge lizard jumped out from behind a gum tree and another appeared next to him. Two more came out of the brush behind their comrades. All four lizards stood in front of Stokley and Slade. The largest of the lizards held the two whimpering puggles.

"Help us," one of the puggle babes cried at Slade and Stokley.

The lizard's malevolent laugh and booming voice shook the leaves on the gum trees above their heads. "We don't need the four of us to take care of these two prickleys." He turned to the dragon lizard standing beside him. "You handle them! Do with them what you will; bring 'em, leave 'em, or eat 'em. Don't matter much to me, but the three of us must head back to the fortress. The sword, I mean, the king, wants us back. We took too much time burning down that useless village. The fun is over. We must return." With that the three disappeared into the forest, the screams of the captured puggle babes fading with them.

"So it's just you and me, you little prickleys!" The remaining lizard took a step toward Stokley and Slade.

"Run!" Stokley yelled. And the two echidnas were off as fast as their little legs would carry them. "Quick, Slade, follow me!"

Stokley led Slade under every broken limb and fallen tree before him. They had the advantage of being small. They could fit into places where a larger creature like the dragon lizard could not follow, but the lizard was close behind. Dried leaves and broken twigs flew in every direction as the echidnas sprinted back and forth across the forest floor. The lizard could not keep his eyes on them.

Stokley grabbed Slade and pulled her down into a burrow deep under a fallen tree.

"Where are ya, ya nasty prickleys? Come out now! Where are ya? I know you're close. I can smell ya! Come out!" The lizard's voice was filled with anger and frustration. He panted as he paced on the fallen tree above them. Beneath him, in the burrow, the echidnas hugged each other tightly.

"You annoying little blighters! Come out!" It was a heart-stopping moment as the lizard stood directly overhead. "Miserable little rodents. I don't have time for ya. I've got to return to the fortress. You're lucky this time. If I ever sees you again, I'll grinds you into chopped meat."

Stokley listened to the ponderous gait of the lizard as it faded away into the woods. Neither echidna moved a muscle as fear gripped them both.

Stokley had no concept of how much time had passed. He waited with Slade under the fallen tree while the forest grew quiet around them. Finally, he gathered all his courage and poked his nose out of their hiding place.

The forest felt dark and dangerous, even though it was mid-day. The wind whispered among the leaves in the treetops as thin rays of light filtered down to the forest floor. Stokley rubbed his snout while he considered whether or not he should try to find their way back. He didn't know which way to go. They were truly lost.

His thoughts were a jumble. He struggled between the choices before him. Should they try to follow the lizards or should they try to find their way home? Following the lizards would put Slade at risk, but what about the puggle babes? Their intention to help the puggles was honorable, but they had acted rashly, and now their situation had become desperate. Nevertheless, he wondered what would happen to the puggles if they didn't follow the lizards to the fortress. He knew in his heart that they had to help the babes, but how? The lizards might still be out there, and he and Slade would be captured, or worse, killed. He tried his best to banish such awful thoughts from his mind, but he couldn't. He imagined fierce lizards outside the small hiding place. In his terror, he envisioned huge growling hounds and long black hissing snakes alongside the lizards, waiting to attack them. His thoughts were running wild when he heard the screech of an owl.

"Quiet, Oswin. We don't want to frighten our small friends any more than they already are."

Slade nuzzled closer to Stokley. He touched her lightly with one paw to reassure her. Raising the other, he signaled her to remain still. As he took a tentative step out of the burrow, a cool mist enveloped him. The forest was immersed in a soft, warm yellow glow. It had become brighter, less ominous than it was moments before.

"Ah, Stokley, my fine young man, you needn't fear me, nor the forest around you."

Startled, Stokley took a step back and looked around. He could not see where the voice was coming from. Slade remained close behind him, hugging him for comfort.

"I don't know who or what it is, Slade, but I don't think it means us any harm. It doesn't sound dangerous."

Slade craned her neck and looked out from behind Stokley.

"Slade! There you are."

"Who . . ."

"Am I?" the voice finished for her. "I am Aldon, Guardian of the Forest, and keeping you and Stokley safe is important to me." He laughed softly before continuing. "I know you're both frightened. You've just had a close call with the dragon lizards, so I need you to listen carefully."

Stokley tried to see through the mist, but his little eyes could not see anyone.

"Soon you will meet two young kowaries. Join them. They will need you and you will need them." Aldon hesitated for a moment. Stokley wrapped his arm tightly around Slade, waiting patiently for Aldon to continue. "Please, come all the way out from there so I can see you better. I promise you all is well."

Stokley, with Slade in tow, crept all the way out from beneath the fallen tree and peered into the churning mist. Rubbing his eyes, he watched as the mist swirled before them. At its center, looming over them, stood Aldon. The noble numbat gazed down at the two echidnas. His eyes twinkled, reflecting the glow from the mist, and a warm smile slowly formed on his face.

"Look, Oswin," he said to the magnificent owl sitting on a branch over his shoulder. "They are coming out to greet us."

"Are you really Aldon?"

"Yes, Stokley, I am."

"You can help us!" Stokley shouted joyfully. "You can tell us what to do! The puggle babes are out there. The lizards have them; we have to catch up to them. Please tell us what—"

"Whoa, whoa, young man, first things first. You must be prepared."

"Prepared for what?"

At this, Slade came out from behind Stokley and shyly said, "We are too . . ."

"Small," Stokley finished, looking meekly at his paws.

"We are too . . ."

"Young," Stokley said as he gazed up at Aldon. "Yes, perhaps we are too young." His words were tinged with sadness as his eyes returned to the forest floor. "I am young and so is Slade. Maybe we should return to Kirby-Doane. Maybe chasing the lizards was the wrong thing to do." He tilted his head back to look up at Aldon again. "But is it wrong to try to help your friends, even if it means putting yourself at risk?" He began to pace back and forth at Aldon's feet. "Slade is frightened, and so am I. Now the lizards have the puggle babes, and we don't know how to help them." He covered his eyes with his paws. He didn't want to cry, but he felt all his confidence drain out of him. He felt confused and conflicted, unsure. The only thing he was sure of was that he had to watch out for Slade. If that meant that they should return home, then so be it. "Can you help me decide what is best?"

"Stokley, you have done your best."

Stokley raised his eyes to Aldon.

"You're frightened, but you have done the right thing. The puggle babes *do* need your help. *I* need you, and so do many others. Size and age is meaningless. It is the strength within your heart that matters." The numbat's voice was soft, but firm. "Always remember, I will be watching over you." The giant numbat bent down on one knee so he could be closer to the two friends.

"Look for two young kowaries," Aldon said, nodding at them both. "You will need each other. Take care of each other." He raised his arm and pointed out the path he wanted them to take. The two echidnas turned and looked in the direction of a fern-covered trail, which cut through the thick forest.

"Go that way. You will meet the others soon." Aldon reached into his cloak.

"One more thing Stokley, I want you to have this." He pulled out an elaborately carved recurve bow made of light birch, inlaid with ebony scrolling.

"Aldon, I can't . . . ." Stokley looked up at Aldon in amazement. "Only the best of our echidna warriors carry such a bow!"

"You're right, Stokley. Please take these as well." In Aldon's paw a quiver of arrows magically appeared. A shower of sparkling light fell from the arrows, evaporating in the air around Stokley. "You have to practice, but I have faith in you. You will become a great warrior."

Stokley was speechless and Slade stood wide-eyed beside him. Stokley reached out and took the quiver of arrows from Aldon.

"Remember what I've told you. There are others who will need your help."

"Two kowaries?" Stokley stood with the bow in one paw and the quiver in the other. "Who are these *others* that you speak of? And what can we do for them?" Stokley trembled a bit. He was aware that it might not be polite to ask questions of Aldon, but his fear of the lizards was great, and he wanted to make sure that he understood everything. "We don't understand."

"Do not underestimate yourselves, Stokley." Rising to his feet, Aldon gazed at Slade. "Do not misjudge yourselves or the power that can be generated when friends are bound together for a just cause. I will always be close by."

The great numbat's voice faded as the mist swirled around him. Soon he disappeared within it, taking the great owl along with him. The deep colors of the forest slowly returned. As the mist evaporated, Stokley looked out into the wood. All was quiet and still. He put the bow and arrows down and reached out for Slade. He gathered her up in his arms and comforted her as best he could. It was then that he heard voices. Someone was approaching.

STOKLEY, THE WARRIOR ECHIDNA

CHAPTER 20

S tokley picked up his bow, slipped the quiver of arrows over his head and strapped it to his back. He climbed up onto the fallen tree and looked down upon two young kowaries heading up the path. They were in the middle of a heated discussion.

"Look, Erik, look at the map. We have no idea where we are. I'm sure we're going the wrong way!"

"Emma, calm down." He sighed and sat down with a thump into a heap of dried leaves. He pulled out the map and began to study it.

"Are you a kowari?" Stokley asked from the top of the fallen tree.

Startled, Erik and Emma looked up.

"Did I finally meet someone who knows what a kowari is?" Erik slapped his leg in surprise. "Now that's refreshing."

Stokley smiled at Erik and Emma. He was very pleased with himself, and surprised that Aldon's instructions were coming together so quickly. "Well, I had help. I knew you'd be coming."

"You had help," Erik said, a bit of skepticism in his voice. "Okay, I give up. Who helped you?"

"Aldon."

Erik stood up. "You've seen Aldon? Where? When?"

"He was just here. He told us you'd come this way and that you'd need our help."

"Need your help?" Erik glanced quickly at Emma. She shrugged her shoulders, and both kowaries stared up at Stokley.

"What's your name?" Emma asked. "Mine's Emma, and this is my brother, Erik."

"I'm Stokley, and this is my good friend, Slade." Slade had climbed up onto the fallen tree and stood silently behind Stokley.

Erik scrambled up the tree, and Emma followed. The four animals stood for a moment, scrutinizing each other.

"What do you mean Aldon told you we'd come this way?" Erik asked. "Did you actually see him? Did you see a great masked owl?"

"Yes, we actually saw Aldon. And we saw the owl too!" Stokley waved his paw toward the spot where Aldon had appeared. "Right over there. That's where we saw him. He told us we would meet you, and that you would need us. He told us to go in that direction." Stokley pointed toward the fern-covered path. "He said you should come with us."

Erik took a step away from the others. "Oh, wow, this is out of control. You saw Aldon himself!" Then he turned and looked down the path that Stokley had pointed out. He jumped off the fallen tree and walked toward the path.

"We shouldn't be doing this," he said under his breath.

"You can't actually be considering this!" Emma rushed to her brother and stood before him, blocking out the view of the path. "We have to go home so we can help mum!"

Erik looked at his sister; he was holding the map Aldon had given him limply in his paw. He opened it up and stared down at it. "Emma, maybe Aldon..."

"I don't care what Aldon says or wants!" Her eyes drilled into his - the determination evident on her face.

"Look, I don't like this either." He let out a loud groan. "I don't understand. This keeps getting more complicated. Are we supposed to stop and help everyone we meet along the way?"

Emma took a step closer to her brother and spoke softly to him. "Erik, think about this." She looked up at her brother, her eyes pleading. "We don't know anything about these two echidnas. We just can't blindly follow two echidnas when we don't even know them!" She began to raise her voice. "What are they doing out here in the middle of nowhere? You can't be sure that Aldon actually talked to them!" She waved her paw and unintentionally hit Stokley, who had quietly walked up to stand beside her.

"Please don't talk as though we're not here," Stokley said, rubbing his cheek where Emma had accidently hit him. "We're here, and Aldon did speak with us."

"And, please, don't sneak up on us like that!" Emma said. "I'm sorry I hit you," she whispered. Then she stomped her foot to the ground, folded her arms across her chest, and turned her back on the small group.

Stokley stared with narrowed eyes at Erik and Emma. He was growing impatient.

"I don't know what's wrong with your mum, but Slade and I have to go on, and we will go on without you, if necessary." Stokley flashed Erik a defiant look. "We have to help our friends." Slade stood beside Stokley, nodding her agreement with each word he said.

Erik tilted his head to the side, looking inquisitively at Stokley. "Your friends?"

"The dragon lizards have carried away Ackley and Amber, and they—"

Erik gasped. "Ackley and Amber? It can't be."

Emma turned, casting a stunned look in the direction of the two echidnas. "Are you talking about two puggle babes?" she asked.

Stokley nodded. "That's our Ackley and Amber. They wandered into the village a couple of days ago. They were lost in the wood. Odelia took them in. Odelia's one of the oldest quokkas in the village." Stokley turned to Slade and licked his lips. "Odelia makes the finest mushroom stew around and those puggles loved—"

"Never mind the stew!" Emma cried, gripping Stokley by the arm and shaking him.

Stokley stopped mid-thought, his mouth open and eyes wide.

"They were carried off by what? Lizards—dragon lizards?" Emma screeched.

Stokley stared back at Emma. "Yes," he shouted at her. "Lizards! Dragon lizards. And we have to help them." Stokley stopped for a moment. "Aldon says we need to help you, too. So, that's what we're gonna do. We're gonna help Ackley and Amber and we're gonna help you too, whether you want it or not. Right, Slade?" Chest out, head held high, bow in one paw and a quiver of arrows on his back, Stokley was the picture of confidence.

"Yes!" echoed Slade boldly. She smiled, a note of authority evident in her voice as she said, "Aldon would not . . ."

"Lead us astray," Stokley finished. Slade nodded her agreement.

Erik and Emma looked at Stokley and Slade, and then at each other.

"How did this happen? Dragon lizards?" Emma said to her brother. "What are dragon lizards? Those little puggles must have followed us into the forest the day we left!" Emma stood nervously wringing her paws as tears formed in her eyes. "This is our fault! We're responsible for this!"

Erik shook his head. "We have to stay calm and think this through. Fault doesn't matter now. I don't know what a dragon lizard is, and I don't care. Now we know what we must do. We can't go home without Ackley and Amber." With that, he started down the fern-covered path. The three others hurried after him. Erik turned to Stokley. "Where does this path lead?"

"I think the dragons are heading back to the fortress. They said something about putting the babes in the dungeon, before having them for dessert, that is."

Emma's paws flew up to her cheeks. "Oh, my! Oh my!"

"Emma, if you don't stay calm, I'm gonna, I'm gonna . . . well, I don't know what I'll do, but I can't think straight when you're like this." He began walking faster down the fern covered path. Erik stopped and turned to Stokley. "What fortress are you talking about? Who lives there?"

"It's the Fortress of Demelza, home of the evil King Cynric. He rules over the dragon lizards, and he has a dungeon under the fortress. I'll bet he's holding other prisoners there."

"How far is it to the fortress?" Erik asked.

"I'm not sure exactly, but I believe that it's in this direction. The way Aldon told us to go."

Slade touched Stokley to get his attention. "It's getting . . . ."

"Late." Stokley patted Slade on her shoulder approvingly. "Slade's right. There's not much travel time left today. Let's get some ground under us before we rest for the night."

"Agreed," Erik said. He turned to Emma. "Bede will know what to do for Mum. We'll get home in time. It will be alright." In the lead, he started down the path, mumbling under his breath, "Dragon lizards, evil kings, and wayward echidna babes. What's next?"

The four companions walked quickly down the path. A large masked owl watched them from a branch high above in the foliage of an aged tingle tree.

CHAPTER 21

Basil and Samuel came running from behind a burnt building. Devon was in quick pursuit.

"I'll never catch up with you, you little scoundrels." Devon stopped and leaned over, resting both paws on his knees. Panting, he looked up to see Sebastian laughing heartily.

"Good luck catching up with the little ones!" Sebastian called out.

The two young ones peeked out at Devon from behind a tree.

"I suppose you can keep up with them?" Devon asked Sebastian.

"Never said I could!" Sebastian said, smiling broadly.

Stella walked up behind Sebastian. "They're quick little tikes, for sure!" She wrapped her arms around her mate. "Your mind is made up, then?" she asked as Sebastian turned to face her.

"Yes, Stella, it is. Someone has to do something. Our families and our homes will not be safe until we do." He glanced around the little village of Kirby-Doane.

Villagers scurried to and fro with tools and building materials; the business of rebuilding the village had begun. Sebastian looked on, beaming with pride. "The villagers spent many years building Kirby-Doane," he said. "They are not likely to abandon it now." He looked lovingly at his mate. "We're going to be fine, Stella, just fine." Sebastian took her in his arms and hugged her tightly.

"Be careful. The boys and I need you."

He brushed a paw across her face. "I need you too. I'll be back soon."

In the distance, a group of villagers worked to gather weapons that had been produced by the village blacksmith. The weapons had been crafted over time, and the villagers never expected that they would be put to any use other than defense. Their paws were familiar with gripping a rake or hoe, not a pike or sword. The time had come to take up arms. No one knew how long it would take to find the rebel army hidden deep in the forests of Demelza, or how long it would be before they returned home. Sebastian kissed Stella on the top of her head, held her at arm's length, and looked down at her.

"I'll return. In the meantime, Noden is in charge. He and the other elders will watch over the village while we're away."

Noden walked up and stood beside Devon. "The men are ready to go whenever you two are." He glanced at Devon and met

Sebastian's concerned gaze. "No worries mate. Everyone here will be well cared for. When you return, you won't recognize the place. Destroyed buildings will be restored, and damaged buildings will be repaired. We have great plans. I will gather the best carpenters in all Demelza."

The two little quolls dashed across the open field. Sebastian knelt to the ground and they rushed to his embrace. He held them close, kissing them on their heads. "I'll be back before you know it," he whispered into their ears. He let them go and they flew to Devon, each one wrapping around a leg.

"Whoa." Devon put his arms out to balance himself. Bending down, he picked up the two babes. "No worries, little mates. I'll keep close watch on your papa. I'll return him to you safely." With that Devon gave each babe a kiss. Placing them gently on the ground, he turned to Sebastian and said, "Are we ready?"

"Yes, I believe we are."

The two walked across the field to join the gathering troop of quolls, quokkas, and echidnas. Pearce met them as they approached.

"We're all set, Sebastian." He glanced quickly at Devon and then at Sebastian. "We've sent the sugar gliders ahead. They will be our eyes when night falls. And we've put a call out for the Gang-gangs. They would be a great help in battle if we can get word to them."

"Good," Sebastian said. Then he looked intently into Pearce's eyes. "Are you certain you want to come along? Yesterday you seemed dead set against..."

"Yes, I am," Pearce said with finality. "No need for further discussion." With a quick glance at Devon, Pearce turned and walked to join the farmers who had now turned into soldiers.

"Load up, men!" Sebastian waved his arm, signaling everyone to lift and position their weapons.

Staff in hand, Devon was taking a last look at the village when a young echidna approached.

"I've told our troop of sugar gliders to scout out ahead of us up in the trees. Is that acceptable, sir?"

Devon hesitated for a moment then said, "That will be fine."

The echidna saluted Devon and walked off. Shocked, Devon thought about how he had reached this point. How had he become one of their leaders? What happened to his solo quest for revenge? How had fate twisted him to seek justice for so many?

Another echidna approached. "Sir, we've left enough weapons here in the village for those who remain – just in case. I assume that was the right thing to do."

"Yes, that's the right thing to do," Devon stammered. The echidna saluted and walked off, giving direction to other echidnas that were waiting for Devon's approval. Devon shook his head. Now he was indeed a leader. They looked to him for direction, for permission. Without vote or discussions of any kind, he had been promoted, and it felt somehow right. He had followed his heart thus far; he would continue to do so.

He looked around the village. It still smoldered in spots, and buildings stood in various stages of ruin, but many were already being repaired. Stella stood before him holding Basil and Samuel. Devon had never felt this way before. What was he feeling? A new mission was speaking to him, calling to him. He was just beginning to appreciate his place in this wild world.

CHAPTER 22

The four companions followed the fern covered path until darkness began to fall. They sat huddled in a hollow log they found just off the trail. The log was well hidden and offered a place to rest for the night.

Stokley sat across from Erik and studied his new friend. His fingers formed a tent in his lap and he tapped the tips together nervously.

Slade looked at Stokley. "How will we . . ."

"Do it?"

She nodded her assent, concern etched on her pointy face. "Your papa said the walls . . ."

"Are high and thick," Stokley finished. "Yes, Demelza will be difficult to get into. We must be strong and clever, Slade." He continued to tap his fingers together as he looked at Erik. "We have to assume that Ackley and Amber are now prisoners inside Demelza, and we must find a way to breach the walls and set them free." Stokley picked up a twig and began to sketch lines in the dirt, representing the walls of the fortress. "Papa spoke a great deal about a labyrinth of dungeons." He drew a circle, adding a smaller circle in the center with an X through it. "The dungeons are directly beneath the fortress, here." He pointed to the center. His gaze moved to each of his companions, meeting their eyes as he spoke. "According to papa, there are many old wombat tunnels that lead to the edge of the labyrinth." He then drew several lines out from the edge of the large circle. "The wombats, who once used the tunnels, have been gone for many years." He rubbed out some of the lines he had just drawn as he explained, "Some of the wombat tunnels may be clear. One may lead to the labyrinth, the dungeons. We don't know for sure. All we know is that the dungeons are located somewhere in the heart of the labyrinth. We have to reach those dungeons if we're going to save the puggles." He ended by driving the twig into the dirt.

Erik considered every word as Stokley spoke. The echidna's eyes glistened in the beams of moonlight that shone through crevices in the old log.

Emma looked sadly at her brother. "I can't stop thinking about Amber and Ackley. I'm afraid that they will not survive long in a dungeon." She trembled and stuttered as she turned and spoke to Stokley. "How close are we to the fortress, Stokley?

Do you really think we will discover a wombat tunnel that leads to the dungeons? Can the four of us do this alone?"

Stokley shook his head slowly. "There are so many questions, so many things we need to talk about. We must plan and plan well. Ackley and Amber are depending on us, and I am pretty sure there are others being held in the dungeons as well."

There was the sound of movement in the underbrush, and the three companions sensed it.

"Be still," Erik whispered.

All eyes remained fixed on Erik as he moved stealthily to peer out from under the log. Small branches moved, and the sound of leaves crunching under foot could be heard nearby. Someone or something moved closer.

"I really dislike these woods at night." A deep, grumbling, angry voice reached their ears.

Twigs and leaves were kicked in every direction. The quiet woods came alive with the animal's movement. In the moonlight, Erik saw a large goanna lizard kicking debris as he came closer. The tall creature wore a plaid sash across his chest, tied at the waist. A long scaly thin arm rested on the pummel of a sword, which hung from his belt. He wore forest-green britches, and high boots rose halfway up his long legs. Mumbling to himself, he looked baffled and confused as he stared up into the foliage of the tree.

"I was never one for scouting," he said disgustedly. "Now I've got myself completely turned around." He looked to his left and then to his right. "Where did I leave my army? Aldon knows I'll never live this down."

Erik cocked his head and listened to the stranger's voice. It sounded so familiar. Then he heaved a sigh of relief as he stepped out from beneath the log. "Uncle Durward," he shouted, with his arms extended wide. "Aces, Uncle Durward! What are you doing here?"

Startled, Durward lost his balance, stumbled and rolled down a slight incline, hitting his head against a tree stump. He snapped up quickly to his feet, rubbing his head and looking disoriented. He blinked; his snaky tongue hung out the side of his mouth. He glanced at Erik with excited recognition.

"Erik, my little cobber," Durward said, "it's been a long time." For a moment Durward stood there looking fondly at his little friend. "The last time I saw you, you were just a boy painting a bridge with Emma and your papa. Heaven's sake, Erik, what are ya doin' so far from Digby?"

The mention of his father caused a lump to form in Erik's throat. He swallowed hard then pointed to his companions as they climbed out from under the log.

"This is Stokley and his friend, Slade, and of course, you know Emma."

"Ah, me bonnie wee nipper! How are ya?" Durward picked up Emma and hugged her tightly. Then turning to the small group, he asked again, "What are ya doin' here?" He lowered Emma gently to the ground and waited for an answer.

"I'm fine, Uncle Durward," Emma said.

"What are *you* doing here?" Erik countered.

"Oh no, I insist. You first, young man."

There was a moment of silence before Erik said, "It's Mum, Durward. We're here because of Mum. She was bitten by a brown snake and Bede sent us out to gather ingredients needed for a potion to make her well."

"I'm so sorry to hear that, Erik." Durward glanced at Emma. Slade walked up next to Emma and wrapped her arm around her to comfort her.

"I didn't know," Durward said. "Have you gathered the ingredients?"

"Yes, we have them. And up until the time we met Stokley and Slade we were on our way home. Now, we are heading to Fortress Demelza, because we believe that two young puggles from Digby are being held captive in its dungeons. We're determined to free them."

Durward's eyes opened wide. "The Fortress of Demelza! Why, that's exactly where I'm headed. How do you guys plan on getting in?"

"It's not going to be easy," Stokley said. "We've been talking about it. My papa knows a bit about the Fortress of Demelza, and he told me that it's heavily guarded." Stokley glanced around at his companions. "There may be a way underground through an old wombat tunnel. There are many of them around the fortress, and one of them may lead us into the dungeons beneath it."

"Ahhh, it seems that some of our plans are in common. I'm here to fight King Cynric and his evil dragon lizards. They attacked Acadia Abbey. And many other inhabitants of Sunderland have been left homeless. Their villages have been burned, crops destroyed..." Durward hesitated. "This must stop, and it sounds like we might join forces. I've heard of the wombat tunnels." Durward's claw scratched his chin as he considered what Stokley said. He locked his claws behind his back and stepped toward Erik, bending close to speak to him. "Finding a tunnel that's clear will be a dangerous task. The perimeter of the fortress is heavily guarded." He unlocked his claws and pointed a bony finger at Erik. "I won't be able to fit in a tunnel. The tunnels are small."

"And so am I." Erik quickly pointed to Stokley. "Stokley's small too. We can do this." Stokley nodded in silent agreement.

"It's a lot to ask." Durward said. "You will need time to find a tunnel, get into the maze, find the dungeons and free the prisoners without being discovered. Whew! A tall order indeed!"

"Yes, it is, but we are determined to free our friends!" Erik began to pace back and forth in front of Durward. Frustrated, he stopped in front of the goanna. "We will need others to stand guard while we search the tunnels. Durward, even with you helping, I don't think there are enough of us!"

"It's Durward you're talking to here, remember?" A sly grin formed on the goanna's face. "Do you think I would try to attack and take revenge on the King of Demelza all by myself?" The four companions looked at each other then up at Durward. "I have gathered an army," he said proudly, bending toward the four friends. Then he looked all around, checking to see if anyone was listening. "They are a motley crew to be sure," he whispered. "There are goannas, echidnas, kowaries, foxes, quokka, and quolls. Many different creatures of the forest have joined me to stop the evil king and his horde of dragon lizards."

"Durward," Erik said quietly, following Durward's gaze into the depths of the surrounding forest, "where are they?"

174

CHAPTER 23

A huge spotted quoll stepped out of the brush, a broadsword at his side. He had a patch over one eye, and one large canine extended over his bottom jaw. Emma drew in her breath, gasping back her fear.

"Who's there?" The quoll shouted as he removed his sword from its sheath in one swift movement.

Erik looked at Durward. Durward smiled and stepped out of the underbrush.

"Afton, put the sword down."

"Durward, I've been looking for you." The quoll swung his broadsword in front of him, and replaced it back into its sheath.

"We became alarmed when you didn't come back. We were afraid you got lost again."

"What do ya mean again?" Durward glanced down at the four companions who now stood at his side. "I haven't been lost in days!"

Afton looked down at Erik and then up at Durward. "Yes, you're right. It has been about a day since the last time." Durward and Afton began to laugh, and one at a time Erik, Emma, Slade and Stokley joined in.

"This is Afton," Durward said, reaching out and patting the quoll on the shoulder. "This here's Erik. He and his sister Emma are like family to me. Over there are Slade and Stokley, their two friends."

Erik straightened a bit, making himself as tall as he could. "Nice to meet you, Afton."

"Afton is one of my commanders," Durward said to Erik. "He lost his entire crop. Cynric's dragon lizards burned it. He fought them off his land, losing his eye in the conflict. His children and wife are hungry. He is determined that this will not happen to another family in Demelza, or all of Sunderland, for that matter."

"It's an honor to meet you, Afton," Erik said.

"I like your sword," Stokley added. "I've never seen a pommel made of ivory like that one."

"A gift from my father" Afton smiled down at Stokley. "Let's head back to camp. We can talk more there." He led the group through the undergrowth. They circled around a rocky hill and on the other side a large camp was laid out. Thousands of forest creatures were gathered there. The camp was busy as many different forest dwellers went about their tasks. A forge was set up and weapons were being made. In another area, ladders and siege engines were being prepared, and in still another, the smell of warm food cooking drifted toward the companions.

"Why, look at this. Just a few steps and I would have been right back at camp." Durward exclaimed. "I wasn't lost at all!" Afton, Erik, Stokley, Slade and Emma, all looked at Durward at once. "Well, I wasn't," he said quietly, scratching the green scales on his head.

Afton cleared his throat, and said, "I'll get a meal ready for the young ones."

"Good," Durward said with authority, and then he grinned at Erik. "Good man, that Afton," he said, pointing at Afton as he walked away. "Let's meet some of the other commanders."

Durward led the four comrades to a quokka sitting on a log sharpening his dagger. "This here's Daegal." The quokka had thick, medium-brown fur and small black eyes. His large rounded ears perked up as the group approached. "I've known Daegal for a long time now, and I can tell you for certain that there is no soldier more loyal. He will follow me into the depths of hell if I ask him to." Daegal and Durward exchanged knowing looks.

Daegal held out has paw to Erik. "It's a pleasure to meet you, Erik." Erik shook the quokka's paw in wonder and admiration. Daegal turned and addressed Stokley. "My pleasure, Stokley," he said. "And you, young ladies, nice of you to join us."

Durward pointed to a huge older echidna standing at attention beneath a large fern. He carried a golden shield in his paw and looked down on Erik and Stokley. He appeared stern, but there was compassion in his eyes. "This is Beldon," Durward said, walking up to the noble echidna. He shook a finger at Beldon as he spoke to Erik and Stokley. "Do not underestimate his power. His strength will surprise you."

"Hello, young men, ladies," Beldon bellowed in his deep strong voice. "Stokley, my friend, I see you carry the weapons of an echidna warrior. We are comrades in arms."

Stokley nodded in silence, grasping his recurve bow tightly to his chest.

"You haven't met all of my commanders, there are many, but each one directs a well-trained, disciplined squadron. We are the rebel army of Sunderland!" he said with dignity as he nodded toward the camp. Then he looked at Erik, Stokley, Slade, and Emma, and said, "We are here in Demelza to put an end to Cynric's reign. We will help you with your plans. We will free the prisoners beneath the fortress."

Erik hesitated a moment. Then he stepped closer to Durward and whispered, "Can I speak with you...privately?"

Erik pulled Durward aside and out of hearing distance of the rest of the group. "How can this be, Durward?" Erik waved a paw in the direction of the rebel army. "Some of these creatures are natural enemies." Erik stared at Durward, eyes narrowed with incredulity. "Surely this won't work. They'll start to fight amongst one another."

"Ahhh . . . I see," Durward said slowly. "Just because they are different doesn't mean they can't be trusted or become your friends. Why, look at you and Stokley, Emma and Slade as well. You're quite different, and yet all of you have formed a friendship and a bond. It's safe to say you trust them. Don't you agree?" Durward looked deeply into Erik's eyes. "A common purpose can be a driving force in bringing a diverse group like this together. Recognizing that we all must work as one to accomplish our common goal is key." Durward poked a claw into Erik's chest. "Common goals and common feelings will make us stand together as one." Durward took Erik's chin in his claw, lifting his face up to his own. "This is your opportunity to trust, and in doing so, we will prevail. You must believe this."

Erik paused as he tried to control his feelings of fear and concern. "Durward, you know what's happened, don't you?"

Durward nodded his head slowly, "I know that your papa is missing, and now your mum is sick. It is indeed a difficult situation for you and your sister to deal with." He put his claw across Erik's back, drawing him close. "The fact that Amber and Ackley have been taken prisoner makes the situation urgent, for you, for us. We're here now, together, in this forest, near the fortress. It must have been a very difficult decision for you to make – to save your young friends in the fortress, or to return home with the ingredients. A courageous decision for sure. I do believe that your mum and papa would support the decision you have made."

"We've lost our father. I don't think we can stand to lose our mum."

"I know what you're feeling, mate. But don't give up on your father. And your mum, I'm sure she'll be well cared for until you return. Right now, right here, we must be brave. Together we can do this." Still holding Erik firmly at his side, Durward squeezed him reassuringly. "It's time to prepare." With his arm wrapped tightly around Erik, the two walked back toward the camp and the rebel army.

CHAPTER 24

D evon, Sebastian, and their army traveled swiftly, covering as much ground as possible before twilight fell. The deeper they penetrated into the forest, the edgier they all became. The surrounding trees closed in on them, falling around them like a heavy cloak. Foliage hung limply from the trees, the air was still, and the ominous feeling emanating from the forest only intensified the group's nervousness.

Devon walked beside Sebastian, his keen eyes peering into the dense undergrowth. "The men are tired, Sebastian. They're tense and hungry. We need to call it a day and rest for the night."

"Yes, you're right; we've come a long way. We will be close to the fortress tomorrow. We may even be able to see it." Sebastian cupped his paws over his muzzle, and, looking up into the trees, he emitted a short chirp.

In an instant, Babble, a sugar glider, appeared in the branches above them. He was quick, and small, and the loose skin under his arms helped him to glide soundlessly from tree to tree. "Yes, boss." He saluted sharply and stood at attention.

"Find Pearce. Tell him to gather the troops and prepare to make camp for the night."

"Orright, sir. I'm on me way!" He disappeared in a flash.

Minutes later, a large tiger quokka stepped out from a willow wattle shrub. "The men are all accounted for, sir. Any further orders?"

Sebastian nodded at his soldier. "Make sure they settle in one area. I want everyone close together." A dark look passed over his face. "Something doesn't feel right. Set up a rotating guard duty. Light a small fire to ward off the chill. Make sure the men are fed and are as comfortable as possible in this gloomy wood. We'll head for the fortress at first light."

The quokka attempted a salute to recognize Sebastian, and then decided to simply nod. They were not formal soldiers, yet their loyalty to Sebastian was strong, and somehow they wanted to express that. With a quick glance at Sebastian, the quokka strode off to carry out his orders.

"These men are just farmers, simple villagers. They are not accustomed to behaving like soldiers, but they are trying their best." Sebastian watched the quokka walking away. Then turning to Devon he said, "Come with me. I need to talk with you alone."

BABBLE

They walked a short distance from where the troops were setting up camp. Sebastian stopped under a giant red gum tree. Leaning against it, he gazed out into the dark forest.

"Tell me, Devon, what do you think of our chances? Getting into the fortress will be nearly impossible. And if we do get in, I'm concerned about our ability to get into the dungeons." He paused, looking down at the dagger on his belt. He pulled it from its sheath. Holding it before him, the moonlight shone off the steel blade and reflected into the soulful eyes of the quoll. "What if our weapons are not enough? What if our army is not able to penetrate the fortress and its dungeons? What if we can't save the prisoners and the puggle babes?"

He sighed deeply as the tone in his voice changed. He waved his paws in an off-handed manner, placing the dagger back into its sheath. "I don't know why I'm expressing my doubts to you. Forgive me."

"You needn't ask for forgiveness, Sebastian. I understand the burden you're bearing. I think we need to remember our strengths." Devon looked up into the trees, as he considered what he should say to his new friend. "The men look up to you and are loyal to you." He looked deeply into Sebastian's eyes and with firmness in his voice he said, "They believe in our cause. If we are lucky, we will find the rebel army and join forces. We must try, Sebastian, and not give in to our fears. I will be beside you no matter what." Devon slapped his paw across Sebastian's back and smiled. "I am convinced the creatures that attacked Kirby-Doane are the same malevolent beasts that attacked my home and killed my family."

"Devon . . . ." Sebastian hesitated over his words. "I didn't know."

"It was a long time ago. I have spent most of my time pursuing an evil thylacine. It killed my mother, my father, and my stepfather. My home, Acadia Abbey in Sunderland, was attacked in much the same way that Kirby-Doane was, with wanton destruction, innocent creatures hurt, and much worse." Devon saw the concern in Sebastian's face and he wanted to assure him, to let him know that he understood his fears. "From everything I've been told, and what I have seen in your village, the root of this evil is the king of Demelza. There was a time that I thought only of myself, of my goals. That's no longer the case. That's why I'm here, Sebastian. I will fight alongside you."

A rustling in the leaves above their heads caught their attention. A moment later, Babble appeared with his cohorts, Jibber and Jabber.

"Weapons down, mates. It's me, with Jibber and Jabber here," Babble said quickly in his high-pitched tone. "These fellas have just returned from this evening's reconnoiter. They report an army of creatures further to the south of us. No way to really know if they are friend or foe."

Sebastian looked at the three sugar gliders. "Good work, friends." Turning to Devon he said, "I think you and I should take a look before we put the entire troop on alert. This close to the fortress, it could be our enemy. We must be certain."

"Agreed. How far off are they, Babble?"

"They's a little way south of us, like I said." Babble stretched his paws out as far as his arms would allow, exposing his gliding flaps. "There's ten hundred thousand of 'em, boss! They's got a camp set up." Babble paced on a tree limb, becoming more and more agitated as he spoke. Jibber and Jabber watched from another limb, their heads moving back and forth in time with Babble's pacing. Their feet moved up and down as though jogging in place. The tree limb shook with their antics. "We must be very cautious, boss. They's looking mighty fierce and all, with them bows and arras. And there's one lizard I caught sight of, he's mighty big. Mighty big indeed!"

"Ten hundred thousand, you say." Sebastian chuckled. Sebastian turned and whispered to Devon, "Babble's prone to exaggeration." He laughed again and said to Babble, "And I'm sure the lizard you saw is quite large. Devon, let's go check out this *huge* army. We'll keep off the main path. Babble, you, Jibber and Jabber travel on ahead as quietly as possible and spread out. We'll follow you."

"Right, boss. This way." Babble, Jibber and Jabber lifted off and glided silently to the next tree.

"By the sounds of it, if there are as many as Babble reports, we should have no trouble seeing them," Sebastian said. "Let's separate. We'll locate them faster. I hope that at this time of the night they are all settled in. Then we can get a look at them and determine if they are forces from Demelza or the rebel army we are seeking."

Devon nodded and the two parted, putting just enough ground between them to ensure that one or the other would come upon the camp. At the same time they kept an eye on the three gliders as they sailed from tree to tree.

Sebastian watched Devon walk over a small hill and disappear from sight.

A little farther along, Sebastian came upon a large boulder. Cautiously, he approached the rock and stopped behind it. His ears flicked as he listened closely to the sounds of the forest. A pebble rolled from atop the boulder and landed on the ground at his feet. He looked up and swiftly removed his sword from its sheath. Above him, the silhouette of a large creature took off from the rock, flew over his head, and landed on the ground in front of him.

With broadswords drawn, the two animals faced each other in the dark. The creature skillfully moved around Sebastian, lifting its broadsword above its head. As their swords met, the clang of steel rang throughout the surrounding forest. Back and forth, the two animals parried. Swords clashed, and the creature stumbled and fell to the ground, but quickly regained his balance. Back on his feet, he struck Sebastian's sword hard, pushing him into the boulder. The force of the impact knocked the sword from Sebastian's paw, and it sailed out of reach.

Sebastian was defenseless. For a moment, everything was still as he looked up into the eyes of his attacker. A glimmer of moonlight sparkled back at him. He watched helplessly as a long scaly arm raised a sword, preparing for the final stroke.

A humming, whirring sound filled the air around them. It was the sound of Devon's staff moving through the air. In a flash, the young fox had put himself between the lizard and Sebastian. As his staff met the creature's broadsword, sparks flew in every direction. The creature shifted from attack to defense, but was no match for Devon and his staff. Devon swung the staff as he whirled in the soft soil beneath his feet. With one final blow, the creature was disarmed, its broadsword landing several yards behind him.

At the top of the boulder, a small shrill voice yelled out, "It's the rebel forces! Lay your weapons down." It was Babble, with Jibber and Jabber beside him.

Devon hesitated. He stared at his staff, stunned by the fact that a simple wooden staff had turned into a weapon as strong as the broadswords carried by warrior echidnas. He looked up from the staff and into the eyes of his opponent. It was a large goanna.

CHAPTER 25

"Well, well, well. Would you look at the wee wooden weapon ya got there," Durward said as he stepped toward Devon and eyed the staff carefully. "Looks like a wooden staff, but it doesn't behave like one, and it seems to have the strength of a sword. Hmm, I got to get me one of those." Then looking from Devon to Sebastian and back again, he said, "Am I looking at recruits, prisoners, or are ya fellas on holiday?"

Devon was speechless, gazing down at the staff in his paw.

In fits of laughter, Babble, Jibber and Jabber rolled on the top of the boulder like marbles tossed in a game.

"Has the squirrel glider got your tongue, young man?" Durward asked Devon. "You can put your fine weapon down now," he said. "Where did you get that anyway?"

"Yes, yes, you're right," Devon stammered, lowering the staff. "I always thought it was just a wooden staff. It was given to me by my stepfather, Colum."

"Didn't know ya had it in ya, did ya, me mate?" Durward asked.

"No, as a matter of fact, I didn't," Devon answered, still astounded.

"What's your name, and where are you from?"

"My name is Devon, and the quoll you were battling is Sebastian."

Sebastian extended a paw. Durward took it, shaking it until Sebastian thought his entire arm would fall off.

"My pleasure, mate! My pleasure! So sorry I attacked you," Durward said as he continued shaking Sebastian's arm. "You can never be sure who you'll come across in the forest these days."

"I can understand that," Sebastian said, rubbing his arm. "We're a bit on edge ourselves. We've come from Kirby-Doane."

Durward finally stopped shaking Sebastian's arm, and said. "I've heard of Kirby-Doane. Isn't that the village that was recently attacked?"

"Yes, that's right," Devon answered. "I guess news travels fast in the forest."

"That it does. What kind of creatures attacked your village, Sebastian?"

"Dragon lizards."

Durward winced. "They are nasty animals for sure. So, are you hunting dragon lizards out here in the forest by yourselves?"

"Actually no, we're not looking for dragon lizards yet," Devon replied. "We are looking for the rebel army first, then we'll hunt dragon lizards."

"Well, you found the rebel army," Durward said proudly.

"Yes, seems we have!" added Sebastian.

"My men and I welcome you." Durward looked at Sebastian inquisitively. "So, it's not just the two of ya, is it? Where are your forces, and how many are they? And are there more wooden staffs like the one this fella has?" He pointed at Devon.

"We've been able to gather two hundred men-at-arms, two squadrons of sugar gliders, and a company of men who are skilled with bows and arrows." Sebastian explained. "We've also called out for reinforcements from other villages and woodland communities. These men are mere farmers and villagers, but they are strong and willing to fight. As for Devon's staff, looks like that's one of a kind. Oh, I must not forget, we have been trying to contact the Gang-gangs. They would be a help as well."

"Oooh . . . Gang-gangs. They're a noisy bunch for sure," Durward said.

From his perch on top of the boulder, Babble bobbed his head. "Yessir, they is. I hear that they throw rocks at their enemies whilst they's making noise!" There was a moment when everyone turned to look up at Babble. Mouth open, eyes round, he nodded excitedly.

Durward blinked twice at Babble. "Fair enough, can't wait to see that." Then to Sebastian, he continued, "We're honored to have you. In the morning we'll all meet. We have a lot to discuss."

"Sounds good to me," Sebastian said.

"Now, to find my army..." Durward said as he scanned the dark wood.

Sebastian and Devon entered the rebel camp with their troops early the next morning. Everyone's spirits were high as word of the two armies spread. The sounds of merriment could be heard everywhere. Some soldiers had formed a group and were tuning instruments. An echidna played a flute. The cheerful tones of the instrument moved on the wind, reaching out to everyone in the camp, touching every ear until the music took hold of them. Several quolls strummed their lutes, while a number of bilbies kept time to the melody by beating a hollow log with sticks. Many gathered to listen, tap their feet, and take in the harmony.

The smell of a morning meal cooking wafted through the air. A large group of goannas stood nearby rubbing their claws together in anticipation of sharing breakfast. Another group of soldiers talked around the fire, grinning and nodding at one another.

"So, how's your appetite this morning, Devon?" Sebastian asked.

"I'm always ready for a good meal," Devon said as he gazed past Sebastian toward the far side of the camp. What he saw surprised him. A familiar kowari was running through a crowd of soldiers. "That looks like..." Devon said to himself.

Sebastian stared at Devon quizzically. Turning in the direction of Devon's stare, he saw the soldiers parting. Two young kowaries pushed through the group, while two young echidnas followed in their wake.

"Ah, I think I recognize that kowari," Devon said with a smile.

"Emma, look! It's Devon. Look at the white star on his forehead. I'm sure it's him. Devon, Devon, it's us, Erik and Emma." He began running toward the fox and waving his paw.

"What are you doing here?" Devon asked as Erik approached. Smiling, he clasped Erik's paw in his. "It's so good to see you again. I thought you would be on your way home by now." Devon smiled at Emma. "How is it that you and your sister have become a part of this rebel army?"

"We met Stokley and Slade on our way home," Erik said as he pointed at the two echidnas. "They told us about the prisoners that are in the dungeons beneath the fortress. Two of those prisoners happen to be young puggles from our village of Digby. We cannot go home without Ackley and Amber." The fire at the center of camp warmed him as he spoke. "We traveled a long way, and we've collected all we need to help our mum, but we have also learned a lot on our journey." Erik smiled at Devon as he spoke. "We met a wolf spider one evening, and he said something that I cannot forget. He said that we are all a part of this forest, and that sometimes circumstances are much bigger than we are. The spider said we may not see everything clearly, and that small things sometimes are more important than they appear at first glance." A look of sorrow came upon him. "We may have thought we controlled events," he said sadly, "but we haven't. Events have controlled us. We had to make a decision, and it wasn't an easy one."

"So now you are part of the army that will attack the fortress."

"That's right. We'll do everything we can to help free our friends."

The fire burned brightly before them, and many soldiers filled their bowls with the mornings meal.

"And your mum?" Devon asked, solemnly.

"Bede is with her, and Aldon promised that she would be alright until we return. We were faced with a difficult decision. I'm learning that it's how we deal with our problem that's important." He paused, taking in all the activity around him. "We're here to fight alongside you and the other soldiers. Durward is not just a good friend, he's like family, and we will stand beside him as well." Erik reached out for Stokley and pulled him toward Devon. "This is Stokley and his friend Slade." Erik nodded at Slade. "All four of us have made a commitment to one another and to Ackley and Amber. We will do everything we can to free them and bring them back to their mum."

Erik rested his paw on Devon's arm, shaking his head sadly. "Many villages have been attacked and burned. We all know now that these attacks are not new. The woodlanders have put up with them for too long, ever since the King of Demelza came to power. Many who have tried to fight the king have been imprisoned. It has to stop, Devon."

"Yes, the king. The evil fox," Devon said despondently.

"I'm sorry it's a fox, Devon," Erik said. "But our mum taught us to judge each woodland animal we meet for who they are, not what they are. We know you, and we consider you our friend."

"Thank you," Devon said looking at the four young friends. "Now, what do you say? Let's all have some breakfast."

CHAPTER 26

The trail up Mt. Olga was steep and winding. A cold wind whistled through the craggy mountaintops. Numerous rockslides had left scree strewn along the path, and only a few gnarled trees lined the way. Mt. Olga was not far from the fortress of Demelza, but it looked like another world. The mountain overlooked the fortress, but its bleak and frigid terrain stood in stark contrast to the lush forestland of Demelza's valley.

"Keep up, you lazy dog!" The thylacine's shorter strides were no match for Gorgon's powerful ones. Gorgon turned and watched as the creature dragged himself up the path. Exhausted, Flitch followed Gorgon, panting and tripping over stones along

197

the way. Gorgon looked up into the ashen sky. A blanket of low-lying clouds churned close to the mountaintop, causing the air to feel thick and wet. A narrow path wound its way to the top. One side dropped off sharply, ending in nothing but jagged outcroppings of rock. Nothing would survive a fall.

Gorgon glanced back disgustedly at the thylacine, and then glanced off the edge of the path. "If Malfoden didn't think you were necessary, I would throw you off this mountain."

"Keep your foul words to yourself. You need me just as much as I need you," He snarled at Gorgon between staggered breaths. "I can roam free. Your wretched fox king confines you. He is a king of naught, false and good for nothing!"

"I am not going to enter into a battle of wits with you." He shot an angry look over his shoulder at Flitch. "You're not worth my time. Once Malfoden is free, all the lands of Sunderland will be under our control. And Demelza will be mine, as promised." Gorgon turned on his heels, grabbing Flitch by the neck, shaking him soundly. "After that you can roam wherever you like in Sunderland, but stay away from Demelza. I will not want to see your ugly fanged snout again." His angry voice drilled into the thylacine's ears. "Malfoden is waiting. Pick up the pace. I need to get back to the fortress. As you so perceptively pointed out, I cannot stray for long." He tossed the thylacine aside like an old used cloak and continued walking. Flitch growled angrily, as he picked himself up and reluctantly followed Gorgon.

Up ahead, tucked between two steep walls of stone, was an opening. The fissure in the mountain dwarfed the two evil creatures as they approached. Gorgon stopped just inside the entry.

Reaching to his left, he pulled a torch out of a bracket that was affixed to the wall. He took a piece of flint from a pack on his belt and lit the torch. The walls came alive with the flickering light. A combination of minerals and water droplets clinging to the rock created a sparkling sensation unlike any other cavern in all of Sunderland.

The narrow tunnel led deep into the mountain. Gorgon strode ahead, the torch lighting the way down the stone corridor. The tunnel suddenly opened into a large cavern. Multitudes of sheath-tail bats hung on the roof of the cave, watching the two strangers pass beneath them. Huge stalagmite pillars stood around the cavern, seeming to hold the ceiling of the cave in place. They glittered in the torchlight, standing like ancient columns from some long forgotten city. A constant drip of water and the occasional flutter of bat wings were the only sounds beside their footfalls.

Gorgon passed between two massive pillars and entered another chamber. At the far end of the hollow space was an arched opening. Numerous lintels surrounded the doorway supporting it. Strange symbols were engraved into each stone, their meaning a mystery.

Gorgon stopped outside the entrance beneath the arch. He looked back to make sure Flitch followed, and then he stepped into the small alcove. The temperature dropped. Gorgon could see his breath. A grey haze filled the enclosed space, and through it, the container appeared. The translucent case was embedded vertically into the stone wall. A shadowy form stood inside it. Gorgon narrowed his eyes, trying to bring the form of Malfoden into focus. The old numbat had been imprisoned here for a long time. Most of his power remained captive within, but Malfoden's desire to be free was still strong. His craving to seek revenge on Aldon and all the other living creatures that Aldon held dear was also still very much alive. Gorgon and the demon would help Malfoden achieve this goal.

"We are here, Malfoden." Gorgon's words echoed off the pillars and walls.

"I have waited a long time, Gorgon. Too long." The sinister voice reached them on a cold wind that seemed to blow at them from the tomb where Malfoden was encased. "My vengeance cannot wait! The plan must be set in motion now. The time approaches."

Through the misty walls of the container Gorgon could almost see the anger and frustration on Malfoden's face. At this moment, he was grateful that Malfoden could not reach out of his prison.

"Gorgon, you must steal the sword of Demelza and return it here." An image of the sword's green stone flashed in Gorgon's mind. "If you are to rule Demelza as I have promised you, the young fox must be eliminated. I have foreseen his rise to power. Cynric will be replaced. If the young fox is able to seize the sword, all I have suffered will be for nothing."

It was quiet for a moment, and Gorgon could hear Flitch's nervous panting behind him. He turned slowly to look down at him. The thylacine was cowering against the wall, his front paws pushing at the dirt floor of the cave. "Flitch, I sent you to eliminate him, and you failed." Malfoden's anger seemed to pierce the rock like a bolt made of ice. Flitch cowered, trying his best to disappear into the rock wall. "How many opportunities have you missed? You let him slip through your paws."

Malfoden's voice grew louder with each reproach. "You will have one last chance to redeem yourself. There is a rebel army converging on the fortress of Demelza as we speak. Your opportunity to seize the sword from Cynric will come when they attack. Beware of small creatures that travel with this rebel army. They are small, but from small things unexpected dangers come."

CHAPTER 27

Asevere thunderstorm rolled off Mt. Olga and threatened to sweep down into the forests of Demelza. The occupants of the fortress had gathered in the great hall for dinner. Cynric sat with a turkey leg in one paw; his other was wrapped around a flagon of mead. Braydon and several commanders occupied the table with him.

Cynric snarled as he scanned the room. Braydon sat across from him, watching with narrowed eyes. Cynric saw distrust and anger in those eyes. All manner of Demelza inhabitants were assembled in the great hall. There were quolls, quokkas, dragon lizards, foxes, bilbies, and many others. Small squabbles broke out like summer squalls sweeping through the stone hall. Claws were raised, and teeth were bared as the diverse group attempted, with little success, to get along with one another. A quokka and a bilby argued over scraps from a discarded turkey carcass. Two kowaries rolled on the stone floor, pummeling each other as other animals passed them, oblivious to the brawl. Cynric sniggered under his breath. The fights taking place around him were his favorite form of entertainment.

A large chandelier hung in the center of the room from a thick rope, bathing the hall in candlelight. Numerous servants ran back and forth from the kitchen to the dining hall as they busily served the evening meal. Several quokka maidens filled and refilled goblets, while other servants arranged various plates of food before Cynric and his soldiers. Bowls of fruits, various platters of meats and forest greens covered the tables. Sweet puddings, candied berries, and other treats were passed to all the hungry creatures gathered there.

As Cynric lifted his flask to his lips, preparing to take a swig of the warm liquid, he spotted Luella crossing the room with a plate of fresh mushrooms. He looked at his quoll commander. Braydon watched Luella as well, and then he turned to face Cynric. His eyes blazed with contempt, and a low growl escaped his lips.

"Does the food disagree with you, Braydon?" Cynric asked sarcastically.

"No, sire, it does not," Braydon replied caustically.

"Then let's not look so sour, mate." Cynric grinned and took a ravenous bite from the turkey leg. "Soon you'll have plenty of time to vent your frustrations. My forest spies tell me the rebels are forming an army and are making plans to attack my fortress."

"Do we know any details?"

"Not yet, but we're working on that." He shook the turkey leg at him. "No creature has ever been successful in mounting an attack against Demelza. This is just another group of malcontents. They're not worth the time it takes to kill them."

Luella, overhearing the conversation, stopped beside Cynric to fill his flagon. "Sire, I believe it's not worth your time to bother with them at all."

"Hmm, you may be right about that. They are insignificant creatures," Cynric said with a smirk. "Your sense of social justice has always fascinated me, Luella. However, your idealistic nature may not be suitable, considering our present circumstances."

"I disagree, sire. It is especially suitable in times like these. We must be aware of how we treat our fellow creatures." She paused with a thoughtful look on her face. "We should be generous, perhaps even benevolent. You must recognize that you not only rule this kingdom, but you are also a part of it."

"Part of the kingdom, you say? It's my kingdom to deal with as I see fit!" he said angrily. The swift wave of anger faded and Cynric waved his paw in the air impatiently. "I'll give it some thought, Luella." He knew that he wouldn't—couldn't—but he wasn't certain why. There was a sort of green haze in his mind. It was like a wall leading him to one clear path. Destruction, pain, and power were the only thoughts he could hold onto for any length of time. All other thoughts evaporated like morning fog.

"Luella, I would like to see you in my chambers this evening. Come as soon as you've finished serving the meal. We wouldn't want our little forest friends to go hungry, now would we?" He gazed around the room, murmuring under his breath, "Disgusting atmosphere of death and decay." Then, as though struck by an epiphany, he stood and pushed his chair back. It crashed to the floor. "You wretched horde!" he shouted. Activity in the hall ceased as all eyes looked up and rested on the angry fox. "How little you know. You live every day not realizing how easily, and without warning you can be struck down."

Silence filled the great hall. He paused for a moment, glaring out over the room. Then, as he turned to leave the dining hall, Braydon stepped into his path. Everyone, including Luella, looked on, certain that a confrontation would ensue.

"Watch your step, Braydon. It's dangerous to threaten me." Cynric's paw grasped the hilt of the sword at his waist. The green stone in the hilt was clear and the candlelight from above reflected off its faceted surface.

"Why don't you just kill me, Cynric? It's obvious you don't trust me."

"Yes, Braydon, you're right. I don't trust you and anger is clear in your eyes. However, you are much too interesting to kill," Cynric said with a slight smile on his face. "Besides, you keep me on my toes. Therefore, I have chosen to let you live. Be grateful for it!" His face contorted with anger as he made this final statement. His words flew forcefully, echoing off the walls of the room. He stepped past Braydon and left the great hall.

Luella hugged Braydon before leaving. She needed to assure him that she was safe and could handle the troubled fox.

"He just needs someone to listen to him," she said softly.

"I hope you are right, Luella. I will be close by if you need me."

"I know you will, and that gives me the support and courage I need."

Walking down the dark stone corridor, she turned her thoughts to the king. The pain that Cynric felt was deep. She could see it in his eyes sometimes when he didn't know she was watching him. If only he could be freed from the anguish he'd created for himself.

Ever since Cynric arrived in Demelza so many years ago, Luella believed there was more to the tormented fox than met the eye. She had spent many evenings trying to draw it out of him, to help him deal with his misery. She had not been successful. However, she did notice that she was like a balm to him, helping to calm and relax him.

She continued on, taking one last glance at Braydon. The candle she carried reflected off the stone walls, lighting her footfalls on the stone floor.

CHAPTER 28

E rik spied the fortress through swaying blades of grass. Deafening booms of thunder rolled overheard, shaking the earth beneath his feet. He had been exploring the meadows, within sight of the stronghold, for most of the day. The rebel army remained hidden in the relative safety of the woods behind him. The commanders had decided that it would be best to free the prisoners before attacking. Then, if their attack failed, the prisoners would at least be released.

He could feel evening approach, but the grey sky made it difficult for him to tell how long it would be before nightfall. The few remaining rays of the sun struggled to penetrate the heavy clouds that hung over the field, like a shroud. The air was charged with electricity, and Erik's fur bristled with it. Brilliant bolts of light flashed across the sky, while on the ground, a warm wind swirled up, causing the tall grass to wave rhythmically around him.

They had collected all the ingredients necessary to help their mum. He knew he should be heading home with Emma, but he couldn't. They were committed now. He and Emma were well aware and afraid that time was running short for everyone, including their mum. How had it all come to this? He didn't know. Circumstances propelled them onward. They seemed to have been caught up in the misfortune that was playing out, reacting as each new dilemma confronted them.

He had tarried too long. He needed to confirm the location of one more wombat tunnel before returning to camp. Once he had its location etched in his mind they would decide how the tunnels should be explored. Erik had volunteered to locate the tunnels because he was small and quick. Everyone agreed he was less likely to be noticed crossing the fields. Nevertheless, there was always a risk. The rebel army commanders had a general idea of the location of the tunnels. He had already located two. There remained one more area to explore. One of the three tunnels was sure to lead to the maze of dungeons under the fortress.

He turned to go, glancing back over his shoulder. The feeling of being followed washed over him. Sensing movement, he came to a stop. The waving grass in front of him crackled and came alive. It parted, and out from between the brown and green blades stepped an amber-colored scorpion with its pinchers held high. Erik knew little of forest scorpions, but he did know two important facts: they were poisonous and they didn't see well.

The scorpion clicked its pinchers over its head. "I hear you breathing, my friend. Come closer so I can see you." The scorpion's voice, a high-pitched whine, vibrated in the air around him, making his ears twitch. "What are you doing here all by yourself?" Its threatening tone sent a shiver down Erik's spine. He didn't dare respond.

"I smell your fear. It gives you away." The scorpion took a step closer to Erik, opening and closing its pincers. Its long spindly legs were attached to an elongated body. Its body ended in a segmented tail, which the creature held aloft. At the tip of its tail was a black stinger. The scorpion lunged forward. Erik dropped to the ground, spun toward the scorpion, and rolled under its belly. In one swift motion, He removed his dagger from its sheath and took a stab at the scorpion. The creature stepped to the side, exposing Erik to its stinger. It came down toward him and stabbed the ground, missing Erik by inches. Erik rolled clear and stood, brandishing his dagger. He jabbed at the scorpion's segmented body, sank the dagger in deep, and raked it along its side with all his might. The scorpion let out a deafening shriek. It lifted one of its long legs and pinned Erik to the ground. The jolt caused Erik's dagger to fly out of his paw. He tried desperately to free himself from under the weight of the creature, but he was caught beneath his leg. The scorpion looked down at him. Erik drew in his breath as its beak-like jaw came closer, snapping viciously at him.

"You'll be sorry you hurt me with your puny dagger. Now you will feel the sting of my weapon!"

Erik could hear the anger and pain in the scorpion's voice. He watched its sharp mouth move slowly toward him. In a final attempt, he stretched out his paw toward his dagger. It was too far away. He looked up at the clouds racing across the sky, resigned to his fate. But just as the stinger came into view, he saw a lasso sail over it, wrapping around it. With a jerk, the stinger disappeared and the scorpion was pulled away. Erik was free.

He jumped to his feet and retrieved his dagger. Numerous echidna warriors came out of the grass and surrounded the scorpion. Each one threw a lasso around it, trying to immobilize it. As they struggled to restrain the creature, its legs snapped and kicked, tossing echidnas in every direction. Erik moved quickly away from its thrashing legs. He saw Stokley step out from between swaying blades of grass with his recurve bow in hand. A flash of lightning lit the sky and a clap of thunder shook the earth as Stokley nocked an arrow and aimed. The arrow flew true, striking the scorpion at the back of his head. The scorpion was now reeling in pain, and Erik saw his opportunity. He ran toward the wounded creature and with a final thrust of his blade, he stabbed the scorpion in its heart. The beast fell over, and its legs flailed and jerked to a stop.

Erik breathed a sigh of relief. "You left the shelter of the forest!" Erik said in amazement. "I'm surprised you did. We all could have been killed here!" Huffing and puffing, eyes wide, Erik stood with his dagger in his paw. "You might have been noticed out here in the open."

"We saw movement in the grass. More movement than a small kowari like you would make." Stokley said quickly. "It just didn't seem right."

One of the echidna warriors stepped up. "We need to move out now." He glanced up at the fortress. "There are dragon lizards walking on the parapet. We cannot let them see us."

Slowly and carefully, they made their way back to the forest. Inside the shelter of the thick underbrush, the thunderstorm seemed to diminish. Yet, when Erik and Stokley looked back toward the stronghold, the storm churned fiercely over the fortification, as though the fortress itself was drawing the storm to its walls and towers.

"Tough day?" Durward asked with a grin.

"Very," Erik answered. Then he shook from the top of his head to his feet. "Whoa! That felt good. I'm glad that's over," he said. "That was one scorpion too many."

"That's it, Erik, shake it off!" Durward said.

"Durward, you should have seen Stokley! We killed that scorpion together. He has become an expert with his bow." Erik laughed with relief. They met and battled a dangerous creature today, and together they had won.

For the moment, there was a feeling of relief, but the job of finding a clear wombat tunnel was not yet accomplished.

CHAPTER 29

"This is it, boys," Durward said to the small troop of commanders before him. "Erik has located three wombat tunnels. We need to explore them as soon as possible. Erik and Stokley have volunteered to go into each burrow until we find one that is clear. Let's hope that we reach the dungeons through this first tunnel. Time is of the essence." Durward looked around at his comrades. They all nodded. "Get in quickly and get out."

Slade poked her head out from behind Stokley.

"You won't go . . ."

"Without you?" Stokley gazed sadly at Slade. "This time, Slade, you must stay here. It will be too dangerous." He reached out and took Slade's paw in his. "Emma will keep you company back at camp," he reassured her. "I promise you, Erik and I will return as soon as we can."

Just then, Daegal came through the thick undergrowth and saluted Durward. "The army is preparing weapons, sir. No word yet from the sugar gliders. The whereabouts of the Gang-gangs are unknown, but the gliders continue to search." His face showed some worry and he shook his head as he looked up into the trees. "Strange thing about our feathered friends. When we need 'em the winged noisemakers can't be found."

"Don't worry, they'll be here," Erik assured him. "For now, Stokley and I have a job to do. We can't mount an attack until our part is accomplished.

"Daegal, would you please see to it that Slade gets back to camp safely?" Stokley asked. Slade trembled where she stood and began to whimper. Everyone could see that it would be difficult for her to be away from Stokley.

"Of course, you can depend on it." Daegal smiled down at Slade with a reassuring look. "Not to worry, little miss. Daegal will take good care of ya, and Stokley will be back 'afore you knows it."

Slade looked up at Daegal with pitiful eyes. Stokley gave her a quick kiss on the forehead and hugged her tightly to his chest. Letting her go, she nodded and reached out her paw to Daegal, who took it gently. With one last wistful look at Stokley, she turned away.

Erik nodded at Stokley, and the pair entered the tunnel. Sunlight quickly faded as they moved deeper into the ancient burrow.

"Pull a torch from my pack, Stokley." Stokley reached up to the pack Erik carried on his back and pulled out a small torch. Erik used his flint to light it. "Stay close behind me. The burrow is narrow and we need to stay together. Let's see how far we can go."

"I'm with you, Erik."

They moved into the dank tunnel. Roots dangled overhead and the dampness increased the deeper they penetrated. Rocks and debris were strewn everywhere along the tunnel floor.

"Take this." Erik handed Stokley the torch. They had come upon a huge rock blocking the tunnel. "I'll try to move the rock." He dropped his pack to the ground. With his back pressed against the rock and his feet firmly set into the dirt, he pushed. It did not move. He paused for a moment to catch his breath.

He glanced at Stokley, and Stokley stared back with wide unblinking eyes. His chest heaved with panting breaths, and the torch shook in his trembling paw. A strange stillness fell around them. Their noses twitched as they caught a momentary whiff of foulness in the air. They looked up at the roof of the passage where the roots were waving, moving inward, toward the dark depths of the tunnel. The damp, chilly air swept around them, causing them both to shiver. An ominous and sinister sound drifted through the tunnel on the cold current of air. It passed by them and floated away into the gloom of the burrow.

Still leaning on the stone, Erik looked at his friend. Stokley's eyes were as large as saucers. Erik shook his head and whispered, "It's nothing, Stokley. Pay it no mind." He pushed again with all his might, and the stone rolled to the side of the tunnel. They had just enough room to pass.

"Come on." Erik picked up his pack, lifted it to his back, and Stokley handed him the torch. They walked by the rock. Behind it, the tunnel curved sharply to the right and Erik moved in that direction. He came to an abrupt halt. Rock and rubble blocked the tunnel. They could go no farther.

"Guess it's on to the next tunnel." Erik shivered, then added, "I didn't like this one anyway."

The two friends walked back toward the entrance.

"What do you think that was, Erik?" There was a tremor in Stokley's voice.

"It was just the wind."

"But where did it come from? It sounded like someone laughing."

Erik stopped and glared at Stokley. "It was just the wind, Stokley. The wind! We have a job to do. Don't think about the sound. But let's just hope it's not in the next tunnel," he murmured.

CHAPTER 30

Cynric entered his chamber. Light from two torches sent flickering shadows into the far corners of the room. A thunderstorm pounded above the battlements, and wind crawled along the exterior walls of the fortress, screeching as it scrambled over stone and moss.

Cynric gripped the hilt of the sword. Slowly taking it from its sheath, he lifted it and held it in his open palms, staring down at it. Flames from the torches reflected off the blade, and an ominous cloud swirled within the emerald stone. He walked to the table and placed the sword upon it. A sense of relief engulfed him, as though a heavy burden was lifted. Then an overpowering sadness enveloped him, making him feel weak and helpless. Thoughts of his long lost son, and his mate, raced through his head. He looked down at his paws, examining them. *Do these paws belong to me? Are they mine? Can I change these dark times and make them light? Where have my days gone?* Searching his soul, he found nothing but emptiness.

A light tap at the door made him look up. Luella stood in the open portal. Clothed in a white peasant dress and sky-blue apron, she was a welcome sight. She walked slowly toward him, the torchlight from the hall outlined her silhouette. Close enough now to look into her eyes, he reached out to her. She allowed him to lean against her, resting his head on her shoulder. She wrapped her arms around him, and he relaxed as though he had returned home after a long, arduous journey.

"Put down the sword for good, Cynric," she whispered to him. "Put down the sword."

"I cannot. It will not let me go. As hard as I try, I am not able to free myself from it."

CHAPTER 31

D urward and Devon sat before the campfire waiting for Erik and Stokley's return from exploring the second tunnel. Nearby, a group of soldiers were telling lighthearted tales about their commander.

"Well, I tell you, men, we thought the bloody lizard was dying the way he was screaming. Sounded just like a squealing pig!" said one echidna to the group. The hearty laughs and knee slapping were exceeded only by the love and loyalty they felt for their commander. Durward and Devon were grinning from ear to ear, enjoying the lively conversation. "And how many times has Durward gotten lost?" a commander quoll asked. "Will someone please give that skinny excuse for a lizard a compass?" The laughs grew louder.

"It was only a temporary condition," Durward responded. "You all are very funny, my friends. Glad I'm good for a laugh."

Devon turned to Durward and smacked him soundly on the back. "In such dark times, it's good to laugh, Durward. Don't feel bad because you are the subject of our merriment. We love ya still!" Smiling, Durward nodded his head as he scanned the faces of his soldiers, his friends.

Durward held up his paw. "Listen! Silence, boys!" He turned to Devon as the group swiftly moved their paws and claws to the closest available weapon. Devon reached for his staff. Rustling underbrush gave way as Erik and Stokley appeared. The two friends were covered in dirt and barely able to carry themselves to the campfire.

"Well, just look at the two of ya!" Durward exclaimed as he walked toward them. "Aren't you two fellas just a sight to behold?"

Devon breathed a sigh of relief as he followed Durward.

Everyone gathered around the two young friends, impatient to hear the result of their latest exploration. Devon reached out and brushed the dirt and roots from the fur on Erik's head. Durward picked clumps of muck and stones from between Stokley's spines.

"Good job, fellas. We can see you are very serious about your work! Now tell us, how did it go the second time around?"

Erik frowned. "Blocked."

Stokley shook his head and looked at the ground. "At least we didn't hear that evil sound we heard in the first tunnel."

Erik groaned. "Stokley."

"Sorry, Erik. It slipped out." "What evil sound?" asked Devon.

Erik raised his head to Devon and Durward, a dark look passing over his face. "I didn't want you to know," he said quietly. "I was afraid you would stop us from continuing. Anyway, we didn't hear it in this tunnel. We only need a short rest before we explore the third. I'm sure it's gonna be clear!"

With concern evident in his face, Durward repeated Devon's question. "What evil sound?"

Stokley and Erik looked at each other. Then letting out a sigh, Erik said, "We were in the first burrow. I was pushing a rock out of the way when we heard a strange sound. It was like a laugh. And there was a cold breeze blowing through the tunnel." Erik shivered, cleared his throat and shifted nervously where he stood. "We didn't let it stop us then, and it won't stop us now. We need to explore the last tunnel soon. The rest of the army is depending on us." He pointed at his friends. "You all agreed that we would not attack the fortress until all the animals are freed," Erik said firmly. "The prisoners might be caught up in the battle. We don't want the blood of innocent creatures on our hands. We have to get them out before the battle begins."

"Yes, Erik. We know what was agreed." Durward turned to Devon. "These young ones need a rest. They've done enough for one day. We'll attempt the third tunnel at dawn."

"We'll rest for a bit," Erik said as he and Stokley settled down next to the campfire. The two exhausted friends, comforted by the warmth of the fire, closed their eyes. Moments later, they were asleep.

Durward pointed at his soldiers. "You three stand guard. You, and you, get a message out to the troops. Update them with the news of the second tunnel. Let them know we will go into the third at dawn, after Erik and Stokley have had some rest," he said. The two friends were sleeping, slumped together and snoring quietly. "Heaven knows, they need it," he added.

The two soldiers disappeared into the dense forest. The remaining soldiers settled down next to the smoldering fire to keep watch over Erik and Stokley.

Durward placed his claw on Devon's shoulder and they walked into the forest.

"The woods are gloomy in these early hours of the evening, don't you think?"

"Yes, they are. I can sense your apprehension." Devon studied the commander's features. "Do you feel that a change in plans is called for?"

"I don't think so. You're right though, I am concerned, but I have faith in Erik and Stokley."

"What do you think it was they heard in the tunnel?" Devon asked.

Durward shook his head. "I'm not certain, but the mind can play tricks on us when we're under stress or frightened. Maybe this was the case with our young friends."

"Maybe you're right, but it's not like these boys to imagine things. They both know how serious this situation is."

Darkness embraced the forest, and the moon peeked between the trees, lighting their way.

Devon came to a sudden stop, nose in the air and ears pricked up. "There is movement among the trees," Devon muttered. "Movement that I can only sense, not see, a shadow perhaps. Something not, not..." Devon struggled to explain his feelings. "Something not solid," he finally blurted out. "Durward . . . to your right."

Durward pulled his dagger from its sheath and turned quickly in the direction Devon indicated. "I don't see anything," he whispered as he peered into the woods.

A cold current of air passed between them. It made Durward flinch, but Devon stood as still as a fence post, his fur bristling. The air carried a low rumbling voice that resonated from tree to tree. "You cannot win," it murmured. A low sinister laugh passed by them on the night breeze and faded deep into the forest.

Durward glanced back at the campfire. His soldiers talked quietly amongst themselves. Erik and Stokley were still sleeping, huddled together.

He turned slowly to face Devon. "No need to doubt them now, mate," he murmured.

Devon swallowed hard. "Right, Durward. No need to doubt them now."

CHAPTER 32

Devon paced anxiously back and forth at the edge of the rebel camp. His feet swept aside dirt, leaves, and twigs as his steps created a furrow on the forest floor. Erik and Stokley had been gone for what felt like ages. They were exploring the third and final wombat tunnel. If this last tunnel was not clear they would attack Demelza whether the prisoners were free or not.

Out of the corner of his eye, he saw Durward approach and sit down on a nearby log. Devon stopped pacing. Then he glanced at Durward. Durward shook his head. There was no news. He returned to the well-worn path he had made in the dirt and continued pacing.

"They've been gone most of the day, Durward. Evening is falling."

"Yes, they have, but there's still a chance they'll succeed. I have faith in them." He tapped his claw on the log, indicating an empty spot for Devon. "Come sit beside me. You'll wear out the pads on the bottom of your feet at the rate you're going."

Devon walked over to Durward and sat down. The two friends stared out into the darkening forest together. Everyone in the camp had been in high spirits when Erik and Stokley left at dawn. Now, with evening approaching, positive attitudes were flagging.

Durward studied the fox and asked, "What's on your mind?"

Devon placed his elbows on his legs, and dropped his head into both paws. "I am thinking, first of all, that I would like to see our two small friends return safely, and soon. Then, I would like to hear that we can enter the dungeons under the fortress before our attack, but I'm beginning to believe that it can't be done." He lifted his head and scrutinized Durward's face. He could see the concern in the goanna's eyes.

Branches in the undergrowth separated as Beldon arrived.

"They haven't returned?" he asked. Devon and Durward shook their heads.

In the approaching twilight, Devon listened to a nearby brook. Water gurgled as it tripped over the rock-strewn waterway on its journey downstream. The lighthearted sound was a sharp contrast to the despair the three companions shared.

An owl hooted in the trees above their heads. Devon looked up. The owl was sitting in the low branches. It hooted at them again, blinked once, and turning its head, peered down the winding trail toward Demelza. It was then that Erik and Stokley could be seen coming up the path. Erik had his dagger drawn, and Stokley's recurve bow was notched and at the ready. Devon and Durward jumped to their feet, anxious to hear the result of the day's venture.

Erik and Stokley put up their weapons; their shoulders drooped as tension left their bodies. Stokley could not raise his eyes from the forest floor.

"We failed," Erik whimpered as he looked up at Devon. His eyes filled with tears. "I'm sorry. We tried. We had such high hopes . . ."

"My small friends, you have done your very best," Devon said. "There was no guarantee that a tunnel would be clear. This will not stop our plans to attack. You can be sure of that."

"Can you tell us what happened?" Durward asked.

Devon placed his paw on Erik's shoulder as he spoke. "Why don't we head back to camp first, Durward? These boys are tired and can tell us what they saw over a nice warm meal."

The small group began the short trek back to the main camp. They walked along the banks of the babbling brook, while over-head the masked owl followed in the trees. It wasn't long before the camp came into view. The soldiers busied themselves ready-ing weapons, reviewing battle plans, and preparing the evening meal over carefully stoked campfires. Many stopped to salute and greet the small group's return.

"Let's sit here." Devon pointed to a small fire surrounded by several flat stones that had been set up as benches. When they settled, a portly old quokka waddled up to deliver warm soup and biscuits for the two hungry lads. Erik and Stokley looked into the smiling, toothless grin of the old quokka and nodded their appreciation. Word of their return spread quickly throughout the camp. Emma and Slade, ecstatic to hear of their arrival, were soon sitting beside them.

"Now, tell us," Devon said. "What happened?"

"It was much like the others," Erik began. "We went in deeper than any of the other two tunnels. Just when it looked as though we had a clear route to the maze beneath the fortress, we could move no farther. It was blocked." Erik rubbed his forehead and covered his eyes, trying his best to get the words out. "Rocks, dirt and wood were in our path. It was the same situation as the other two."

"We felt that strange wind in the tunnel again," Stokley said. "We heard that sinister laugh again, and this time it spoke. It said, 'You cannot win.'" Stokley shook his head. "I don't understand. It's as though someone can see us, but there's no one there."

Erik heaved a sigh and looked up from his bowl. "Stokley's right. You feel the presence of something. You can sense movement, as though there's a shadow drifting nearby. I admit, it's difficult to describe, unless you experience it yourself."

Durward and Devon glanced at each other in silent understanding.

Emma pounded her fist on the stone bench beneath her. "There must be something we can do!"

"There is, Emma." Devon cleared his throat as he stood up. "We will attack the fortress as planned. There may be some way that we can access the dungeons during the battle."

Durward reached out and touched Devon's arm. "Have you considered the consequences, Devon?" He scanned the camp, looking around at the soldiers. "It will mean that many men will be taken away from the fight to try to locate the dungeons."

Devon stomped the ground. "So be it!" he shouted. Then he stopped. He clamped his eyes shut in a painful wince, and his muzzle moved, but no sound emerged. When his voice returned, he said in a flat, emotionless tone, "The sword is quiet tonight."

The group stared at Devon. Erik moved to touch Devon, but Durward stopped him with a shake of his head.

"Devon, what is it?" Erik asked in a whisper.

"This shadow. It seems to drift through the forest, carried on the wind, as though it's waiting for us. I believe it's dangerous, perhaps more dangerous than our evil king. I don't know why I know that. I feel it." Devon broke free from his vacant stare and looked around at his friends. "The sword, I can almost feel it, and I can sense the presence of this shadow."

"Devon, Durward!" One of the great quoll warriors came sprinting toward them. "Babble reports movement on the eastern side of the camp. You should come right away."

CHAPTER 33

I n no time, Devon and Durward mustered a group of soldiers, including Stokley and Erik. When they arrived at the far side of the camp, two quolls and an echidna warrior were waiting for further orders.

"What's happening here?" Durward asked.

"Over there, sir." The echidna pointed toward a row of rocks that formed a low wall across the forest floor. The wall was broken at one point where a path led further into the depths of the forest. "There is movement. Babble and his crew have been watching it for some time. It's coming toward us and we have been waiting. I think it's coming up the path between those two rock walls."

"Quiet everyone." Devon waved his paw. "Let's see what arrives."

A rumbling sliced through the air, along with the crunch of leaves and twigs, as an unknown creature approached. Erik and Stokley peered out into the darkness from behind a large tree stump.

"I hear it," Erik said as he turned and looked up at Devon.

"Yes, I hear it too. I think . . . I think it's singing!" Devon said.

Erik gasped. "Yes, it *is* singing!"

The singing stopped. Around the bend in the path, at the very point where the low wall was broken, appeared a huge wombat. Straddled on the wombat's neck was a black-faced kowari. The kowari held reins that were wrapped around the muzzle of the wombat. He was a fine kowari, wearing a green, pointed hat with a red band around it. A white feather stuck out of the band. The hat was tipped over one ear, nearly covering his left eye. He wore a gold velvet sash, and a quiver of arrows and a bow were strapped to his back.

"Whoa, Lazlo! Whoa!" The kowari pulled on the reins, and the wombat stopped with a low grumble. The kowari's ears twitched and his nose sniffed the night air. His eyes peered into the darkness as he dropped the reins and reached for his bow. He nocked an arrow, and said sharply, "Who's there? Come out or there'll be hell to pay!"

Erik stepped out boldly from behind the rock before anyone could stop him. "A kowari!" he exclaimed with surprise. "You're just a kowari."

"Just a kowari?" the stranger asked indignantly. "Last time I checked that is indeed what I am. And you! I suppose you're not *just* a kowari, right?"

"Oh, I'm sorry, sir. I meant no offense. What brings you this way?"

Showing no signs of fear, the kowari slowly stood, balanced himself on the wombat and pointed his bow directly at Erik. "I guess I could ask you the same question, young man!" With that, the kowari slowly lowered his bow.

"Yes, you could," Devon said as he walked out from behind the stump. The black faced kowari snapped to attention; bow at the ready. "Whoa! Lay down your weapon. We mean no harm. What are you doing in the woods of Demelza?"

The strange kowari slowly lowered his bow and shrugged. "I'm simply traveling through on business of my own. I will not interfere with you or your friends," he said as he tipped his head toward Devon and the others. "Just passing through."

Devon gazed at the wombat. It was huge. Larger than any he had ever seen before. Around his neck he wore a band from which a star shaped stone hung. It glowed with a purple light that cast beams on the ground in front of him. Devon walked toward him, examining every inch of the large animal, its small rider and the unusual stone.

"The name's Devon, and this bold little kowari is Erik."

Erik looked up at Devon and then at the rider. "What's your name?"

"The name's Byrnie," he said as he removed his hat from his head and performed a low sweeping bow. "Byrnie's my name. And this here's Lazlo, my trusted friend and transport. Lazlo and I go way back." He patted the wombat on the head. "Don't we?"

BYRNIE & LAZLO

Lazlo grumbled.

"He doesn't say much," Byrnie said. "But when he does ya better listen up! Right, Lazlo?"

Lazlo grumbled again.

Byrnie replaced his hat, and reached out a paw to Devon, who clasped it, shaking it firmly.

"Glad to meet you, cobber!" the strange kowari said.

"Might I ask if you'd be interested in a meal?" Devon asked. "Before you travel on your way, that is."

"Whatcha serving?"

"We were just getting ready to enjoy a bowl of hot soup when you arrived."

Erik looked up at Devon, and Devon returned Erik's look and winked.

Byrnie's eyes lit up at the mention of soup. "Soup, okay. Soup sounds good. Where you got the soup?"

"Our camp's just over the rise." Devon pointed back toward camp. "But, before we head in that direction, I am concerned about the stone your wombat friend wears around his neck. Glowing the way it does, it could give away our position to enemies here in the forest. Maybe he should remove it, until we get to camp, that is."

Lazlo growled loudly. "It was grandpa's." The wombat grumbled his first few words with a deep voice. "Never take it off."

"OK. It does look very important," Devon offered. "What does it do? Why does it glow?"

"Not sure," was Lazlo's brief answer.

The black-faced kowari looked intently at Devon and Erik. "Enemies? I'm not sure what's happening here, but Lazlo will not remove his stone. It was a gift from his grandfather, and he has worn it ever since his grandfather died." Byrnie shook his head slowly. "I would not ask him again, and there is no need to have him remove it." With that Byrnie pulled the band that held the stone. When the stone reached his paws he tucked it underneath Lazlo's thick brown fur. Then he picked up his reins.

"That should do it," he said. "Lead on, lead on. We don't want that soup to get cold."

The wombat lumbered forward.

CHAPTER 34

Byrnie paced before the campfire holding his hat in his hand and sweeping it through the air with a flourish as he spoke. "My mum's family descended from the Sunderland kowaries. We're a little darker furred than our cousins living near the Pinnacles Desert."

Emma smiled. "We've been to the Pinnacles Desert."

"Ya have!" Byrnie exclaimed. "A desolate place indeed. Did I say I have cousins there as well? Descended from the Cape Kowaries, twice removed cousins on my father's side. They're a rowdy bunch for sure." He stopped walking and, scratching his head thoughtfully, he said, "As I recall, they're hard to find when you need 'em, but family nonetheless. I once heard tell the story of a distant—"

"Ahem!" Durward cleared his throat loudly. "I don't mean to cut you short, Byrnie," Durward said. "Such an interesting story, for sure, but we have a desperate situation here in Demelza."

"You know," Byrnie said, putting his hat down and picking up his bowl of soup and spoon. "I was gonna ask you about that. Seems you got a lot of soldiers here." He continued to speak in his quick jaunty style as he slurped great spoonfuls of soup. "Are you planning some kind of attack?"

Devon realized that the kowari knew nothing of the king, the dragon lizards or the dungeons of Demelza, so he took a few minutes to enlighten the newcomer. Byrnie's jaw dropped as Devon described the dragon lizards' terrible attacks. His eyes widened when Devon spoke of the prisoners in the dungeons, and of the plan to find a wombat tunnel to enter the dungeons and free the prisoners. Finally, Devon told Byrnie about the evil king who reigned over the fortress with his wicked minions.

"I had no idea. How could...I mean, did...? Where are—? It's unspeakable!"

"It certainly is!" Devon said.

Byrnie began pacing. With his soup bowl in one paw, he continued shoveling spoonfuls of soup into his mouth. Drops of soup dripped to the dirt from the coarsely carved wooden bowl. "Best soup I ever—hey! Wait a minute, now!" He stopped and pointed his wooden spoon in Devon's direction. "You are trying to find a wombat tunnel to get into the dungeons. Isn't that what you said?"

Devon and Durward nodded in unison at the comical creature, their grins growing wider and wider with each nod.

"Well, we can help," Byrnie continued, pointing at Lazlo with his chin. "We have a wombat right here!" With a flourish, the black-faced kowari, forgetting the bowl of soup in his paw, flung his arms out in Lazlo's direction. Soup spilled out of the bowl like a small wave heading toward shore, the warm liquid landing squarely on Lazlo's muzzle. Lazlo had been minding his own business, watching the flames dancing before him, until the soup splashed into his face. Eyes as wide as they could be, Lazlo licked his lips once, and then again.

"Yum, pea soup. I love pea soup!" Lazlo said with a grumble. As he continued licking his lips, he muttered, "I know a tunnel."

"Lazlo, pay attention," Byrnie said as he bopped the wombat on the head with the wooden spoon. "This is serious!" Byrnie stopped and peered intently at Lazlo. "Did you say you know of a tunnel?" Byrnie turned to the group. "I am so surprised. You see, Lazlo says very little. He hasn't spoken this much in six months. The last time he spoke was when we were in the high country, and he swallowed a fly. That really upset him, and..."

"Ahem," Durward cleared his throat one more time.

Byrnie stopped and stared at Durward, "But don't you see, Durward, me boy?" Byrnie exclaimed. "He knows a tunnel!" With that, Byrnie leapt into the air and landed in front of Lazlo. Bop, bop, bop! The wooden spoon came down on Lazlo's head three times. "Now! Tell! Us!" Byrnie's words were synchronized with the spoon tapping the great wombat. "Where's this tunnel?"

Slowly, the wombat's clawed paw reached up, grabbed hold of the spoon and yanked it from Byrnie's paw. "Grandpa's tunnel. In the woods."

Devon and Durward looked at each other with surprise. "There are possibilities here," Devon said. Then, in a most earnest tone, he asked, "Where exactly is the tunnel?"

Byrnie turned to the crowd. Every critter leaned toward Lazlo, anxiously waiting for an answer to Devon's question. Byrnie's little arms extended out as far as they could, bowl in hand, soup dripping to the ground. "Yes, and it's in the woods, my fine friends. It's in the woods!"

"In the woods," Erik repeated. "We would never have thought to look for a hole in the woods. That will mean the opening of the tunnel is a long way from the fortress."

Lazlo cleared his throat, and for the first time he looked up with eyes shining and a satisfied smile on his face. Everyone turned in his direction. "Sometimes," he said, in his slow, deep voice, "the longest path is the best path."

"Yes," Erik agreed. "But is it clear?"

"We won't know until we try," Stokley answered.

Durward stood outside the entrance to Lazlo's tunnel. Although the entrance was hidden behind broken tree limbs, dead leaves, and rocks, it appeared to be much larger than the others. Erik, Stokley, Byrnie and Lazlo, were preparing to enter. Erik and

Stokley secured their weapons to their backs. Byrnie climbed up onto Lazlo, taking up the reins in his paws.

"Looks like we're all set," Erik said to Devon.

"Good," Devon said confidently. "I'll go back to camp and gather some soldiers to come with me."

"But you will not enter until we know it's clear," Durward said to Devon. "There's no sense putting an entire troop of men into the tunnel right away. And you'll need to have someone stay at the entrance to signal the rest of the army once Erik sends word that the tunnel is clear. Then we'll commence the main attack on the fortress."

"Wait a minute." Emma slipped in between Devon and Durward, Slade following close behind. "They can't do this alone. We're going in with them. We'll come out and report to Devon."

"Oh, I don't know, little miss," Durward said hesitantly. "This is dangerous business."

"Yes..." Slade said.

"We know that," Emma said. "But we've come this far. We will not sit on the side and watch anymore."

"It's Ok, Durward," Devon said. "I'll be ready to go in as soon as I get the word from Emma. Once we go in, we'll see to their safety."

"Alright," Durward said hesitantly. "But you'll be very careful and you'll come out and report to Devon as soon as you can. Right?"

"I promise, Uncle Durward." Emma reassured him.

Durward then looked at Erik and Stokley. He rested his claw on Erik's shoulder and said, "Explore this tunnel as you did the other two. Our hopes are high that this one will be open. Devon and I will return to camp. He will bring his troops back here, and Sebastian and I will remain behind to prepare for the main assault."

"May the luck and protection of Aldon go with you," said Durward to the five young friends and their wombat companion.

CHAPTER 35

Erik was excited. Lazlo's tunnel appeared to be clear. *Things just might go our way*, he thought. Debris, dirt and rocks were strewn about, but the large wombat easily pushed it all aside. The tunnel was moist and ominous, as frightening as the others. Their torchlight lit their way, and its larger size and greater length made for a longer, yet easier walk. Byrnie stood on Lazlo in his usual manner, reins in paws. Somehow this tunnel *felt* different. They had encountered no strange voices or unexplained wind. Still, an eerie feeling of menace filled the air, as though something waited, biding its time.

As they turned a corner, Erik spotted a door. It appeared to be very old. The wood was faded and splintered in places. Bugs crawled in and out of tiny cracks, and thick layers of mold covered it. The top was rounded, and large rusted metal hinges held it in place. Silken threads covered the door. Connecting strands ran along the ceiling of the tunnel and down the dirt and rock-encrusted walls. The threads glistened in the torchlight. In the dark corners, near the roof of the tunnel, two spiders, as big as Lazlo, sat clinging to their web. They appeared to be sleeping.

"Well, we have walked into a bit of a sticky-wicket here," Byrnie said in a low voice. "These blighters are huge. I've never seen the likes of them before."

The small group of intrepid friends stopped well away from the door. Byrnie and Erik wedged their torches into crevices created by large rocks on the walls of the tunnel. Erik eyed the spiders warily, his heart beating so hard it felt as if it would explode from his chest. Emma and Slade clung to each other behind him.

"They're not moving," Byrnie whispered. "Nasty creatures, they are." From his vantage point, Erik could see their long, sharp fangs hanging over their bottom jaws.

Stokley stood alongside Erik, with Emma and Slade behind them. "What should we do now?" Stokley asked.

Emma shook her head. "Erik, these spiders don't look like Perry, the wolf spider. First of all they are a hundred times bigger than he was."

"You're right," Erik confirmed. "These spiders are different. What do you think, Byrnie?"

Byrnie clucked his tongue and narrowed his gaze at the two creatures. "No, these are not wolf spiders," he said, concern and dread in his voice. "These spiders are much more treacherous. These are funnel-web spiders. They are very nasty, very poisonous, and very dangerous especially in this tight area. Let's get Emma and Slade out of here right now. They can let everyone know the tunnel is clear and that we need help with these creatures!"

"But it's not clear, Byrnie!" Emma stared up at him with a puzzled expression on her face. She pointed her paw at the spiders. "You think that's clear?"

Erik turned to his sister. "Look, we cannot go looking for another tunnel. This is it—that door is the way in. We're making our stand here!"

"He's right," Byrnie said. "They will either let us pass peacefully, or they'll have a fight on their hands. You go with Slade. Tell them the way in is here."

Stokley fiddled with a small dagger on his belt and shifted his feet nervously. "I agree. You two must go back. That's what was agreed."

Emma put her paw on Stokley's as he began to pull his dagger from its sheath. "Don't do anything foolish." Emma said, glancing down at the dagger. "It took us a long time to reach this point in the tunnel. We'll be back with help as soon as we can."

Slade came forward and in a trembling voice choked out three words, "These spiders

are . . ."

"Deadly," Emma finished. "They can kill with those fangs. You must wait for the troops to get here before you attempt to get any closer to the door. Promise me you'll wait."

It was then that the spiders awoke and began to move forward on their silken threads. Erik watched in terror as the front legs of the spiders began to undulate and wave, pulling the glistening threads of their web with each motion. A thick milky liquid dripped from their fangs, falling to the ground, creating small noxious puddles in the dirt.

"Run, Slade! Run, Emma!" Erik's yell echoed off the dirt walls of the wombat tunnel.

With one last look at her brother, Emma grasped Slade's paw and both began running. Erik watched as they made the turn in the tunnel and disappeared from sight. *At least they will be safe.*

"Lazlo!" Stokley nocked an arrow, but he was afraid he would not get a clean shot. "Back up, Lazlo! Back up! Watch out! That spider is coming closer." The spiders separated, one moving toward Byrnie and Lazlo, while the other headed toward Stokley and Erik.

Byrnie drew his bow and arrow from his quiver. "Stokley, watch your side of the tunnel. The other spider is heading your way." He dashed up onto Lazlo's head. "I'll take care of this one!" Lazlo had dropped back a few steps, but Byrnie halted his movement and yelled as he pulled on the reins. "Stand, Lazlo, stand," he said as he pulled his dagger from his belt and began to slice through the silken threads over Lazlo's head, hoping to slow the spider's approach.

Erik drew his dagger and moved closer to the spider on his side of the tunnel. In that split second, the spider in front of Lazlo touched a black hairy leg to the wombat's head. Lazlo shook in an effort to knock the spider's leg off, throwing Byrnie forward toward the horrid creature. The spider grabbed Byrnie with its front legs and wrapped him quickly in thread. It scurried back along its silken highway toward the door, with Byrnie tucked tightly underneath him.

Erik attacked the spider in front of him. He slashed at its legs over and over again. The spider let out an ear-shattering screech as Erik sliced a knuckle on one of the spider's legs. The spider reared up over Erik and Stokley, the shadow of its black body engulfing them. Erik quickly ran under the belly of the creature, darting to avoid the milky ooze dripping from its fangs. As the spider fell toward the ground, Erik held his dagger over his head tightly in both paws. The dagger pierced deep into the spider's abdomen. Screaming in pain, the spider rolled against the tunnel wall, kicking wildly. One leg connected with Stokley, sending him flying across the tunnel, hitting the opposite wall with a thud. Erik stabbed at the injured spider one last time. Finally, it lay motionless on the tunnel floor.

Erik ran to Stokley and helped him to his feet. "Are you all right?" Erik asked as he lifted his friend.

Stokley gasped and pointed above them. "Erik, look at what the spider is doing to Byrnie!" The remaining spider was swiftly spinning threads, attaching Byrnie to the rock wall of the tunnel.

"We have to do something," Erik yelled as he secured his dagger in his belt. Turning to Stokley he said, "Quick, follow me. We'll get up on Lazlo. We have a better chance against the spider from up there." Erik grasped the fur on Lazlo's thigh and climbed up onto his back.

"I'm right behind you, Erik!"

As he and Stokley reached the top of Lazlo's head, Erik shouted, "Release him or you will die like your companion."

The spider stopped securing Byrnie to the tunnel wall, and turned to Erik. Its eyes glazed over as a low sinister laugh came from him. It sent chills down Erik's spine, and he trembled all over. The laugh filled the tunnel around them, and a voice said, "You cannot win. You and your friends have no power here!"

A trembling paw touched Erik's shoulder. "Erik, it's the voice we heard before."

"Go back to where you belong," the cold dead voice shouted at them. "Go back!"

The spider moved slowly toward Erik and Stokley.

Lazlo growled as he moved forward with determination.

"You will not . . . harm my friends!" Lazlo's low grumbling voice bounced off the rock wall as he emphasized each word with an earth-shattering stomp.

CHAPTER 36

Erik and Stokley gripped the fur on Lazlo's neck as the wombat moved forward with determination toward the oncoming spider.

"Steady yourself, Stokley," Erik said. As he rose to his feet, he pulled his bow from his back and nocked an arrow. Stokley did the same. The two small friends did their best to balance themselves as Lazlo began to move. A blast of cold air swept down the tunnel, swirling on the dirt floor, creating whirlpools of dust and small rocks. With each step Lazlo took, the air moved faster and more violently. Dirt and debris filled the air in front of them. Lazlo's head dropped to the ground as he tried desperately to move, but the cold torrent became stronger and held him back. Fissures opened in the rock walls. Black slime oozed forth, flowing slowly to the dirt floor like thick oil. The familiar laugh grew louder as the movement of the cold air and the ooze increased.

"We have to take a shot!" Erik yelled above the sound of the wind rushing through the tunnel.

Stokley took hold of Lazlo's fur with one paw to steady himself. "We can't! Our arrows will never fly true in this wind!"

Both friends crouched against the wombat's back—each with one paw gripping Lazlo's fur and the other paw holding their weapons. Rocks flew in all directions, pounding them. The sinister laugh filled the air. The oily slime took on a life of its own as it moved down the walls and crept across the floor of the tunnel, its oily fingers clawing at the dirt as it moved.

The dark ooze reached one of Lazlo's legs and twisted around it, bringing Lazlo to a stop. It inched up his leg towards his chest as he bit at it furiously. In his efforts, he spun himself around, falling to his side, tossing Stokley and Erik to the dirt floor. Thin threads of slime slithered menacingly toward them. Black tendrils reached out and coiled around their legs and chests, pinning them to the ground and choking them.

The cold air rushed over them, but as they struggled to free themselves they could see a warm yellow mist slowly rotating above them at the roof of the tunnel. The mist caught flying rocks and dirt within its currents. Wispy yellow fog, like liquid sunshine, swirled to the tunnel floor, grasping the oily ropes that had captured the three companions. It tore away the slime and pressed it back towards the walls, forcing it into the open fissures from where it had come.

The sinister voice screamed, causing the rock walls to vibrate. "Get out! Get out! Do not interfere here! You have interfered too many times."

"Malfoden," a soft voice said, "your viciousness knows no bounds. I will not allow you to harm these creatures!"

There was a moment when the air was as silent as death. Then the sinister voice spoke in a low, but malevolent tone.

"Aldon . . . my brother, I promise you will pay for your interference!"

The voices faded away with the wind and the mist.

Free now from the slime, Erik and Stokley ran and leapt onto Lazlo's back. Lazlo was already up and on the move toward Byrnie. Secure on top of Lazlo's back, the two young friends glanced at each other one final time. They both dropped to one knee and nocked an arrow. Taking aim, they let their arrows fly. The arrows struck the spider, and it fell from the rock wall to the tunnel floor.

"My turn," Lazlo growled. With a thunderous gait, the wombat moved toward the spider as it struggled to stand. Raising his heavy body off the ground as high as he could, Lazlo threw all his weight at the spider. He came down on it with tremendous force. The crushing blow killed the spider instantly.

"Hurry, Lazlo! We must get Byrnie down," Erik screamed, urging Lazlo forward. Lazlo moved under Byrnie's body where it was wrapped and pinned to the rock wall.

"Is he all right?" Lazlo grumbled.

"We'll know in a minute," Erik answered.

Stokley began slicing through the threads as fast as he could. With one last slash,

Byrnie's body fell to the tunnel floor where Lazlo began nudging him with his muzzle.

"Byrnie," Lazlo murmured.

Scurrying down Lazlo's back, Erik and Stokley ran to Byrnie. Carefully, the two cut the spider's threads away.

"Byrnie, say something, please!" Erik brushed the web from Byrnie's face, placing his head in his lap.

Finally, Byrnie took a deep breath, blinked and said, "I hate those ugly blighters. Surely, I do."

Stokley and Erik looked at each other and smiled. "He's gonna be all right," Erik said. "No worries, Lazlo. He's okay. Let's get him loose from this web."

Erik, Stokley and Byrnie stood before the door. Lazlo kept nudging Byrnie lovingly.

Stroking the great wombat's muzzle as he spoke, Byrnie said, "I'm okay now, Lazlo. I'm okay."

"What now?" Stokley asked as he stared at the great wooden door.

"Well, let's just give it a try." Erik grasped the handle, pulling it down. Nothing happened, not even a noise. "That's weird." A quizzical look formed on his face. "So, how do we open this door?"

"Let me give 'er a try." Byrnie stepped forward to try the handle. As before, nothing happened, not even a noise.

Stokley shook his head. "There must be something more to it." He scratched his forehead thoughtfully. "There's something we're missing." Walking up to the door, he inspected all the parts—the door handle, the hinges and the brass plate beneath the door handle. The brass plate was covered in dirt and webs. Stokley brushed it with his sleeve. The clean plate revealed a carving of a moon and sun.

"Nice, but not finished," Lazlo grumbled.

"Why is it not finished, Lazlo?" Erik asked.

"Moon and sun. Need a star."

"He's right!" Stokley shouted. "We need a star!"

Erik stood looking at Stokley, shaking his head in disbelief. "A star, we need a star. I don't get it."

As though the thought had come to them all at once, they looked at Lazlo. The stone hung loosely around his neck, casting its purple light onto the dirt floor of the tunnel.

"Star," Lazlo said slowly. "Grandpa's star."

"Well, I never," Byrnie exclaimed. As he reached for the star stone on Lazlo's neck, it began to glow brighter and brighter, until the entire tunnel was bathed in a purple hue. "Bend down, Lazlo." Lazlo's head dropped low enough so Byrnie could pull the band over the wombat's head. "Don't worry, Lazlo. I'll give it right back." Byrnie held the glowing stone in his paws. "Ok, so we have a star. How do we use it?"

Stokley examined the door all over—above the hinges, above the handle, to the left and to the right. Finally, he put his paw against the brass plate. It moved ever so slightly. Stokley pushed at it again, and again it moved.

Erik stepped forward and looked at the door's brass plate.

"Maybe it will move sideways," he said.

Stokley took a deep breath, pressed his paw to the plate, and pushed it to the left. With a screech, the plate began to move. Beneath the plate was an indentation in the shape of a star. Byrnie gazed at the star stone in his paw. Slowly he walked to the door and placed the star stone into the depression. There was a clicking sound and a tumble of gears as the handle moved down and the door creaked open before them.

CHAPTER 37

E rik and his brave companions stepped back as the door swung slowly open. The other side of the door was covered in rock and dirt.

"Stokley, look," Erik said in astonishment. "No one on the other side would ever have known there was a door here. It looks just like the walls of the cave!"

Byrnie examined the rough, rocky surface. "Yes, it is interesting, but we're wasting time." Grabbing a torch from the wall, he confidently walked through the doorway and his companions followed close behind.

They saw several tunnels leading in different directions. The high pitched chirping of bats surrounded them, and their leathery wings buzzed by their heads and ears, causing them to duck.

Stokley waved his paw over his head at a low-flying bat. "Shouldn't we wait for help before we go farther?"

Erik shook his head. "Time is short, Stokley. We need to find the prisoners and set them free. We're here now. This may be our best chance. Anyway, Devon and his troops will arrive soon enough." He peered down each tunnel. "Byrnie, hand me the torch. I think I see a light flickering at the end of that tunnel. That's the way we need to go."

"Wait a minute." Byrnie turned back to the door and removed the Star Stone from its place beneath the brass plate. "Ya never know, we may find another use for that purple rock."

At the end of the tunnel there was a narrow, moss-covered stairway heading downward. Slowly, step by step, they descended while the light at the bottom became brighter and brighter. When they reached the bottom, a wide hall opened before them. Torches were held in brackets on the walls along the way. The end of the hall appeared to fall away, and an opening to their right revealed another stairway leading upward. A metal gate was open and stood against the rock wall.

Byrnie examined the iron gate and the stairs. "Erik, this stairway may lead up to the main fortress."

"Hey, do you guys hear that?" Stokley asked. "It sounds like moaning."

Erik cocked his head and listened.

"Yes, I hear it," Erik said. Turning away from the stairway, he looked down the corridor. "I think it's coming from that direction. Let's go that way."

A wide set of steep stairs at the end of the passage led down into a large circular room. Erik headed down as the others followed close behind. Stokley set his burning torch into an empty bracket, and they all paused to take in their surroundings.

The room was dimly light by torchlight, which revealed numerous doors lining the walls of the chamber. Two corridors on the far side of the room led to inky blackness. Each door had a small barred opening, and at the center of the room a cage sat atop a raised platform. A large kowari was imprisoned within it. Huddled in one corner, the kowari appeared to be sleeping.

Erik stared in horror. "We've reached the dungeons," he murmured. Sounds of stirring came from all around. The face of an echidna appeared in the small barred opening in the door closest to Erik. Eyes wide with surprise, the prisoner's paws gripped the bars tightly and peered out at them.

"Who are you?" the captive echidna asked. "You're not from the fortress, that much I can tell."

Stokley, Byrnie, and Lazlo walked toward the echidna, but Erik turned to the kowari in the cage. *Somehow,* he thought as he approached the cage, *I must find a way to free that kowari.* On the platform next to the cage sat a bucket of water with a ladle in it. Erik lifted a ladle full of water. "Take a drink," Erik said. Kneeling, he offered the ladle through the bars, examining the kowari closely.

The kowari stirred, reaching out a trembling paw to grasp the ladle.

"Thank you, my dear boy," he said weakly.

Erik's paw began to quiver. He grabbed the ladle with his other paw to steady it. Both paws raised the ladle to the lips of the prisoner. Tears filled Erik's eyes as a lump formed in his throat. He tried desperately to control his emotions.

Is it possible? He put the ladle back into the bucket and gently placed his open paw beneath the chin of the kowari and lifted it slowly. "Father?"

The kowari opened his eyes. The dimness that Erik saw in those eyes slowly cleared as pain and weariness gave way to recognition. The kowari smiled at Erik.

"My son, my son." Great sobs escaped from Farrell as Erik threw his arms between the bars of the cage and tried to wrap them around his father's neck. Pulling his father close to the bars he buried his muzzle into his father's fur.

Wiping tears from his eyes, Erik said, "I'll get you out, Papa! I'll get you out!" He removed his dagger from his belt and began to work on the lock that held the cage door shut.

"Byrnie, Stokley, give me a hand here!" Erik was frantically stabbing at the lock, tears rolling down his face. Stokley reached out his paw and placed it on Erik's.

"Stop, Erik," he said calmly. "That won't work. The lock is much bigger than your dagger. You'll only succeed in breaking your dagger. We have to find another way."

"He's right, you know," the voice from behind the barred door said. "The hinges cannot be broken. Neither can the locks on these doors." He paused for a moment, and pressed his face closer to the barred opening of his cell. "This dungeon is no ordinary place, it was built by Cynric. It is a place of torment and sadness where only one lock and one key can release all." His small eyes scanned the large circular room. "The locks are sealed together, and they can only be opened at one place with one key. Only Cynric knows how to open these doors."

Erik ran a paw across his muzzle and shook his head. "You're speaking in riddles. How can you know this anyway? You're a prisoner here. If you know so much, tell me, where is the one key? Where is this one lock you speak of?" He angrily strode up to the barred door and stared at the echidna on the other side. "Speak! We need an answer now!"

"I was once a soldier in the king's guard." The echidna's sad eyes sparkled in the torchlight. "I angered Cynric. He threw me in here. I know this dungeon, and I know you can't get us out. Not without the one key. Only Cynric can free us."

"Tell him about the plaques!" a voice shouted from the other side of the dungeon. "They may be the answer. We don't have all the answers."

Erik turned to Stokley, Byrnie, and Lazlo. "Plaques, what plaques?" Erik gazed across the room to the cell where the voice was heard again.

"The plaques may hold the key?"

"This is ridiculous nonsense. One key, one lock, opens all doors. How can this be?" Erik hesitated for a moment, and then turning to Lazlo he asked, "Do you think you can break the cage?"

"Maybe," Lazlo said in his low grumble. "But, I may hurt your father. I don't think that's best."

Frustrated, Erik turned back to the echidna behind the bars. "Where's the key, and where are these plaques that your mate across the way is shouting about? And why are there no guards here?"

"The guards have been called away. They are preparing for battle. A rebel army has gathered in the forest outside the fortress."

Erik stole a glance at Stokley. "They know," he whispered, fear racing down his spine.

A small grin crossed the face of the echidna as he spoke through the bars, "Yes, they know, and, now, so do you. What will you do? That's what counts."

"Again, more riddles," Erik spat out. "I have to think." He paced in front of the cell. "One key, one lock, plaques. Everyone! Spread out, look around."

Many hopeful faces appeared from behind the barred doors; kowaries, quolls, goannas, and more. They watched as the small group frantically searched the enormous room.

CHAPTER 38

I t was time for the attack on the fortress of Demelza. The sky darkened as black clouds rolled in. The wind whipped through the trees bending branches violently toward the earth. The sun had rushed from the heavens, as though it feared the events to come, and as evening approached, the moon refused to come out from behind the angry clouds.

Devon's momentous day was turning into an unforgettable night. He would neither fail his forest friends, who he had come to admire and love, nor himself. Today he would be his father's son; strong, tenacious, and wise. He would be a kind leader and a force for peace. Peace, it was this elusive condition that Sunderland and

Demelza so desperately desired. He quickly gathered up his staff, put on a black cape, pulled the hood over his head, and confidently strode into the center of the rebel encampment.

Devon peered out from beneath his hooded cape. The camp was a beehive of activity. Slade and Emma had returned from the tunnel with both promising and horrifying news. The news was promising because they had found a door at the end of the tunnel, but horrifying because there were two giant spiders blocking it. Devon must get his troops into the tunnel as soon as possible.

"Devon!" Pearce came up from behind, and Devon turned to face him. "You're on your way back to the tunnel?"

Devon nodded. "Yes. Erik needs our help right away. We must get back there as quickly as possible."

"I'll go with you!"

"Good. We're off immediately." Devon knew that Pearce hadn't accepted the fact that a fox was a commander. Nevertheless, Pearce was one of the strongest quokkas in the rebel army, and Devon needed him. Devon wanted to trust him, and he wanted to win Pearce's trust as well.

He looked up into a nearby tingle tree where Babble sat chattering with Jibber and Jabber. "Babble, are you ready to go???"

Babble saluted. "Yessir!" He scampered up a nearby gum tree and promptly collided with a low hanging limb. Stopping to rub his head, he looked down at Devon and Pearce. "I'm okay, I'm okay." Devon grinned and shook his head as he watched Babble disappear into the treetops.

"Step up, men," Devon shouted over his shoulder as he moved swiftly through the undergrowth. "This is no time to dawdle. Our little friends may be in danger."

The troops stepped up their pace, and by the time the moon had risen in the night sky, the entrance to the tunnel came into view. Devon halted his troops well away from the opening. They remained hidden in the underbrush as Devon listened to the night sounds and scanned the area around the tunnel to insure that their way was safe.

"All right," Devon whispered to his commanders. "This is how it will be done." The soldiers huddled together, listening attentively to the young fox. Pointing to two echidna warriors, Devon said, "You two stay hidden here and guard the entrance, and wait for word from Babble."

Cupping his paws around his muzzle, and looking up into the trees, he whistled for Babble.

Leaves rustled and fell from above. "Yessir, boss." Babble appeared overhead, hanging from a branch.

"Babble, follow behind me. As soon as we're through and have found the entrance to the fortress above, you will return here to tell the guards. The guards will send a message to Durward that we're through. Is that understood?" Devon looked into the faces of everyone surrounding him.

"Yessir, boss!" Babble said.

"You can count on us." The guards nodded in agreement.

"Good!" Devon turned to the two remaining commanders and signaled them to follow. "Pearce, are you with me?"

"Let's do our part!" Pearce said. With those words, Devon and his men stepped out from the dense undergrowth and moved quickly toward the tunnel, disappearing into its blackness. Babble followed close behind, clicking and chirping to himself as he scuttled along.

Erik and his companions were exhausting all possibilities that there might be one key and therefore one keyhole in the dungeon. They searched every cranny in every rock, and so far had come up empty.

"Erik, look at this." Stokley stood in front of the rock wall between two cells. The creatures within those cells angled their heads in an effort to watch Stokley. Their eyes shone expectantly from between the barred openings. Stokley pointed to a large circular stone embedded in the wall. "It's a perfect circle. How many stones are perfectly circular?" he asked out loud. He reached up and touched the stone, splaying his paw over it. After a moment's consideration, he rubbed the stone. A dull shine appeared beneath the thin film of dirt and dust. "It's not a stone, that's why!"

Spinning on his paws, Erik shouted across the room at Stokley. "What are you talking about?"

"Look at it! It's a brass plaque, Erik. It's not a stone at all." Stokley finished cleaning the plaque with his paw. The letter "N" engraved on it was now revealed under a film of dirt.

Stunned by this revelation, Erik looked around the room. "There are others!" he yelled exuberantly. "Find them all. Clean them. Let's see what we have here. It must be a clue. It must mean something. Let's see if we can make any sense of this."

CHAPTER 39

A rumbling, thunderous sound came from above their heads. The walls of the dungeon began to shake. Small bits of stone and dirt fell loose from the walls and ceiling and landed on the dungeon's floor.

"What's that?" Stokley asked, looking up.

"I don't know," Erik said.

Warm air moved in from the dark tunnels that connected to the central circular chamber. It swirled and spun around the room, blowing away the last bits of dirt and dust that covered five brass plates—the five letters were now shining. Erik watched as the plates radiated while the warm wind swept them clean.

"I don't get it," Erik said. "A bunch of letters, D, E, N?" What's that supposed to mean – a den, like a fox's den?"

"And we have an O, V. Maybe, dove? But what of the N?" Stokley cast a baffled look across to Erik.

Concentrating on trying to puzzle out the letters, Erik did not notice a tall thin figure appear at the top of the stairs. Wrapped in a black cape with a hood covering its head, the creature stood still, staring down at the small drama playing out in the central chamber. The shuddering and shaking from above continued, and debris fell around the cloaked creature.

Finally sensing its presence, Erik turned, lifting his eyes to the tall animal at the top of the stairs. In a second it all became clear to him. "It's Devon!" Erik's shout of elation reverberated off the walls of the dungeon. As the name left his lips, he flew from one brass plate to another. Pushing each plate with his paw, he spelled out D-E-V-O-N.

"It's Devon!" He shouted again with such unbridled joy that everyone around him was stunned and shocked. Erik ran from wall to wall. When he hit the fifth brass plate, completing the spelling of Devon's name, a hidden compartment opened on the platform where the cage sat.

Stokley ran to the platform and looked in. A star shaped depression was set into the compartment.

"Lazlo, we will need Grandpa's star stone one more time." Lazlo bent his head toward his friend, and Byrnie slipped the band off his neck.

The pounding of hundreds of paws approaching was heard.

"The troops are arriving," said Pearce as he arrived and stood beside Devon.

They watched from the top of the stairs, as Stokley lowered Lazlo's star stone into place. Stokley gave Devon a nod, and Devon acknowledged him with a smile. The sound of tumbling gears and the lifting of levers now joined the rumbling from above. Over and over again the gears churned and the levers lifted as cell doors unlocked, chains dropped and barred gates flew open.

Prisoners stepped out from their cells, unshackled after their dark days within the dungeons. Lastly, the lock on the cage fell to the platform. The warm wind swirled around the circular room. It touched the walls and swept slowly down every corridor and tunnel of the labyrinth. It entered each cell as if it had a task to complete, as if it was checking to insure that everyone was free.

As cells were emptied of their prisoners, the warm wind slammed the iron doors shut. It continued on until every door was closed with a resounding crash. From the tunnels, hundreds of freed prisoners poured into the central chamber. They gathered around Erik, Stokley, Byrnie and Lazlo. Looks of gratitude and appreciation were evident upon their faces. The warm wind arrived again and transformed into a yellow mist.

"Look at it, Erik," Stokley said in amazement. "It's just like the yellow mist that saved us in the tunnel."

They stood mesmerized as the mist wrapped and swirled about the prisoners. The prisoners gazed at one another in astonishment as the yellow mist churned around them. It enveloped everyone of battle age, and dressed them in the finest gear, arming them with gleaming weapons. They would now stand side by side with Devon and his troop of soldiers.

The echidna Erik had first spoken to when they entered the dungeon walked up to him. The mist had dressed him in the armor of a great echidna warrior, and the armor shone brightly in the torchlight. He turned to Stokley, a grin lighting his face, and spoke in a whisper, "We're free." Then turning to face the crowd, he lifted his sword above his head and shouted, "We're free!" A chorus of many creatures, holding their weapons aloft, joined him.

"We're free! We're free!"

Stokley helped Farrell to his feet, and together they stepped away from the cage and off the platform. A hush fell over the chamber as Farrell straightened himself as best he could and walked slowly to Erik. Eyes glistening, they embraced, holding each other close. Erik looked up at Devon over his father's shoulder.

"They're free," Erik mouthed at Devon as tears soaked his muzzle.

Devon nodded silently and raised his paw, saluting his young friend.

Everyone looked up at Devon as Erik climbed the stairs with Stokley and Byrnie in tow. Lazlo lumbered up close behind taking his place next to Byrnie. As they reached the top, screams of triumph and delight resonated from the farthest edges of the chamber.

The joyful throng parted as a young vixen pressed her way through the crowd carrying two puggle babes. As she looked up at Devon, he pushed his hood from his head and smiled down at her.

Erik and Stokley instantly recognized the puggles and ran to them. "Amber, Ackley! Thank Aldon you're all right!" Turning to the female fox, Erik said, "Thank you, thank you so much."

"I took care of them," she said. "They are a handful," she admitted, smiling up at Devon as she spoke. Amber reached out for Erik and she climbed into his arms, snuggling against him. The fox set Ackley down on the ground at Erik's feet.

"She did, Erik. She took real good care of us, me and Amber," Ackley said pointing to the fox. "Amber was real scared until Richelle came to take care of us. Amber stopped whimpering and shaking when Richelle held her."

"I don't like this kinda place," Amber said, her paws holding Erik's muzzle while she stared adoringly into his eyes. Erik's face beamed as she gently caressed his snout. "We was frightened! This is no kinda place for a puggle."

"It certainly is not," Erik agreed, smiling ear to ear.

"Awe, silly, silly, Amber. I always knowed that Erik would come to get us. I always knowed that. Right, Erik? You'd never leave us, right?"

"That's right, Ackley. I'd never leave you." Still holding Amber tightly in one arm, he knelt down and wrapped his other arm around Ackley, pulling him close.

Erik stood beside Devon and gazed down at the circular plaques. "I wonder why your name is on the plaques, Devon?"

"I don't know." Devon scanned the walls of the dungeons with a confused expression. "But we don't have time to think about this now. There's still a battle to be won."

"Yes, and that's what we're here to do." Erik passed Amber back to Richelle, and looking down at Ackley he said sternly, "I'll be back, ya puggles. Now don't you go wandering off again!"

Erik pointed down the hallway. "There's a stairway heading up. Let's find out where it leads."

Devon glanced behind him. Babble sat on the shoulder of an echidna warrior. "Go, Babble. Get word to Durward and Sebastian that we're on our way."

Babble scampered to the floor and swiftly headed down the corridor to the wombat tunnel.

Erik and Devon led the troops and the newly freed recruits away from the dungeons.

CHAPTER 40

Cynric stood as still as a statue on the rampart of the fortress. Oblivious to the frenzied activity around him, he stared out into the night, looking across the field toward the forest. Flaming arrows whizzed by his head, and stone projectiles narrowly missed him. Fires broke out within the courtyard, and sparks from the flames rose on heated air like thousands of fireflies. The warm wind ruffled his fur, and the smoke forced him to squint.

He watched as the rebel troops mounted their attack. Hundreds of forest creatures were visible on the field. They carried weapons of all kinds, swords, battle-axes, and more. Some carried ladders fashioned out of branches and vines. *They will try to climb the curtain wall,* he thought absentmindedly. He refocused on the tree line. *Was that a movement at the edge of the wood?*

Above his head, menacing clouds coiled angrily in the night sky. Bursts of lightning and explosions of thunder soared across the heavens. The noise of battle mixed with the rainless storm. The clash of swords, the twang of arrows leaving their bows, the stones striking the wall of the fortress, and the shouts of the dragon lizards as they commanded his troops, echoed through the air. But even the cries of the wounded did not disturb his vigil. He could barely see it, but just inside the forest's mantle he glimpsed a mist swirling at the base of the trees. Every so often, it seeped out onto the field, only to retreat back toward the trees and bushes.

A blazing arrow flew toward him as a strong claw grasped his arm and pulled him down behind the wall. The arrow passed overhead and fell to the courtyard, striking a wagon below. The wagon burst into flames, which sent numerous creatures scurrying to and fro with pails of water in an effort to put out the fire before it spread.

Cynric looked up into Gorgon's scarlet eye.

"You should keep your head down, sire," Gorgon said sarcastically. "Someone may want to kill you."

Snapping back to reality, Cynric sneered at Gorgon. "Don't worry about me," he snarled. "Worry about yourself, and make sure the forces remain in their positions."

"Yes, sire," Gorgon muttered under his breath as he waved his claw toward the battle on the field. "We are in control. I believe we outnumber the rebel army. We will subdue them and prevent them from entering the fortress. I am sending out a force from the hidden gate. They will go behind enemy lines to destroy the siege engines."

"Good. Make certain the rebels do not get in, Gorgon. Don't disappoint me."

Gorgon cocked his head at the fox. Then he gazed covetously at the Sword of Demelza strapped to Cynric's chest. The king held it close with one paw. The green stone in its hilt was dark.

Another blast of stone slammed into the curtain wall, followed by a shower of flaming arrows. "Shut down those siege engines, Gorgon," Cynric hissed as dragon lizards raced along the walk. Gorgon nodded at the fox then gave the order to fire. Hundreds of arrows rained down on the rebel troops in the field below. A dragon lizard standing beside Cynric suddenly jerked back. Pierced by a rebel arrow, the lizard pitched toward him. Cynric quickly sidestepped the falling lizard as the creature's limp body hit the wooden railing, breaking it, before plummeting to the courtyard below. Cynric and Gorgon watched as the lizard hit the ground with a thud, a cloud of dust rising up around the lifeless body.

"It's been rather dry this season," Gorgon commented as the dust settled. His voice was void of all emotion.

"Yes," Cynric agreed, looking at Gorgon. "And yet the skies have threatened us time and time again. There is no relief. Maybe tonight." Cynric slowly lowered his eyes to the dead dragon lizard lying in the courtyard. Then he looked at Gorgon. "Carry on, Gorgon. Carry on." He turned, strode along the wall walk, entered the tower, and headed down the stairs to the courtyard.

As he walked out into the courtyard, Cynric took in the scene before him. He had witnessed many feeble attacks on his fortress in the past, but this one was different. This time the attack was more organized, more purposeful, and more intense. He glanced up at the angry sky and then at the hundreds of inhabitants racing back and forth across the courtyard.

The creatures were engrossed in all manner of activities. A wounded quoll was being carried on a stretcher by a pair of echidnas. Several quokkas were filling baskets with various small weapons and arrows. The baskets were tied to ropes and pulleys. The dragon lizards on the parapet walk lifted the baskets up and replenished their weapon supplies as quickly as they could.

Cynric felt a tug on his red velvet cape. He looked down on a frightened little goanna who gaped up at him, his face contorted with fear. "Mister Fox," he said in a tremulous voice.

"What is it, young man?" Cynric asked as he dropped to one knee and looked into the green eyes of the tiny lizard. "Don't be afraid," Cynric said with a smile. "It will be all right."

A deafening clap of thunder shook the ground and the walls of the fortress. Frantic creatures in the courtyard stopped and looked up. The little goanna at Cynric's paws wrapped himself around the fox's leg, shaking uncontrollably. Cynric stared down at him. Memories of his son flooded his mind. He could still feel the paws grasping his fur as they traveled through the forest together. He could feel the small body of his young kit as he hugged him close to his chest, comforting him, sharing his heartbeat as he cut through the underbrush that grew in the forest near his home.

Another tug on Cynric's cape and a blast of flames nearby captured his attention. Slowly, ever so slowly, his paw lifted off the Sword of Demelza and drifted down to the trembling youngster. He stroked the spines on the top of his head and looked up into the night sky where the clouds continued to boil.

"It will be all right," Cynric assured him. "I promise, it will."

Just then, a goanna flashed across the courtyard and swept the small babe up into its arms.

"Mama, Mama, the nice fox said it will be all right."

The female goanna pressed her baby tightly to her, and giving Cynric a startled look she said, "He did now, did he?" She backed away from Cynric one step at a time. Cynric continued to watch the young goanna in her arms. With a smile on his face, his eyes locked with Cynric's.

"It will be all right. I promise," the king said softly. The baby nodded toward Cynric as his mother turned and scurried across the courtyard to the safety of the keep.

CHAPTER 41

Lightning struck the ground, sparking small fires on the battlefield, as Durward's soldiers desperately tried to hold their positions. At the edge of the forest, Durward and Sebastian watched as their army struggled against Cynric's forces. Durward's thoughts were not only on the battle before him, but on Devon and Erik. He thought of the wombat tunnel, hidden in the undergrowth. Somewhere underground, another battle was being fought. Babble had safely returned, and Durward knew that Devon had reached his goal. Now, his army needed to take the fortress and help win the battle.

Durward glanced up. He watched as the wind raked fiercely through the trees ripping the leaves from the boughs. Babble's troop of sugar gliders clung to the branches waiting for orders from Durward or Sebastian.

"You're thinking of our young warriors and of Devon as well. Am I right, Durward?"

"Yes, Sebastian." Durward nodded. "Devon and Erik are determined, each having their own reasons for their courage. We know they were able to enter the dungeon. Perhaps, by now, they are entering the fortress from below with our secondary troops."

Pounding paws vibrating the ground around them interrupted the two commanders. Beldon's huge frame burst through the battlefield's smoke as he ran toward Durward and Sebastian. He held his recurve bow at his chest. He was flanked by two quoll guards carrying battle axes.

"Durward!" Beldon was visibly exhausted from battle. His bow was held tightly in one paw, the other extended out to clasp Durward's claw. He greeted Sebastian in the same manner.

"Give me an update, Beldon." Durward said.

"Cynric's forces are strong," Beldon said. "The wall walk is lined with dragon lizards. Flaming arrows are raining down on our men and lighting fires in the dry grass. We are returning their fire, but they have many more archers than we do. At this point, it's difficult to assess their numbers, but from what little we can see, it appears theirs are greater." He shook his head and turned to look back across the field. "The ground is littered with the wounded, and the smoke from the fires is mixing with this confounded fog, making it difficult to see. Many soldiers have taken cover behind boulders, and they are holding their positions." He exhaled deeply as he met Durward's eyes. "Our siege

J. E. ROGERS

engines continue to bombard the walls, and we're going to try to scale them. Daegal is on the field coordinating a group of soldiers. We will attempt to raise ladders against the walls and get in. Somehow, we need to open the main gate."

"Yes, we must get in. It's the only way we will be able to take the fortress," Sebastian said firmly, his paw forming a tight fist around the hilt of his sword.

"Sebastian is right." Durward said, his face filled with hope. "Devon must get through the dungeons. If he accesses the fortress from below it will give us the advantage we need from the inside. Surely Cynric's lizards will not be expecting that. Still, we need to open the gate so our main force can get through."

"Even if Devon does get through," Beldon offered, "we may still be outnumbered. We need to call up the reserve army."

Before Durward could respond, a loud shriek caught his attention. Looking out across the field, he spotted two small animals running quickly toward them through the smoky haze.

"Oh my!" Babble shouted from above their heads. "It's the little Miss Emma with her friend Slade." Babble ran down the trunk of the tree and sprinted up Durward's leg, taking a post on his shoulder. "Oh my, oh my! The wee dears are all outa breath, and shaking like the leaves on these here gum trees!" Babble paced nervously back and forth on Durward's broad shoulder.

"Uncle Durward!" Emma ran toward him while pointing back in the direction of the fortress. "They're coming out, Uncle Durward. They're coming out of the fortress!"

Stunned, Durward flashed a look at Beldon and down to Emma who stood huffing and puffing at his paws.

"What do you mean? Coming out from where? I can see the main gate through the smoke and haze. It's still shut!" Durward cast an astonished look at Beldon and Sebastian. He fell to one knee to speak to Emma face to face.

Emma shook her head, took a deep breath, and continued, "Me and Slade were watching the battle on the far side from behind a log." Emma pointed back at the fortress again, while Slade, standing beside her nodded. "Then we saw the king's troops. Dozens of them lizards! They came from the south side of the fortress." She trembled all over. Her paws nervously rubbed her eyes then moved up to her head and scratched her ears. "There's another gate there. You can't see it at first. It's hidden behind shrubs and bushes," she said frantically.

Durward reached out to her and rested his claw on her shoulder. Babble used the great goanna's arm as a bridge and he quickly crossed over to Emma and gently brushed her cheek with his paw. Raising her head, she stared wide-eyed at Durward. "They're coming out," she said, her voice trembling with fear. "I tell you, Uncle Durward, they're coming out!"

Beldon, Durward, and Sebastian looked at one another. For a moment no one spoke. Then Durward took a deep breath, and with renewed determination, he said, "I don't know exactly what this force of lizards will do, but we must act swiftly. Beldon, go into the forest and get Afton. I had hoped we would not need him this soon. Take command of the last reserves with him. We will meet on the field."

"Yes, sir!" Beldon quickly headed off into the forest, the two guards running swiftly beside him.

Durward, still kneeling before Emma and Slade, spoke to them firmly. "You two stay hidden in the woods. Do not come out until we return for you. This is no place for wee ones like yourselves. Do ya understand me now?"

"But, Erik, Stokley, Byrnie . . ." The three names fell from Slade's mouth like a torrent. Her eyes filled with dread.

"There'll be no arguing with Durward," Sebastian said with finality.

Durward gathered Emma and Slade into his arms, kissing them on their heads. "Your safety is what's important now," he said as he returned them to the ground. "Do as I say." He stood, removing his sword from its sheath. The sound of the steel blade rang in the night. Laying his free claw across Sebastian's back he said to him, "I have an idea. Babble, you're going to open the main gate."

"Me, sir?" Babble said, eyes wide with expectation. "Of course, sir. What do you want me to do?"

"Take your gliders across the field through the tall grass. I want you to climb the great gate and gnaw the ropes that hold the door in place. It's held by a counterweight. Once you gnaw through the ropes, the gate will go up. Then our troops will be able to enter the fortress."

"Consider it done!" Babble snapped to attention, saluted Durward, and ran up the old gum tree to gather his troops for their task.

Durward and Sebastian ran onto the field together. The light of the flames before them outlined their bodies until they disappeared, swallowed up by the smoke.

Emma and Slade walked in the direction of the forest, away from the battlefield. Emma turned for one last look. Without warning, a small lizard appeared from the forest with a dagger raised over his head. Emma saw the menacing look in his black beady eyes and quickly pushed Slade to the ground falling on her to protect her. Emma winced, waiting for the thrust of the lizard's weapon. Instead, an owl's shrill cry echoed overhead as a wave of mist flowed out from the undergrowth. The mist wrapped around Emma and Slade like a blanket, its glow bathing the air around them.

Emma and Slade looked through the mist into the face of the lizard. The lizard stared at them in disbelief.

The owl screeched again.

"What is that?" the lizard stammered, has claw tentatively reaching out to touch the swirling haze.

"Why are you threatening us?" Emma asked. "How could you do such a thing? We mean you no harm. We have no weapons!"

"I, I..." the lizard stuttered, incapable of answering.

Slade slowly rose to her feet. She put out her paw, helping Emma off the ground. She gathered all her strength, all her resolve, as she said to the lizard, "You don't know what you're fighting for, do you?" Slade spoke slowly. "What are you hoping to gain?" Her voice rose as she continued, "You blindly follow the order of the king. Haven't enough innocent creatures of the forest been hurt?" Trembling all over, she realized what she had done. She lifted her paw, covering her mouth. Emma, shocked that Slade had found her voice, wrapped her paws around her friend and held her tight.

The lizard's jaws dropped as he watched the two friends, swathed in the mist, disappear into the forest.

CHAPTER 42

Leaves and twigs crunched beneath their paws. Beldon and his two guards trampled new paths as they ran through the forest toward the reserve army's encampment. They burst through dense underbrush into a small clearing and came to an abrupt halt before a blazing campfire. Beldon looked across at Afton, who stood before the fire surrounded by his men. His armor gleamed and the spear in his paw was firmly planted into the ground. Its shining brass tip pointed towards the stormy sky, and a red and white-striped triangular flag topped it. The flag snapped as a strong wind rushed through the trees.

Beldon stepped toward Afton. Both creatures saluted each other. "You are needed on the battlefield immediately," Beldon said.

The treetops came alive with the cries and squawks of countless Gang-gang Cockatoos. As Beldon took another step closer to Afton, one bird fluttered down and landed on Afton's shoulder.

Beldon gazed at the bird in recognition. "Ah, good, I see you've decided to show up, Hector," he said, grinning with relief.

Hector cleared his throat, tucked his wings behind him, leaned toward Beldon and said, "Oh yes, I have indeed shown up, and I have brought my avian brethren with me." He raised one wing and pointed to the trees. Beldon looked in the direction of Hector's wingtip. There, on the topmost branch of a tree, sat the largest eagle he had ever seen. Hector tucked his wing behind himself once again, met Beldon's eyes and whispered at him, "The eagle has brought some cousins as well."

Afton let out a hearty laugh, shaking all over as he did so. Soon, Beldon was laughing with him. Then the cockatoos and Afton's soldiers joined in the rousing sound. Above the laughter, Afton's voice shouted, "Follow me, men!" Suddenly things weren't so desperate.

A cacophony rose from the forest as thousands of cockatoos prepared for flight, and hundreds of Afton's troops grasped their weapons and fell in behind their leaders. The forest floor shook with the movement of soldiers heading toward the battlefield, led by Afton and Beldon. The eagle launched himself into the night sky, and hundreds of others followed him.

Emma and Slade found an old log covered with fallen branches and leaves. They settled in to await Durward's return.

"Do ya think we'll see Stokley and Erik again?" Slade asked solemnly.

"Don't speak like that, Slade. Of course, we will. This will all be over soon. You and Stokley will return to Kirby-Doane. Erik and I will return to Digby." She paused for a moment, furrowed her brow, and wrung her paws. Finally, she looked up at Slade and said, "Yes, all will be well. Erik and I will arrive home in time to help our mum," she said with determination, choking back her tears.

Slade put her arm around her friend. "You're right, Emma. We've come so far and we've accomplished so much." She patted Emma gently on her back. "Stokley and Erik are strong. Soon we'll all be heading home."

Emma nodded in agreement. The two small creatures sat huddled together when a sound made them look up. Through the swaying leaves and gaps in the branches, Emma saw birds flying—great numbers of them. The sight of the birds was accompanied by the sound of splintering twigs and the crackling of leaves. Louder and louder it became until it surrounded them. Instinctively, they tucked themselves deeper into their hiding place. It was the sound of pounding paws, and it came from every direction. Quolls, echidnas, goannas, foxes, and many others flashed past them and over them at top speed.

"They are coming from inside the forest," Emma shouted over the din. "It must be the reserve army, and they're heading toward the battlefield!"

Babble, Jibber and Jabber scurried down the old gum tree. Scores of sugar gliders followed close behind. On the ground, the troop—too many to count—stopped in a tight "v" formation with Babble, Jibber and Jabber forming the point. The sugar gliders flattened themselves against the ground and started slowly up the sloping hill toward the fortress.

Every so often Babble would stop. His troop would stop as well, becoming motionless. Babble rose on his back paws to see over the top of the tall grass to determine their position. The shortest distance to the main gate was his goal. He returned his front paws to the ground and glanced behind at his gliders. They were alert, watching every movement on the battlefield. Flashes of lightning and roars of thunder echoed around them. Fires burned everywhere, and the noise of the battle raged on all sides. Babble raised one paw, waving it in the direction of the fortress, and moved stealthily forward. The gliders followed, moving as if they were one creature blanketing the ground.

A figure loomed overhead and a fierce cry blared in their ears. Looking up, Babble saw the body of a large lizard falling toward them, an arrow imbedded in his chest. The gliders quickly adjusted their direction, avoiding a direct hit as the lizard collapsed to the ground. Its armor exploded with the impact, and pieces broke off, flying in every direction. The spear the lizard was carrying fell alongside him. The flag at the top fluttered to the ground over the gliders as they quickly assumed their original formation and continued on toward the main gate.

Moments later Babble halted his troops before the gate. He turned to face them, standing tall on his hind paws, and said,

"We know what we need to do!" He nodded once. Half the troop headed forward to the left, the other headed forward to the right.

Babble, Jibber and Jabber watched the progress of their companions as they climbed on either side of the gate. They craned their necks to look up to the very top, watching their forces scurrying up the wood frame. Babble let out a high shrill whistle, and the troops went into action. On the right side and on the left side of the portcullis the tiny gliders climbed the wooden frame and squeezed into the fortress between the steel bars at the top of the gate. When Babble was satisfied that all his gliders were in place, he gave a sharp nod to his two comrades. With another shrill whistle, his troops began gnawing the thick ropes that held the gate in place.

CHAPTER 43

Braydon stood on the balcony outside the entrance to the keep. The central tower of the black fortress of Demelza rose overhead. Clouds raced furiously in the sky as dawn tried to penetrate their fierce progress across the heavens.

His steely gaze dropped to scan the courtyard. Through the frantic activity, he spied Cynric speaking with a tiny goanna. *What could this be?* He continued to watch with narrowed eyes, taking in the sight and straining to hear the conversation between the two creatures. His concentration was broken when the light touch of a paw rested on his shoulder. He turned to see Luella standing beside him.

"What is it, Braydon?"

Braydon turned to look back at Cynric and the small goanna. Luella's eyes followed his gaze.

"He is not what you think, Braydon." Luella smiled softly.

As they watched, a streak of lightning flashed overhead, and a booming clap of thunder shook the ground. A goanna ran across the bailey, plucked the babe up into her arms and hurried back to the keep.

Braydon turned to Luella. "You should be in the keep, Luella. It's dangerous out here."

Shouts from below caught Cynric's attention as a frightened lizard came scurrying across the bailey toward him. "Sire! Sire! The dungeons sire."

"What! What about the dungeons?" Cynric yelled.

"The dungeons sire." The exhausted lizard's chest rose and fell as he tried to catch his breath.

"Explain yourself!" Cynric's paw shot out and gripped the lizard by the throat, lifting him off the ground. The lizard's feet dangled in the air as Cynric drew him closer and peered into his eyes. "Tell me," Cynric said through gritted canines. "Exactly what is happening in the dungeons?"

"The prisoners, sire," The lizard gasped. "They're free. Somehow they've been freed."

Cynric dropped the lizard and looked up to the balcony where Braydon stood with Luella.

"Braydon!" the fox shouted up at him. "Send troops down to the dungeons. Find out—"

The crash of the main gate striking the stone walls of the fortress brought all activity to a standstill. Above the gate, great numbers of sugar gliders scurried along the stone walls and crawled up the scaly legs of dragon lizards on the ramparts, harassing them like a swarm of angry insects. The lizards tried batting away the critters with their claws, but the gliders were too quick and too numerous. Many of the lizards leapt to the courtyard with swords in hand, shaking off the harassing gliders. Fierce combat commenced as Demelza's army met the incoming soldiers of the rebel army.

Braydon watched Cynric turn toward the gate and remove the sword from its sheath. A deep pulsating sound emanated from the blade, as the stone in its hilt shot out a beam of green light. The light flashed from the stone on the sword's hilt and bounced off the walls of the fortress, dousing everything in a strange green glow. It ricocheted up to the thick grey clouds and back down to the battlefield outside the walls. On the field, the light spread, immersing every soldier, friend or foe. It was then that the dragon lizards in the field headed back to the fortress, answering the call of the sword.

The reserve army, led by Afton and Beldon, arrived in time to see the battlefield drenched in green light. They took the field quickly, chasing dragon lizards as they raced toward the fortress.

"Look up!" Beldon shouted at Afton. "It's Oswin!"

The great masked owl led an eerily quiet flock of Gang-gang Cockatoos, while above them flew a company of wedge-tailed eagles. The cry of the owl was the only sound as the eagles plummeted, like feathered missiles, toward the dragon lizards. With wings tucked in tightly against their bodies and eyes narrowed, they aimed for their targets. The eagles attacked the lizards, pecking at their eyes with their hooked beaks. The cockatoos dropped stones in great numbers, pelting the animals mercilessly and thwarting their progress. Oswin's mighty talons easily ripped swords from the claws of lizards who were forced to run unarmed toward the fortress, their claws covering their heads as their eyes scanned the skies.

Inside the fortress walls the battle raged on. The two forces clashed in every corner of the courtyard, on the ramparts, and on the balcony of the keep. Braydon shouted orders to his troops, directing them as they entered the courtyard from the keep.

"Move, move!" he exclaimed. "Luella, you must get inside, now!" As he spoke, he saw Gorgon moving swiftly along the rampart in their direction. His sword was held aloft and he dispatched small creatures as he came, tossing them over the balcony to the ground. Many were heedlessly trampled under claw. Braydon and Luella were in his path. Bellowing as he rushed onto the balcony, he headed directly toward them.

"Get out of my way!" Gorgon's clawed arm slashed the air, striking Luella as she tried to avoid him. She was thrown toward the railing, arms flailing, fear etched on her face; she tried to grasp it. One paw caught the rail. She shot a pleading look at Braydon. He reached out to her, but she slipped away before their paws could meet. Sliding off the rail, she dropped to the ground below.

Braydon's anguished cry echoed throughout the fortress. He drew his sword as he stepped in front of Gorgon. Their blades met in a deafening clang, sparks flying off the steel. Creatures moved from the balcony as the two dangerous combatants locked in battle. Gorgon took several steps back, surprised by the vicious attack. Braydon rushed at Gorgon over and over again, slicing the air before him as he came. Gorgon stepped back again to avoid Braydon's blade and his spine hit the stone wall of the keep. He kicked out with one clawed leg, hitting Braydon in the chest. Braydon stumbled as he tried to regain his balance. Gorgon pushed away from the stone wall. Centering himself, he planted his huge legs like stone pillars on the balcony and roared. Braydon answered with a mighty growl from deep inside and lunged at Gorgon again.

CHAPTER 44

Devon burst out into the courtyard from the tunnels below; his troops followed like a living wave. Numerous entries to the main courtyard had been discovered in the dungeons. The prisoner army and Devon's troop flowed up from all of them. Devon surveyed the battle before him. The main gate was open and sugar gliders were climbing from the gate to the battlements, attacking the lizards. The lizards shot arrows down at the freed prisoners and the rebel troops as they entered from the gate.

"Secure the battlements!" Devon shouted as his army spilled out onto the courtyard. "We will have no more attacks from that quarter!"

The cry of an attacking dragon lizard made Devon pivot. Erik, who stood beside him, reacted quickly. He drove his dagger into the lizard's leg as Devon slammed his staff across its back. Doubling over in pain, the wounded lizard dropped his axe, flashing a look of anguish and surprise at his two attackers. He rushed down the closest stairway to escape their next assault.

"Good work!" Devon said, patting Erik on the back. Both companions moved forward together. Working as one, they met every attacking creature in their path, deflecting every sword, axe and mace.

Devon looked up and, touching Erik's shoulder, pointed to the sky. It was filled with flocks of birds. On the highest tower of the fortress, Oswin extended his wings to their full length, his piercing cry calling out over the fortress and beyond.

A scream from a balcony across the courtyard caught Devon's attention. A quoll hung by one paw to the balcony railing, while a huge quoll tried but failed to reach her. She fell to the courtyard. Devon and Erik rushed to her side. Devon dropped to his knees and lifted her head off the ground, cradling her in his arms. Her eyes fluttered open.

"You're going to be all right," Devon said.

She stared back at Devon. There was a look of astonishment on the quoll's face as she stammered, "Who-who—"

"There," Erik said to Devon as he pointed to a sheltered corner deep underneath the balcony. "She'll be safe there." Devon picked up the quoll and carried her to the spot.

"You'll be fine here," he assured her as he leaned her gently against a stone wall.

She narrowed her gaze at him. "You look like . . .." The quoll slowly raised her paws and pushed Devon's hood back away from his face and off his head. Devon watched as she drew in a quick breath and looked deeply into his eyes.

"I can't stay here with you," Devon said. "Erik will stay by your side." He nodded once at Erik. "Keep her safe." For a moment he stood looking down at Erik and the dazed quoll; then he lifted his paws, drew the hood of his cape back over his head and ran into the fray, scanning the bailey as he ran.

A flash of green light filled the courtyard, followed by a rush of dragon lizards pouring in through the main gate. Across the courtyard near the gate, Devon spotted Sebastian and Afton, each one locked in battle. Atop his friend Lazlo, Byrnie shot arrows in quick succession at any dragon lizard entering his line of vision. Pearce battled with dragon lizards near the center of the courtyard.

"Follow me!" Pearce yelled as he directed a large group of soldiers toward the tower stairs. Movement from behind Pearce caught Devon's eye. It was the thylacine. Snarling and growling, Flitch flew through the air, landing squarely on Pearce's back. A flash of white canines drove deeply into his neck.

"No!" Devon screamed. Pearce fell to the ground, the thylacine standing on his back. Flitch lifted his head. With his mouth open, Pearce's blood dripped from his teeth to the injured quoll beneath his paws. He flashed a wicked grin at Devon and ran off.

Kneeling beside Pearce, Devon looked down at the quoll in panic. He could see the wound was deep. Devon rolled Pearce over and he opened his eyes and smiled weakly at Devon.

"I doubted you, just because you are a fox. I was wrong. It was an honor to fight alongside you." His eyes glazed over and he was still.

Tremendous anger welled up inside Devon as he peered through the turmoil that surrounded him. The thylacine was nowhere in sight, but in the center of the courtyard, he noticed an enormous fox. Devon could see the strength in his limbs as he swung a heavy sword. Waves of green light flowed off the sword, flooding the courtyard. The fox's red cape swirled around him as he moved effortlessly, confronting each creature that came near him. Devon knew immediately this was the king, the source of all this death and destruction.

Devon gripped his staff tightly and rushed toward the fox. He raised the staff over his head, preparing to strike. The king immediately spun around, his sword slashing the air and meeting Devon's staff with a clang. Devon's simple wood staff was now a weapon as powerful as steel. Surprised by the quickness and agility of the mighty fox, Devon staggered. Regaining his balance, he lifted his staff once again, meeting the king stroke for stroke. The two opponents moved in a deadly dance, each one trying to gain the upper hand. The king's sword hummed, growing louder with each stroke, and the green light flashed from the blade as it clashed with Devon's staff.

Braydon and Gorgon were locked in battle on the balcony overlooking the courtyard.

"You are a worthless creature, Gorgon!" Braydon shouted, as his sword clashed with the immense dragon lizard. "You are worthless to yourself and the creatures of Demelza. I have had enough of you. This is where it all ends. It ends with me!"

Gorgon threw his head back, exposing his saber-like teeth, and let out a sarcastic laugh. "You are right, my friend. This will end here, but not with you."

As he shouted at Braydon, Gorgon grabbed hold of the railing on the balcony and hurled himself to the courtyard below. Braydon moved to the railing and watched Gorgon as he headed across toward the gate. From out of the shadows, Flitch followed Gorgon's footfalls.

"You won't get away!" Braydon shouted after him. Reaching over his head, he grasped his bow and an arrow from his quiver. He raised his bow and nocked an arrow. Taking careful aim, he released the arrow. It flew directly toward the lizard, but Gorgon turned away abruptly. Braydon gasped in horror as the arrow sped toward the center of the courtyard where Cynric was locked in combat with a young fox. The young fox had fallen to the ground under one of Cynric's blows and Cynric was preparing to deliver his final stroke.

Braydon gripped the balcony railing as Cynric lifted the Sword of Demelza over his head. It was then that Braydon's arrow struck and drove deeply into the great fox's chest. The force of the arrow caused Cynric's body to stiffen and his arm to swing up, sending the sword soaring skyward. Over and over again, the sword spun in the air as it rose. It seemed to move in slow motion, and every creature within sight of Cynric and the young fox stopped to watch.

A flash of lightning lit the sky. For a split second the court-yard was bathed in light. A crack of thunder made all the creatures in the courtyard tremble. A streak—a thin tendril of yellow mist—ripped across the heavens and grasped the sword. Surrounding the sword, the tendril held it above Devon in the darkened sky. The mist caressed it, spinning it in the air. Touching the point of the blade, the mist moved down the length of the still-spinning sword, reaching the stone in its hilt. In one swift movement, the tendril fashioned itself into a point, and rearing back, it gathered and coiled and thrust itself through the green stone.

Another crack of thunder, louder than the first, roared. It shook the fortress to its very foundations. The sound moved along the walls and between the frightened creatures. They stood motionless in a circle around the king and his young opponent. But the growling thunder began to fade as the yellow mist moved through and around the sword. The stone was changing.

Devon watched in amazement as the color of the stone began to change to a golden glow as bright as the sun. The sword turned, and, with hilt pointing down, fell back toward the earth.

A cry came from the ramparts. "Get up, Devon. Get up!"

Devon leapt to his feet as the sword descended directly above him. He looked up and his hood fell away, revealing the white star on his forehead. He gazed across to the great fox, who now stood with Braydon's arrow in his body. His paws grasped the shaft as his chest heaved and his eyes stared at Devon. Devon stared back. It was then he heard the great king whisper his name.

"Devon."

Startled, Devon dropped his staff. He looked up to the sky and watched the great Sword of Demelza fall toward him. In one movement, he raised his paw and grasped the hilt of the falling sword, and caught the injured king with his free arm. A flash of brilliant white light shot up from the sword. Devon held it tightly in his paw as he lowered the king's body to the ground.

Now, looking into the eyes of the King of Demelza, a pain of a different kind welled up from Devon's gut and filled his chest. The weight of a great sorrow enveloped him as he recognized his father. He lowered the sword to the ground and wrapped both arms around the dying king.

Lifting him, to hold him close, the years melted away in the space between them. He was a young kit again. His mind raced back to the days with his father. He felt the deep red fur in his paws as he gripped tightly to his father's back. He felt the rush of the forest air as they ran through the trees together. It was a fleeting and loving memory—one he had always cherished. Now he held his father in his arms, and felt his father's paws grip his fur to hold him close once more.

Devon looked up; all his companions had gathered around him. Erik was there and his father, Farrell, stood at his side. Durward was there, his arm wrapped around Farrell. Beldon, Byrnie and Lazlo were also there. Finally, Richelle appeared with the puggles in her arms. Sebastian, Afton and all the troops stood there, in the courtyard, silently looking on. The female quoll whom Devon had rescued stepped through the crowd and knelt beside Cynric. A silence marked the end of the battle.

"Luella, you will look after my son, now," Cynric said, looking up at her.

"Of course I will, Cynric. He is strong. He is his father's son," she said with great dignity. "He will rule as you truly intended."

Cynric nodded. Luella looked into Devon's eyes and smiled. "We will be here for you," she said.

With an expression of confusion and disbelief in his tear-filled eyes, he shook his head.

"Devon," Cynric whispered.

"Yes, Papa, I'm right here." Lowering his head, he rubbed his father's muzzle lovingly. Grief gripped him as he thought about all the love lost and how things could have been.

"I'm sorry, my son. My grief was so great that I could not overcome the pain. The power of my sorrow was overwhelming and took control of me. I did not intend for all this to happen. Do you believe me?"

"I believe you, father." Devon held Cynric, the great evil King of Demelza, until his body became still. Then, Devon cried.

The sword continued to shine as it lay on the ground beside Devon. Morning had arrived and the sun slowly revealed itself in a clearing sky. Its rays joined with those from the sword, filling the courtyard with a brilliant light. Dragon lizards woke from their sword-induced daze. They crawled and slithered out and away from the fortress, and the influence of the sword. Now, the intention of the sword was changed. All those who witnessed the transfer of power knew it was no longer necessary to fight. And it began to rain. The rain and the sun occupied the sky together,

as a rainbow formed over the tops of the trees in the forest surrounding Demelza.

In the distance, at the edge of the forest, the yellow mist stirred,
rotating upward and then swirling back to the ground. Aldon
stood in the clearing mist. Beside him, at his feet, Emma and
Slade stared up at him.

"Go," he said smiling. "Join your friends. They will need you."

He looked up and followed the movement of two creatures as
they hurriedly ran toward Mt. Olga. Aldon knew that they had
not seen the last of Gorgon and Flitch. A rumbling drifted down
from the mountain and angry clouds continued to swirl directly
over its peak.

CHAPTER 45

E
rik, Emma and Farrell rushed home to Digby with the
puggles in tow. They had crossed the red and blue bridge
quickly, barely noticing the scene. The stream rippled and
swirled round the mossy stones. The sun shone down between
the leaves, its rays tripping brightly across the surface of the clear
water. All was lost to them as their thoughts centered around one
thing only, Mum.

As they hurried down the path toward their home in the
ancient tingle tree, Ackley and Amber spied their mother Aida
sweeping the walkway to her front door.

"Mama," they shouted, racing toward their mother.

Aida dropped her broom and knelt to the ground, arms open wide to embrace her babes.

"Oh my, oh my!" Aida said as she petted and kissed the puggles, tears flowing freely. "Just wait till your papa comes home from work. He'll pluck your little spikes. You'll learn not to go wandering off ever again." She squeezed them close. "Oh no, oh no, he won't touch a spike on your wee heads. I don't know what I'm saying." She laughed as she flashed a smile at Erik and Emma. Then noticing Farrell, she drew in her breath, and gasped, "Farrell, goodness, Farrell." Aida rose to her feet and walked slowly toward her neighbor.

"We thought we'd never see you again," she said, then quickly added, a bit embarrassed by her admission. "Well, I never lost hope, ever."

"And I thought I'd never get home!" Farrell said as he reached out and gave Aida a hug. "But now we really must attend to..."

The door to his home opened and Bede stepped out, closing the door behind him. His eyes were smiling at the sight of Farrell standing before him, but he could not hide his concern.

"Farrell, my dear friend! I have prayed I would see you again." The two old companions embraced. "We will celebrate your homecoming after we attend to the business at hand." He turned to Erik and Emma. "Do you have the ingredients?" he asked.

"Yes," Erik said as he quickly removed the pouch from around his waist and handed it to Bede.

"May I see her?" Farrell asked, tears welling up in his eyes.

"Let me administer the potion," Bede said. "It will be alright. Please wait here." He reached out and touched Farrell, squeezing his paw reassuringly. Then he turned and disappeared into the house.

"I don't know if I can stand the wait," Emma moaned. "Maybe we took too long. We should have come home immediately. We should have..."

"Stop, Emma!" Erik said angrily. Farrell placed a paw on Erik's shoulder.

"Don't be angry with your sister, Erik." Turning to Emma he said, "The decisions have been made, Emma. We cannot change them." He hesitated a moment. His lower lip quivered as he continued. "You and your brother did what you thought was best at the time. There will be no negative thoughts, and there is no blame."

"Father, you're shaking. Let me help you." Erik walked his father to the stone bench beside the walkway. He and Emma sat beside him, wrapping their arms around him to comfort him.

"Bede knows what to do," Aida said as tears welled up in her eyes. She picked up Amber who reached up and wiped a tear away as it rolled down Aida's face.

"It's OK, Mama, it is," Amber said in a sweet whisper.

Ackley walked to Farrell and looked up at him, touching his leg lightly with his paw. "Don't worry, Mr. Grassley. Bede's a great healer. Mama always said so. Right, Mama?" Ackley glanced up at his mother with a pleading look in his eyes.

"That's absolutely right, Ackley."

Farrell smiled down at Ackley, nodding slightly. "Yes," he whispered. He ran his paw over the quills on Ackley's head. "It will be alright."

"Come now, Ackley," Aida said, coaxing Ackley with the wave of her paw. "Let's leave Mr. Grassley alone. He needs time with his children, and you and Amber need a bath and a nap."

"Aw, Mum," Amber moaned as they entered their home.

Farrell turned to Erik, studying his son carefully. "You have grown, Erik." Then he smiled at Emma. "And you are even sweeter than I remember, if that's at all possible." He pulled them close to his side. "You two helped to rescue me. You helped to free the prisoners from the dungeons of Demelza. You helped to end the reign of King Cynric. I do not believe it was all for nothing!" he stammered. "Aldon would not let her die." He dropped his face to his paws and cried.

The door opened and Bede stepped out. Erik, Emma and Farrell cast expectant looks at him.

"I've given her the potion," he said solemnly. "We can only wait. You can all come in now. She is resting quietly."

They gathered around Edlyn's bedside; Farrell sat with her paw held tightly in his. Emma and Erik sat quietly beside each other at the foot of the bed.

Hours passed as they waited patiently by Edlyn's side. Farrell, exhausted from their journey, had fallen asleep in his chair next to the bed.

"Please, Mum," Emma whispered, squeezing her mother's paw, "I need you, we need you. Papa's come home. Please, Mum, come back to us."

A warm yellow light filled the room, and a soothing voice filled the air. "Have faith, young ones."

"Aldon," Erik whispered as he peered into the yellow mist. "What happened, Aldon? We did everything we could. Everything we needed to do."

"Yes, you did. You and Emma were courageous and loyal. Your bravery, the bravery of your friends, your devotion to those friends, your thoughtfulness and concern for others, and your strong desire to do the right thing shone through, even in the most difficult of circumstances." The warm glow intensified, seeming to hug them as the voice of Aldon continued. "You made your decisions; you were steady, strong, and willing to accept the consequences of your actions. That's what happened. All these things happened, Erik."

Erik thought for a moment about all they had accomplished and turned proudly to his sister. "We did this together, Emma, didn't we?" Into the surrounding glow he said, "I couldn't have done it without Emma and all the other friends we made along the way. And Devon, will he be all right?"

"His story is not over. He faces many trials ahead, but he is young and resilient. He knows what he needs to do, and he has the strength and faith to do it. Devon has something that I spoke of when your journey began. He has friends. Friends are a most enviable thing to have, and to be." Through the warm glow, Erik thought he could see the face of Aldon smiling tenderly at them. "The value of friendship is one of the lessons I am certain you have learned," Aldon said.

"But what of Mum?" Erik pleaded. "We couldn't have done all that for it to end this way." His mother's face was peaceful, her eyes closed, her breathing even. "She can't die."

Emma gripped her brother's paw tightly as the warm glow intensified and Farrell stirred and woke. Blinking, he looked at his children.

"What's happening?"

The glow began to fade around them as Edlyn's eyes fluttered and opened slowly. Erik and Emma leaned in closer to their mother on one side of the bed, Farrell on the other. Bede walked to the foot of the bed and smiled.

"Mother!" Emma cried, wrapping her arms about her mum's neck.

"Oh, my dear, Emma," Edlyn said weakly. Edlyn's eyes blinked as she struggled to focus. "Farrell! Is that really you?"

"Yes, my dear. It's really me. I've come home to you!" As he reached for her paw, the glow flowed to the edges of the room, lingering there. Edlyn's eyes shone with joy.

"Thank Aldon!" she said. With tears of happiness, she reached out for Bede and he walked to her side, talking her paw in his. "Bede, you were always with me, weren't you?"

"Of course, Edlyn, and I'm not leaving yet." He couldn't stop smiling. Then he finally added, "I've stopped by for some berries and cream!"

The End

GLOSSARY

Australian Masked Owl

The Australian Masked Owl is closely related to, and looks very much like a barn owl. It is listed as 'least concern' on the International Union for Conservation of Nature and Natural Resources (IUCN) list and can be found in much of the non-desert areas of Australia.

Bilby

The bilby is a desert-dwelling marsupial (see below) found in Australia. There used to be two species, but one became extinct in the 1950s. The term bilby comes from an Aboriginal word meaning long-nosed rat. It is sometimes referred to by the nickname, pinkie. It is listed as 'vulnerable' by the IUCN.

Billabong

A Billabong is a small lake, usually located adjacent to a small river. The water in a billabong is usually quite still.

Brown Snake

The Brown Snake can be found all along the east coast of Australia. Even the venom of a baby brown snake can kill a human. This snake is responsible for most snakebite deaths in Australia. I have taken liberty by using this snake in my story since the bite Erik's mom received would certainly have killed her.

Dragon Lizard (Gippsland Water Dragon)

This lizard is also known as the Australian Water Dragon. It is an arboreal (lives in the trees) species of lizard. They have long powerful limbs for climbing and a strong tail for swimming. This Australian lizard is quite common and therefore not endangered.

Echidna

The echidna is a monotreme (see below). It is also known as the spiny anteater. According to the IUCN, the short-beaked species is not endangered. However, the long-beaked specie is about to become extinct due to loss of habitat. The echidna is named after a creature found in Greek mythology that is half woman and half snake. Eek! She was considered the mother of all monsters.

Funnel Web Spider

The funnel-web spider is one the world's most deadly spider. They are found in coastal and mountain regions of eastern Australia. They live in burrows in the ground that they line with silk threads. The funnel web spider is not an insect, but an arachnid, related to scorpions, mites and ticks. Their venom is highly toxic.

Gang-gang Cockatoo

The Gang-gang Cockatoo lives in southeastern Australia. The red crest of feathers on their heads easily identifies the males. The name Gang-gang is derived from the Aboriginal language. Due to loss of habitat, the Gang-gang is now considered vulnerable in Australia, but the IUCN lists it as 'least concern.'

Ghost Bat

The Ghost Bat lives in Western Australia, the top end of the Northern Territory, and scattered throughout the Queensland area. It is also known as the False Vampire Bat. It is called a Ghost Bat because of its very thin wing membranes. It is listed by the IUCN as 'vulnerable.'

Goanna

The term goanna refers to a varied group of lizards that live in Australia. There are a great number of species ranging greatly in size. The goanna is prominent in Aboriginal mythology and Australian folklore.

Golden Wattle

Golden Wattle is a flowering tree, and Australia's floral emblem. It grows in areas across the southern states of Australia, and can also be found in South Africa and California.

Gum Tree

Gum Tree is a general term that covers a number of different species of tree, including the Eucalyptus trees, which Koala's love to eat. Most Gum Trees are found in Australia, but there are also some, which occur outside the country.

Kangaroo Paw

Kangaroo Paw is a perennial plant found in southwestern Australia. The tubular flowers, which are covered with dense hairs, form a claw-like structure hence the name of the plant.

Kowari

The Kowari is also known as the brush-tailed marsupial rat. That alone says a lot about the appearance of this little creature. It is a carnivorous animal that lives in the dry grasslands and deserts of central Australia. It is listed as 'vulnerable' on the IUCN list.

Loosestrife

Loosestrife is a common name for many different species of flowering plants.

Magnetic Termite Mounds

The Magnetic Termite Mounds are located in Litchfield National Park in Australia. They can be as tall as 6 to 12 feet high. They are called magnetic because their edges point in a north south direction.

Marsupial

A marsupial is a kind of mammal that has a pouch. Their babies are born in a very immature state and mature inside their mothers pouches attach to her nipples. The babies will stay inside their mother's pouch for weeks or months, depending on the species.

Monotreme

A monotreme is the most primitive mammal. There are only two monotremes on the planet, the echidna and the platypus. These two mammals lay eggs. Then once the babies hatch the mother nurses them with milk.

Numbat

The Numbat is a small colorful marsupial, which is also known as the banded anteater. It has a finely pointed nose and a bushy tail. Once upon a time, it could be found across the southern regions of Australia. However, now its range is restricted and it is considered 'endangered' on the IUCN list.

Pinnacle Desert

The Pinnacles Desert is found in Western Australia in the Nambung National Park. The Pinnacles are limestone formations consisting of broken down seashells combined with sand. There are still ongoing discussions about how these tall natural structures were formed.

Puggle

A puggle is a baby echidna.

Quokka

The Quokka is a marsupial that is about the size of a cat. It is nocturnal (comes out at night), and it is herbivorous (eats plants). It can be found living on several islands off the cost of Western Australia. It was one of the first animals seen by the Europeans who first set foot on the shores of Australia. It is considered 'vulnerable' on the IUCN listing.

Quoll

The Quoll is a marsupial that is carnivorous. It will eat small mammals, birds, lizards and insects. Its numbers have declined since Australia was colonized, and one species has become extinct. Urban development and poison baiting are the major threats to the Quoll. Depending on the species, they are listed as 'threatened' and 'endangered' on the IUCN.

Sugar Glider

The Sugar Glider is a marsupial. It is a small tree living omnivore (eats meat & plants). They look a lot like a squirrel, but are not closely related to them. The Sugar Glider can be found on the mainland of Australia and also on Tasmania. It is listed as 'least concern' on the IUCN list.

Thorny Devil

The Thorny Devil is a spiny lizard that looks quite prickly. A frightening display of spikes cover the entire body and helps the creature defend itself. It is also known as the Thorny Dragon. It lives in the desert areas of central Australia. It is not an endangered species.

Thylacine

The Thylacine was a very interesting animal, but we can only see them in pictures because they are extinct. The last living thylacine was seen in the 1950s in Tasmania, which is an island off the coast of southeastern Australia. This mammal was a wolf marsupial, a very strange combination indeed!

Tingle Tree

The Tingle Tree is a species of eucalyptus. There are many species of this type of tree. They are also known as Gum trees, or eucalypt. There is a giant tingle tree in Australia that is considered the oldest living eucalypt in the world.

Willy-Willy

The Willy-Willy is the Australian term for dust devil. The word willy-willy is believed to originate from the Aboriginal language. In Aboriginal myth, they represent scary spirits. Many parents warn their children that if they are not good, an evil spirit will appear from the spinning dust and whisk them away.

Wingecarribee Swamp

Wingecarribee Swamp was once a significant ecological system in Australia. In 1998, this unique peat swamp collapsed and it will take many years to restore it. It was, at one time, rich in endangered plants and home to the Giant Dragonfly. Peat mining in the swamp was the cause that led to its collapse.

Wolf Spider

The Wolf Spider is a scary, hairy looking spider. However, they are not aggressive arachnids unless they are disturbed, then they may defend themselves by biting. They are very hardy spiders and can be found in different areas of Australia, feeding on insects, crickets, and lizards. They are called Wolf Spiders because they 'hunt' their prey much like wolves do.

Wombat

There are three main species of Wombat. The Northern Hairy-nosed Wombat is 'critically endangered' on the IUCN list. Two other species are of least concern. It is a short-legged marsupial that lives in burrow systems. It has powerful front claws and rodent-like teeth. Interesting fact: the Wombat's pouch is backwards so that it doesn't get dirt into it while digging.

Dear Readers,

Australia (OZ) is home to some of the world's most unique forms of flora and fauna, containing approximately ten percent of the world's biodiversity. There are sixteen thousand species of plants in OZ that are found nowhere else on the globe. Eighty percent of the mammals that live there are found nowhere else in the world and there are over seven hundred species of lizards unique to the continent.

Why did Australia develop such unusual plant and wildlife? The story begins millions of years ago when there were two super-continents. The most southern continent was called Gondwana. The huge continent began to break up and about fifty million years ago a chunk of land separated and drifted slowly away. That piece of land is now Australia. Since it was not connected to any of the other major land formations, the animal and plant life developed entirely separate from the rest of the world.

I hope, as you read the story, you enjoyed learning about different flora and fauna that live, and grow in Australia. I also hope I have piqued your interest enough that you will do some research on these and other endangered animals around the world. Remember, we share this planet with many living creatures and we depend on each other ecologically. That is why it is so important to protect our environment.

J.E. Rogers
December 2012

Visit: warriorechidna.blogspot.com

COMING IN 2014

Another Australian Fantasy Adventure

The Gift of Sunderland

CHAPTER 1

In the northern lands of Acadia, deep in the realm of Sunderland, there once stood an ancient gum tree. The ancient tree had fallen so long ago that the event was no longer a part of the forest's memory. Over the years the fallen tree had become a comfortable and cozy home for a regal line of numbats named Ayers. Roland Ayers' family history was a source of pride for the great marsupial. He was patriarch of his immediate family, advisor to his extended family and the forest community in the surrounding lands. Above all, he was the Guardian of the Forest. The creatures throughout

Acadia, and the lands beyond, recognized his strength and the power of his sorcery. He was well loved.

Roland sat at his great oak desk in his library. The walls were lined with shelves. The shelves were filled with volumes containing histories of the lives of the ancestors, and the ways of the forest. The Book of Memory was open before him. He referred to it when he had a problem, a concern or needed a potion for various ailments that might befall the forest creatures. He was deep in thought when Waylond entered. The lamplight cast Waylond's shadow across the floor and over the page of Roland's book. Roland lifted his paw and set it on the book, then slowly moved it across Waylond's shadow to the bottom of the page.

"Ah, my son. How are you this evening?" he asked, slowly raising his head.

"I'm fine father, except..." Waylond hesitated. He would be entering prime this season and Roland was proud of him. He was a strong, tall numbat. His prominent stripes, especially the black stripe that ran from his ears over his eyes to his pointy nose signaled his maturity. It was always a bittersweet moment to recognize that one's children had grown and would leave their home to set out on their own. Waylond's time was drawing near.

"Except what, son?" Roland leaned back in his chair, resting his paw on the arm. He peeked over his reading spectacles at Waylond, examining the concerned look on his son's face.

"We had another disagreement, Father."

"I thought that might be the problem." He turned back to his book and picked up a cup of tea that sat at his right paw. Taking a sip of tea, he said, "Sit down, Waylond. This is a problem that we need to discuss."

Waylond walked across the room and sat in the ladder-back chair next to his father's desk. Roland placed his teacup on its saucer, reached into his red velvet vest pocket and pulled out his pocket watch. He flipped open the brass cover to check the time, closed the top and placed the watch back into his pocket. "It's getting late," he muttered under his breath.

He sighed, looked up at his son and said, "Soon the book and all its secrets will be passed to you, son." He reached up and removed his reading glasses, placing them beside the book. "You'll need to carry on the traditions. You'll need to guard the book and use its contents for the good of Acadia and all of Sunderland."

"I understand, father, but..."

Roland raised a paw, stopping his son in mid-sentence. "There is no 'but', Waylond. The secrets contained in the book, the power contained in the book, must be kept safe. You are to be the keeper of the book. It has been written."

"Kailond does not see it the same way."

"Kailond is a rash young numbat. Furthermore, your twin brother was not chosen." He pointed a claw at Waylond. "You have been chosen," he admonished. "The book has spoken and its words are final." He let out a heavy sigh. "I am growing old, Waylond. I am not as strong as I once was." He stood, closed The Book of Memory and lifted it slowly from his desk. Embracing the book, he looked down at his son. "You must accept this responsibility. Your time is approaching. Do not allow your brother to restrain you, or divert you from your destiny."

Waylond looked up at his father. Roland saw the puzzled look in his eyes, the questions, the fear, but most of all he saw potential greatness. Was his son ready for everything that was to come? That was the question that plagued him.

The door to the library opened with a crash. Waylond looked up and saw his brother, Kailond, standing in the entry. His eyes flashed with anger.

"Father, tell me why this...this *weakling* has been chosen." His paws balled into fists. He appeared to Waylond as a tightly wound spring ready to snap.

"We've gone over this before." Roland wrapped his paws around the Book of Memory, bringing it closer to his chest. "The word of the Book is final." He placed the book on his desk. Turning to Kailond, he said with finality, "There is nothing more to discuss. You must accept the word of the book."

"The word of the book..." Kailond repeated his father's words with a snarl. "Waylond cannot handle the forces within the book, especially the power of the sword. And you Father, you are afraid to complete the sword!"

"The sword is to be completed in its proper time or it will fall into the wrong paws."

"Brother," Waylond stood and took a step toward his brother. Kailond's paw moved to his belt, removing a dagger from its sheath.

"Don't even bother, Waylond. You're a coward!" Kailond shouted. "You wouldn't know how to handle the sword!"

"Put the knife away." Roland said in a calm tone. "We are family. We will not allow such discord to control us."

"I am sick of your foolish philosophies and lectures, Father," Kailond growled. "The power of the book will be mine." He glanced at the book on the desk, and rushed at his brother, his dagger held before him.

Waylond moved forward to meet him, but Roland stepped between the two. It all happened in a flash. Thrusting the dagger with all his might, Kailond struck. Eyes wide with surprise, Waylond caught Roland as he slumped to the floor.

"What have you done?" Waylond shouted. Kailond stood over Waylond and his father. His father's blood dripped from the dagger that he held in his paw.

"He shouldn't have interfered," Kailond growled.

Waylond rose to his feet, eyes fixed on his brother. With all his fury, he lunged at him and threw him against a wall of bookshelves. The dagger flew from his paw. Books fell, hitting the floor and creating a thunderous noise. The two brothers rolled over the books, gripping, clawing and biting each other. Kailond reached out and grabbed his brother by the throat. Gathering all his strength, Waylond brought his right arm around, landing a powerful punch to the side of Kailond's head. Dragging and lifting his brother to his paws, Waylond pushed him against the bookshelves and held him there with his forearm across Kailond's throat.

"Get out of here," Waylond hissed into his brother's face. "Get out, and never come back!" Grasping him by the throat, Waylond flung his brother out of the library.

Gasping for breath, Kailond reached for the doorframe to steady himself. "You think this is over," he roared, eyes flashing with hatred. "It's not over, Waylond!" He spat out his brother's name as though it were poison on his tongue. Turning, he limped away.

"Father," Waylond whispered. Roland's eyes fluttered open as Waylond lifted him gently into his arms.

"Waylond?"

Waylond lowered his head to his father.

"You must not allow this to alter your course." Weakly, he raised a paw to touch his son's arm. "Take the book." Roland's words sputtered out between breaths. "Go to the hidden cache. Take the stone and complete the sword in its time. Be strong my son." His eyes closed, and he was gone.